CASH AND GRAVITY

CASH AND GRAVITY

A NOVEL

PERRIN PRING

DIVERSION
BOOKS

Diversion Books A division of Diversion Publishing Corp.
www.diversionbooks.com

For more information, email info@diversionbooks.com

First Diversion Books Edition: May 2026
Trade Paperback ISBN: 979-8-89515-117-4
e-ISBN: 979-8-89515-118-1

Design by Westchester Publishing Services
Cover design by Alan Dingman

Printed in the United States of America
1 3 5 7 9 10 8 6 4 2

For Mom and Dad

ONE

CHEVY

Chevy doubled over in her hammock, her hands instinctively going to her stomach. The punch had been quick, and the feeling of the marine's knuckles lingered on her intestines.

"Get up. It's my turn to rack."

Chevy opened her eyes. She did not see the bunkroom walls of Orbital Station 17-B. Instead, she saw a hulking man, his shoulders rounded forward from too much benching, tattoos crisscrossing his bare chest, hair buzzed so a clear diagonal slash ran from one ear to just above one eye. This is what stood over her, monopolizing her field of vision.

"What the fuck is the matter with you?" Chevy swallowed so she wouldn't puke. "You punch people to wake them up?"

"You should have been out by now," the marine said. "Get up on time, and I won't have to."

Chevy unzipped the hammock and groped for her phone. She'd overslept by ten minutes.

"You could've asked." She swung her legs to the ground.

"I did."

Before she'd taken a step, the marine was in the hammock, zipping himself in.

"I hope you sleep like shit."

He didn't respond.

Chevy moved through the bunkroom. The dull red deck lights that guided her in the darkness turned to harsh overheads once she made it to the hallway. The hall's sterile brightness only reinforced to Chevy that she was in a fragile tin can in the endless void of space.

They'd moved her briefing back, so she now had just under two hours to kill. It would have been nice to sleep longer, but space was tightly controlled on station. She'd hit the shower then head to the chow hall, even though she was still pretty gravity sick and couldn't imagine eating. You usually slept the first eight or so hours on station, and that's what she had been doing before being unceremoniously assaulted. She knew that given enough time the nausea would fade, but she didn't expect to be in orbit all that long. Launch Tech, L Tech to the Marines, didn't send grunts to space to have them just sit around. She would be dropping back to Earth soon, that much she knew. No doubt her briefing would tell her when and hopefully why.

Inside the locker room, Chevy grabbed a clean sponge. Like most of the marines on station, she was a big human, standing at a full six feet and two inches and weighing in between 227 and 232 pounds, depending on the day and her salt levels. She was no lard ass, though. While corporations like L Tech ran their marine corps differently than the government did, the one thing all marine corps had in common was the physically fit grunt. Chevy's muscles had muscles.

Smearing the sponge from armpit to armpit, she stretched her achy body and lifted her right arm. The L Tech marine tattoo on her bicep, her first, didn't come near eye level. On her best days

Chevy couldn't touch her toes, but now her body was about as flexible as her issued armor plates. It was always that way after arriving on station. She pushed the arm higher. Her neck popped. She stopped. Space messed with your joints in weird ways. That was enough stretching for the day. She rubbed some soap on her half-shaved skull then massaged the foam through what short hair she did have. She imagined she was in a hot shower.

Closing her eyes, she thought of Lake Winnipeg. She could almost smell the freshly grilled catfish, cooked on the dusty sand. She could *almost* taste the tang of lemon on the blackened skin, the sylvan odors of the surrounding trees settling between the pepper stuck in her teeth. The endless stretch of the water that was Lake Winnipeg, its beauty and danger, reflecting the red rays of the sun, sinking below the horizon. But try as she might, her mind wasn't buying that she was anywhere other than in another BO-filled locker room on an L Tech Station orbiting Earth. Here, all you got was a clammy sponge and tepid water.

Finished with her sad excuse for a bath, she dried herself, chucked the sponge and the towel into the recycler, pulled on a standard issue set of BDUs, and set out for the chow hall. The chaos of the room hit her the moment she slid open the hatch. Marines yelled and joked with one another. The sounds of steaming pots, clattering utensils, and rushing dishwashers wove between the elevated voices. Then there were the bulkheads.

One bulkhead showed the latest Ace Games on Channel Z. Major Hernandez, one of Chevy's favs and a six-time recipient of the Gold Trident, was representing L Tech in a bi-wing obstacle course. Chevy paused, hoping to watch her complete her run, when an ad for the L Tech's university system interrupted the feed. Another bulkhead showed a team of Aces building a house in what looked to be a tornado damaged area back on Earth. The Aces, all women under five foot three and built like fitness models, pushed a wall frame to vertical, their arm muscles gleaming in the sunlight. Chevy stared at the feed, captivated by the way these noble, chosen women moved. They seemed to dance across the construction site, every step, every arm bend, every tilt of their heads intentional and beautiful. Not like Chevy, who moved like a wrecking ball through a retaining wall. But that was one of the reasons she made a great grunt. Up here, on this station, with the other marines, a lack of elegance didn't matter. She could never be an Ace, but that didn't mean she didn't dream about it.

Chevy avoided the chow line and went straight to the coffee station, waiting patiently while a marine with sleep-crusted eyes slowly poured himself a cup. Once he finally figured out this mystery skill, she filled her own plastic mug, found a table, and let the coffee's steam warm her face. She watched the bulkhead with the bi-plane comp, but Major Hernandez still hadn't flown. Chevy's mind wandered. Her two weeks of recent shore leave had been nice, maybe too nice. She really didn't want to be here now.

"CHEVY."

Fetia and Kimo lumbered at her. Both from Hawaii, although Chevy could never get the island names right, they were giants, even by marine standards.

"Hey, guys." Chevy heard how tired she sounded.

Fetia sat next to her, the table's bench groaning under her weight, more chow than Chevy could even think about eating heaped on her tray. Kimo dropped onto the bench across from her, the plastic making a desperate noise. Kimo had one of those megawatt smiles. Chevy imagined he had charmed many a woman during many a tropical sunset. He beamed it at her now and all she could think about was that her bra wasn't sitting right at the seam. She pulled at it.

"You hear the scuttlebutt?" Kimo dug into a mountain of eggs.

"I've been awake for less than fifteen minutes." Chevy twisted the elastic flat. *Fucking finally.* She sighed. "So, no."

"A big op," Fetia said. "Sounds like EXO did it."

Kimo pushed away his tray. "These eggs taste like dishwater. Why the fuck do chow hall eggs always taste like dishwater?"

"Because they make everything from the same protein paste. They just add a little soap to color things." Fetia gave Kimo a flat stare then turned to Chevy, her voice low. "Word is Exoterra pulled off something big."

"Fusion, but mobile. Like battery-sized," Kimo said through a mouthful.

Chevy let out a whistle. Exoterra was Launch Tech's main competitor among the Big Six, the six mega corporations that had risen to world dominance after the former superpower governments tumbled, or at least stumbled. "I thought they quit fucking with that shit after half of Vegas was vaporized . . . What was that, in forty-two?"

Ever since Chevy could remember, fusion was the great white whale of the Big Six. It was true science fiction shit, on the shelf with flying cars or going to Mars, except that with fusion, those things could actually be possible. The talking point of every political cycle, always promised and hoped for but never enacted, like universal health care, basic income, or free universities. It was the cure for cancer and the fountain of youth. It was everything and nothing. It would remake humanity, as soon as humanity figured out how to fucking make it.

Kimo nodded. "Some time in the forties, yeah, when they thought it would save the ice caps."

Fetia skewered a soy sausage on her fork. She bit off half and pointed the rest at Chevy and Kimo. "But not this time. Turns out people plus fusion *usually* equals slagging everyone in a major metropolitan area, but . . ."

"Not this time?" Chevy asked.

Kimo nodded, having moved on to a dumpy-looking muffin. "Kinda funny to think about, yeah? Finally, it's not disintegrating people. And it's self-contained."

"Allegedly." Fetia gnashed the other half of the sausage between her teeth. "Allegedly."

"Huh." Chevy felt stupid for not having something more profound to say. This was actually a real moment in human history. And Exoterra no less. She blinked dumbly at Fetia, but all she could focus on was her sudden hunger. It seemed her gravity sickness had subsided. She stood.

"I'm gonna grab some chow."

"Don't get the eggs," Kimo said.

"Noted."

Chevy walked past a bulkhead showing the news. A blond woman in a garish suit jacket spoke. Subtitles below her read, *Today, the American government is voting on several "traditional America" laws. Senator Rob McLeonard states that realigning America with the founding fathers' visions is a strong move for democracy. Senator Taylor Park states that America has more important things on its plate than deciding if it should, once again, be illegal for women to wear pants.*

Chevy sighed and shuffled into line behind a stocky bald man. The United States would not stop squabbling over bullshit that was totally irrelevant. This was one of the main reasons she'd joined up with L Tech. America was done. Those too stupid to realize it were on Earth arguing over the same crap their parents and grandparents had argued over. Anyone with balls and a brain was in space or doing their best to get to space.

She'd grown up in a small town in Mississippi. Her parents were distrustful of the government, outsiders, and a nonbinary world. They believed in the superiority of the white race. But when she'd joined L Tech, Launch Tech had sequenced her DNA. The test placed the Ivory Coast markers in her genome as originating from sometime between 1811 and 1840. Chevy never told her father she was part Black, not because she didn't want to see the look on his face, but because her parents had disowned her the day she signed her contract.

Launch Tech was Chevy's savior. That sounded extreme, that a company was Chevy's idol, but it was true. Without L Tech, Chevy would be back in inland Mississippi, married off by now, as an aged twenty-four-year-old—assuming her dad could convince a man to marry a woman of her size—pregnant, ignorant, struggling to feed and raise a horde of dirty children, surrounded by people like her parents. No women in her family worked or lived outside of the home. They did what their husbands said, when they said. L Tech had given her a way out, and for that she would fight for L Tech until her dying breath.

And like any good L Tech grunt, Chevy knew, a self-contained fusion device could change everything. *If* humanity had access to endless, free, clean energy, people could literally do anything. Sure, they could kill each other with it, but if L Tech had it . . . Well with infinite energy, L Tech could leave Earth, forever. They could colonize the stars, which was what they were trying to do. But a fusion battery would make it happen *now.* Humanity could restart. And that's really why Chevy was here. She believed L Tech would be the company that pulled it off.

Someone bumped into Chevy.

"Brent!"

"Mustafa!"

A marine pushed past her and grabbed the bald man in front of her. The men embraced, thumping each other on the back. They smiled wildly. Chevy's mind wandered back to Winnipeg. She wondered what Kenji was doing right now.

"Get a fucking room!" someone yelled.

The line bent around Brent and Mustafa, the two men too absorbed in their chance meeting on a random space station to care about breakfast. She watched the reunited marines laugh, then one of the bulkheads caught her attention. It showed a promotional video of an L Tech doctor checking the eyes of a dirty, shoeless kid. The video transitioned back to the Aces rebuilding houses.

The noise in the chow hall suddenly fell, and a single, clear voice sang above the tables.

"*Earth can't contain us, progress is our destiny, but only if the brave, the brave of us are free . . .*"

Chevy sighed. The singer, a resonate baritone, who even Chevy had to admit had talent, paused, and then a chorus of voices cried, "*LAUNCH TECH MARINES ALWAYS LEAD THE WAY, snow, sand, or zero G, doesn't bother me.*"

Chevy closed her eyes. Was this better or worse than being punched in the womb while sleeping? She was a patriot, but couldn't a woman just enjoy her breakfast in peace? She *would* fight until she died. But why did people love the Battle Hymn so much? Everyone thought it was normal to always be performing.

Chevy started to box breathe, doing her best to derail her annoyance. They taught it in boot as a way to control one's emotions. Mad at your spouse? Box breathe. Shot in the leg? Box breathe. Taking a promotion test? Box breathe. Teaching your snot-nosed kid how to read? Box breathe. It was apparently the answer to everything. She looked at one of the news feeds.

A panel of spray-tanned people discussed the current political state of the Big Six—Launch Tech, Exoterra, Tsiolkovsky, Jinzhan, Lua Um, and Alpha Orbital—referred to colloquially as L Tech, EXO, Til-what, Jin-who, Um, and KOed by her fellow marines. But the only two that really mattered were L Tech and EXO. The other four were content to align their business relationships behind one or the other depending on how the energy market cards landed each quarter.

Chevy focused on reading the subtitles, doing her best to block out the now cheering marines. The fact that L Tech had so many grunts in space at once meant something was up. Going to space was rare. Yes, it was a big reason why anyone joined the Marines. But most of the battles were fought on Earth, jockeying for raw materials to further the victor's space race objectives. When L Tech dropped marines from orbit, they were used as a quick assault force. For a few, dangerous, heady, scary, and so, so, addicting moments, it would just be Chevy and her platoon against the world. As much as she knew she wasn't supposed to love that, she did.

In reality, Chevy wasn't built to be a space fighter. She was built to live and fight in Earth's gravity. The actual space fighters were the Aces. Aces were small, almost exclusively women, and they spent their entire active lives in space. They were elite super soldiers who specialized in space-based hand-to-hand combat. They lived in plush suites on special stations, ate real food, and were paid more per mission than Chevy could hope to make in a year.

Aces had a fifteen-year retirement. If they survived, they often transitioned into something on the world's stage. Everyone loved Aces, no matter what corporation you signed with. Many retired Aces became pro-athletes, representing their corporation in sold-out sporting events. Some did relief work, their star power a philanthropic boon. Everyone had a favorite Ace, and when she did something, you paid to support her or see her. Retired Aces had clothing lines, challenge coins, perfume, you name it, an Ace had already done it.

The one time Chevy had gone to an L Tech recruiting fair, a retired Ace had been there, Major Kim, telling stories and showing off her scars. With Chevy's size, the major didn't even bother to show Chevy the recruitment paperwork, but despite that, Major Kim's confidence and power had captivated Chevy. Never had she met a woman like that. Her mom, sisters, and aunts, they were meek and subservient, just as she was trained to be. Not Major Kim. She was outspoken, strong, and intimidating. She made Chevy want to be her.

As an enlisted marine, Chevy got sent to an infantry station, where she hot racked, tried not to puke, and worked out and ate as much soy chow as she could. This wasn't the life L Tech had promised her. But when she was able to think objectively about it, she knew her life was way better as an L Tech grunt than it would have been had she stayed home. Still, there were a lot of marines up here. Chevy's stomach tightened, maybe a remnant of the wake-up punch, maybe not. Maybe she should box breathe some more.

When Chevy arrived at the briefing room, most of her platoon was already there. She'd been recently promoted, despite her best efforts, and was now what her buddies termed "a big-time corporal." Mostly it was a big-time headache, but she did like her newfound rank's negligible ability to protect her unit. Luckily, she wasn't high enough up the ladder to be responsible for a platoon brief, so she made herself as comfortable as possible in one of the hard chairs and munched on a sausage link while PFC Gonzales and PFC Williams had a mock dance-off at the front of the room.

At twenty hundred hours on the dot, her lieutenant walked in. Also a large woman, Bernice Quinn had a no-nonsense way of plowing through a room to get straight to the point. She kind of reminded Chevy of a dinosaur, if a dinosaur constantly had a prehistoric stick shoved up its ass. Chevy stood at attention until the lieutenant gave them the at ease command. Everyone slid into their seats, and the lieutenant started to talk, no preamble, just direct, grouchy information spit straight at their faces.

"Alright," she began, the bulkhead behind her lighting up. "We are launching a multi-front assault against several Exoterra mines in Nevada. We will initiate a siege of the Zola mine, which is a rare Earth element site in the southwestern part of the state."

Chevy took in the lieutenant's brief. She spoke for nearly fifteen minutes straight, no pausing, no questions, just a wave of information crashing over them. They were attacking a mine. That was it. The lieutenant said nothing about a fusion device.

When the lieutenant stopped talking, Chevy's heart sank. She knew she would be in a dozen more meetings, planning and leadership briefs, but the entire premise of what was going on was unsettling. It was strange for L Tech to be so . . . aggressive. Most attacks they executed were predicated upon another event, and Chevy doubted this was any different. Since nothing public had recently happened, it was suddenly plausible that the fusion device did in fact exist, and Fet and Kimo weren't just regurgitating rumors. If it did, this offensive was probably related to capturing that tech. Chevy knew for a fact though, that if fusion did exist, it wasn't at a mine in southern Nevada. In all likelihood it was in space, since it was easier to defend a station in orbit from capture, although not destruction, than it was to defend a mine on the ground. And if she was being sent to a mine in Nevada, that meant . . . Well, Chevy wasn't paid to have opinions about the tactics. She was just paid to execute them.

Still, Chevy's nausea returned. She had a bad feeling about this.

TWO

DOLON

Dolon took a sip of his coffee and considered the sky. Red with streaks of blue and fuchsia, the morning colors didn't disappoint. He knew, though, that the day would be hot, hotter than he wanted. But that was the way of the world now. It was already ninety-two degrees, and the sun wasn't even up yet. September in Nevada was no joke.

He shifted; his right hip was tight. The tablet on his lap slipped. He caught it, cursing. When he was a kid, a few print newspapers were still in circulation, but now *everything* was digital. He had memories of his grandfather drinking coffee and reading the paper when it was on actual paper. Dolon had been born in the wrong century.

The tablet flashed today's dramatic headline. There was yet another scrape between Launch Tech, Exoterra, and the American government. Washington, DC, was still clinging to whatever semblance of power it could muster to stay relevant, but it had been functionally replaced. The Big Six were the ones with the actual power now. Everyone knew it, including Dolon, who did his best to stay out of world events.

Lifting the mug again, he let out a sharp cough. The air quality hadn't been great lately. Fire was just part of life in western Nevada, and even after years of it, his body had never really adjusted.

He dragged a calloused hand across his jaw. His beard, grayer than not these days, was at that point he hated. He needed to trim it. His fingers drifted up from his beard and into his rapidly thinning hair. Too bad the hair on his head didn't grow with the same ferocity as the hair on his face. At least the hair on his head was still mostly brown.

The hair on his face . . . He touched his beard again, and then his fingers found the crow's feet that blossomed from the corners of his eyes. He knew what he would see if he looked in the mirror, his skin weathered from a life in the sun and wind. When had he become an old man? Really, it didn't matter. He wasn't looking to impress anyone. Besides, sixty was the new forty, or so he'd been told.

Dolon lived on a little slice of land just west of Dyer, Nevada. Nestled against the eastern foot of the White Mountains with Leidy Creek burbling at the far end of his property, he lived an isolated, and in his opinion, wonderful existence. This was the kind of place where if a paper newspaper did still exist, he could have read it in peace.

He'd built his cabin by hand nearly thirty years ago and made his living as a handyman for a variety of the ranches and agricultural outfits in Dyer and in the Fish Lake Valley. He didn't need much money—technically he didn't need any money—but he preferred an honest living. So he continued to work, even though a lump sum of more than he could ever hope to spend landed in his bank account each month.

Today, he had a list of chores to perform around his property. The eastern fence had been run down by wild mustangs, again. His tomatoes needed picking. He was going to shave Captain Picard, the fluffy cat who'd apparently adopted him, once more before winter. He didn't look forward to dealing with Captain Picard. The cat liked his matted fur, but Dolon knew from experience if he didn't shave it, a host of creatures, including fleas, would colonize the interior of his house. It was easier to shave the cat than try to tell the cat he couldn't come inside anymore.

Dolon watched the sun rise and finished his coffee. Once the colors had faded and the sky was a warm yellow, he stood. He'd start on the fence and try to make headway before it got too hot to work. Pulling open the screen door, he stepped inside.

The house itself was small, but he'd built it well, a stacked log design that wasn't dark like most cabins. His wife had insisted he put in windows that accentuated the natural light. At the time, he'd found the request amusing, but like most things, she'd been right. The windows lit up the space. When light filled the cabin after a long night, he felt her, even if just briefly.

He moved to the kitchen and went about rinsing his mug. He set it in the metal drying rack and turned to the fridge, pulling out a carton of eggs he'd collected from his hens. He drizzled some oil on the cast iron, turned on the stove, and cracked in an egg, the yolk a dark yellow. He tossed the shell into the compost, and then a sound he'd never heard split the air.

He searched around for the source behind a stack of books by the wall and pulled a black cell phone from behind a sci-fi hardback. It was still plugged into the wall, as it had been since he'd first gotten it from Launch Tech years before. He couldn't believe it still worked, the design so old even he recognized it as out-of-date. The angry noise repeated itself, and he realized it wasn't an incoming call, but a text.

Eidolon DaTerra,

You have an assignment.

Keep this phone with you for the next forty-eight hours. You will get a call with instructions. You will follow the instructions, and if those instructions include getting an object to a location, you will do that as expeditiously as possible, using minimal technology. You will be tracked. Go totally off the grid.

Dolon flipped the egg with a spatula then cracked his neck. He felt extremely tired despite having just drunk a cup of coffee. He set the spatula down and used both thumbs to mash the unfamiliar keyboard.

Will this end my contract?

The screen showed a symbol Dolon assumed meant someone was composing a reply. Then it came through.

I am not at liberty to discuss that. Complete your mission and someone will address this question.

Dolon rolled his eyes. He wanted to chuck the phone into his compost pile, but he knew that would ruin the compost. After a few deep breaths he typed, Roger.

Keep this phone with you and charged until you get another message.

Dolon scooped the egg onto a chipped plate. He managed another question. What kind of object?

You will be told when you need to know.

END COMMUNCATION

Dolon stared at the screen. He had been both dreading and waiting for this day, when his favors were finally called in. He'd waited nearly fifteen years, and now, just like that, it was all coming to a head.

He cut a piece of bread and added it and a few tomato slices to his plate. He began to eat, his mind swirling with all the things he'd spent years trying not to remember.

THREE

THE CRANE

The Crane checked his retinal display. He was on a 5:40 mile pace, but his heart rate was higher than he wanted. He took a deep breath, the pounding of his legs echoing up his body, the St. Louis pavement hard under his feet. He focused. His pulse dropped a beat. Then another. His pace didn't flag.

He smiled, embracing the three A.M. darkness. Yes, he was a military man, but he occasionally thought in civilian terms. Three A.M. was a time when most of the world was tucked into their beds, relaxing into the illusion of safety. And that repulsed him. It pushed him to train harder, to run faster, to never stop. Because, if he stopped, that kind of thinking would catch him. It was infectious. He was not the kind of person who snored into his pillow at *three A.M.* He was the kind of person who trained at *oh-three-hundred.* He was the predator, not the prey. The early morning streets of St. Louis didn't scare him. He was of them.

His heart rate dropped another beat. He was a hunter. He was the alpha predator. Another beat. He was at the top of his game. The Crane rounded a corner, his legs pushing him down another shadowy street, his heart rate now settled where he wanted it. A machine. He was a machine.

A call alert popped up on his retinal feed. He flicked his eyes to activate the communication chips modded in his cochlea.

"Crane."

"Are you on a secure line?"

The words were disembodied and slightly robotic, which was textbook Exoterra. The Voice vibrated against his cheeks and jawbone.

"No."

"Get to one and call back."

The Crane had intended on making this a semi-long run, fifteen miles, but he banked to his left and ran back toward his quarters, pushing himself and dropping his pace to a five-minute mile.

The Crane was a standard Exoterra soldier when he'd joined up, but he'd quickly risen up the ranks before his capabilities landed him on their black ops teams, then beyond and into a position without an acknowledged classification. Only two people knew the Crane existed: the one he'd just spoken to and the Banker.

He'd first met the Banker a few years ago, in a back alley in Poland running a lucrative scam, convincing drunks and transients to sign away the rights to their organs. His specialty was skin, which had a longer shelf life if "banked" appropriately. To do so required that, when the Banker performed the delicate removal surgical procedure, his donors were still alive. And he never used sedation, but that was just his personal preference. It was brutal and efficient. And in the Crane's world, brutal efficiency was a must.

It was good to have a partner who shared this understanding. Over the years the Crane and the Banker had deployed for the most urgent and specialized missions. They both knew their way around a computer and a rifle. Each could track, hunt, locate, and kill their quarry without a trace of technology, but bio-implants put them as close to the tip of the human evolutionary spear as a modern human could be.

The Crane finished his last two miles at a 4:45 pace and jogged up the stairs to his seemingly mundane second-story apartment, an Exoterra safe house. The building housed an impressive array of weapons and surveillance technology and was designed to turn to slag if the Crane flicked his eyes in the correct pattern, which made it safe for the Crane alone. He was ready to deploy to anywhere at any time. All he needed was a location.

The Crane linked into apartment 3C's biometric security system with his internal retinal display and plugged in his code to get inside the door. The interior was utilitarian, neutral-toned, and hard edges. He walked straight to his desk chair, toggled on the computer, and hit a button. Foxtrot Delta, the Voice, answered on the first ring.

"Taking your time?"

The Voice was always modulated, never human enough to be recognized in case the mission became a political nightmare.

"I was on a fifteen miler."

The Voice wasn't interested. "We did it."

The Crane opened his newsfeeds. Nothing caught his eye.

"The Non-Radioactive Generator is operational."

The Crane sat back at the news. The fusion battery. If Exoterra had done it first, the ripple effect among the rest of the Big Six would begin immediately. The Crane's thoughts jumped to the issues more immediate than global war.

"Where?"

"EX-10."

"Educate me."

"It's a research station. Low odds, high gains work."

The Crane had already pulled EX-10 up on the Exoterra database, a detailed holographic green print of it rotating in three dimensions in his retinal display. Technical specs, coordinates, and personnel detail spilled down around it like textual waterfalls. It was a backwater station in orbit, built nearly a decade and a half ago. When Exoterra had been rolling out its trillion-dollar orbital infrastructure initiative, EX-10 had been cutting edge. It still was, at least in the sense that it hadn't fallen Earthside. Now it was still in service but had very little expectation to go with the investment. Still, there was always a chance that one of Exoterra's God Machines, one of which was on EX-10, produced something spectacular for all the shot-in-the-dark research tasked to them. Now one had randomly made a working fusion device.

"We scuttle the device and rebuild it in an area with legitimate security," the Crane said.

His eyes continued to scan the schematic. EX-10 was a zero G station with a life support system that was capped at five people. There was *no* ground security there. Yes, the standard network of defense satellites surrounded it, and it came with the normal company-mandated physical security measures—cameras controlled by an operator on Earth, external station weaponry also controlled by that same operator, alarms and sensors that could be triggered by any atmospheric imbalance. All five of the station occupants' biometrics were sent back to Earth every seven minutes, fed into a computer in real time, and analyzed for any irregularities. It was a totally inappropriate defense network for something as powerful and world altering as mobile fusion.

"We can't scuttle it," the mostly robotic Voice said.

"Why?"

"The God Machines generate output randomly. I've been assured reverse engineering and re-creating it aren't as simple as messaging the outputs to Earth."

That sounded ridiculous to the Crane, but he wasn't a scientist. And he now saw why he was being called. "Then we have to move it. You're sure it's stable?"

"More than we could have ever dreamed. That's not the issue."

"I see . . ."

Exoterra would blow up their own station before they let an enemy seize it and take the device. Anything was preferable to letting the device fall into enemy hands, no matter the cost. The Crane rubbed his chin. They had to play the odds here. Ideally, the scientists figured out how to duplicate the technology quickly from EX-10. The problem was, even with only a few people knowing this secret, the other companies would find out. Be it from hacked communication, an undetected monitoring net, or just loose lips, Exoterra had been handed a ticking time bomb. Either they moved the device under heavy guard, shouting to the world a secret they didn't want anyone to know, or they moved it quietly, gambling nobody would catch wind. Both options were fraught with major issues and bad odds.

Relations between the Big Six were more strained than they'd ever been. Skirmishes between enemy marines were so common they no longer made headlines. Territory maps were never up to date. One company was always assaulting another, and then the inevitable retaliation that came only further disrupted who had what and where everyone's pieces were. In some ways, the constant warring made the Crane's job complicated, but in others, it made it simple. If Exoterra wanted to attack Jinzhan, for whatever reason, they didn't risk political fallout. It was simply expected that everyone involved would win some and lose some.

"The scientists have requested at least forty-eight hours to attempt a reverse engineer. Their nutrient supplements have been augmented with amphetamines, so they shouldn't have to sleep in that time." The robotic Voice was too level. "They will crash at some point though, and then it's up to biology on how fast they recover."

"Forty-eight hours from when?"

"Zero three hundred hours CDT. Zero eight hundred hours Zulu."

"So we give them until zero eight hundred their time on Thursday, and then we move it."

"That is your suggestion?"

The Crane didn't hesitate. "Yes."

"*You* are the contingency. *If* we lose the device and there is even the slightest chance it is not scuttled, your team will retrieve it. Only if things go sideways will you be deployed. I suggest you prepare for the unexpected."

"Yes, sir."

And the line went dead.

The Crane stared at the blank screen for several moments, letting the silence in the apartment wash over him. If a competitor stole the device, he and the Banker would finally have a mission commensurate to their skillset. This was the best news he'd gotten all year. Nothing went according to plan. He *knew* he would be deployed.

And he would not fail.

FOUR

CHEVY

Chevy walked quietly through the station halls, rifle in hand, her trip to visit Kenji at the Lake Winnipeg Valhalla on her mind. Chevy had been more relaxed than she'd ever been, and that made her want to retire more than ever, even though she was nowhere close to finishing her time.

She and Kenji had spent their days lounging by the lake, paddle-boarding up and down its coasts and napping on blankets in the sand. In the evenings, they wandered into town to find something to eat. They weren't dating, but it wasn't that complicated either. It had been a blissful two weeks, but the logistics of the world prevented it from being more. And that was okay. Now, Chevy held on to the image of the Manitoba sunset, the sky hazy from forest fire, her head on Kenji's chest, the moment liminal, but real. Grounding and real.

She wasn't concerned about dying on this mission. According to their intel, the Zola mine only had a handful of privately contracted guards. Her platoon was one of many that were assaulting a host of minimally guarded EXO sites. All the target mines were poor producers, which she knew because she'd pulled up the stats on each mine's net worth and average yield. She'd captured various low-level mines before. It wasn't difficult. The marines dropped in, stormed the site, overwhelmed the security. The miners knew the drill and would sit with their hands visible and wait.

Once the mine was secure, Chevy's platoon would start the process of putting the miners on their books. The entire switchover process was boring and administrative, but it could be done within a couple of hours. Then the miners would start work again. New bosses, new contracts, same job, same day. War could be so bureaucratic, just another Tuesday. But this day seemed weird. There were so many resources on this op.

They were to land at zero eight-fifty Zulu tomorrow.

It was now zero one hundred Zulu. The only marines awake were the leaders who had loose ends to tie up before the assault. Since there weren't enough racks for everyone, marines were sleeping on every available surface, from the mess hall decks to the briefing room tables. Many had the best sleep of their lives before a mission. But Chevy always had anxiety to bleed, and boundless energy to go with it. So she looked for places to put that energy.

She reached the hatch and hit the entry button to the armory. It was set up so that the tech sat behind a plastic partition, like a bank teller. The woman at the counter came off as sharp and bony. Chevy supposed she could have been attractive in some light, but from the entryway her cheeks looked like daggers. Chevy steadied herself.

"Hi, Corporal Cole with Ugly Two. One of my privates damaged his XM90 optic, and I need a replacement. We ship out in a few hours." Private Whitehead had given her a massive loose end to fix this late in the game.

The PFC lifted a manicured eyebrow but didn't say anything.

"I've got it here." Chevy held up the rifle.

"That's a major replacement, Corporal." The PFC's voice was barbed. "We don't take that kind of damage lightly." She looked directly at Chevy. "Because it reflects poorly on the squad's leadership."

"I understand." Chevy's voice was even. "That said, I would be a poor excuse for a leader if I didn't do everything in my power to unfuck the situation. I don't need to tell you that the XM90s are temperamental. I cannot afford to have even one private with a faulty optic. That would be unacceptable."

Chevy inhaled and counted to four. Box breath. She knew telling the PFC that her men might possibly die while she sat safely on the station would not get her what she needed, and that was where her little speech was headed.

"Is there any way you can help me?" She purposely edged her voice toward pleading.

The PFC's emerald eyes, the unnatural color an obvious and cheap tint job, were flat and so green that Chevy felt a little sick in their gaze. The woman didn't seem to blink.

"We're on a station. It's not like I have access to a full armory. We have limited supplies."

"I understand. But you must have replacements?"

"Let me see what I can do," she finally said, her voice ice.

Chevy nodded and thanked her. She took the XM90 to the clearing station, demonstrated both chambers were empty, and then slid the rifle across the counter and under the plastic window.

The PFC picked up the rifle with practiced hands, and despite her nearly inch long fingernails, checked it was clear, then considered the optic.

"Come back in an hour."

"Yes, ma'am," she replied, only too happy to get out of the armory.

The PFC disappeared from the desk, and Chevy slipped back into the hallway. She walked toward the room where her platoon slept, working through her mental checklists. She considered grabbing a few minutes of sleep before she returned to get private Whitehead's XM90, but then her mind wandered to the logistics of her upcoming fight.

Their overwatch was taken care of. The gunship Stefanovich, a.k.a. the Stef, would be their shepherd while they dropped to Earth. The orbit of the Stef would sync with the brunt of their attack, meaning that for the battle, their primary overwatch would be the Stef. This calmed Chevy. She had dropped with the Stef protecting her many times, and she had always lived to talk about it. On paper, this mission's overwatch was a formality, but Chevy knew having a low orbit gun ship on your side was never a formality.

Chevy pushed herself toward the staging room where her marines' gear waited. The anxiety was creeping up on her. She needed something else to do and checking gear seemed appropriate.

What were they getting into, and why?

FIVE

DOLON

Dolon drove the fence line, his eyes scanning the wire, his mind on the text. He'd known, all those years ago, that he'd sold his soul to the devil and this day was coming. Strangely, the feelings he'd expected to feel—the pain, the anger, the injustice of it—they all hit him, yes . . . But, while he drove, the window down, the smell of sage breaking under his tires, he felt like a lake at dawn. The wind wasn't blowing, yet. Everything was still, for now. The chaos would come, of course. But in this moment, this instant, he was deadly calm.

Fifteen years ago, he'd gone to Launch Tech and told them he would do anything if they poured every conceivable resource into curing Flora's cancer. They said they would, on one condition—he become a phantom. His palms still got sweaty when he thought of that day. Until that point, in Dolon's world, phantoms were nothing but cultural lore—off-the-gridders that the Big Six recruited but rarely used. They had no social media, no info for the algorithms. They knew things like how to smell blood on the wind and how to navigate by the stars. They were figments of the past stuck in the present.

Dolon often thought of himself as a man stuck in the wrong era, so he made it make sense, had to. When Launch Tech put that contract in front of him, he signed it without hesitation. Launch Tech would pull out all the stops and do everything possible to save Flora. Regardless of her survival, he owed them one job, as a phantom, and then his debt was cleared. The payment didn't matter, only Flora did, and in the end not even Launch Tech could save her. Still, it had been the right choice then, and it would be the right choice now. His debt was now due, and he would pay them back because that is what he said he would do. The equation was simple, no need to complicate it with morals.

He saw one of the sections of fence he needed to fix. A twist of wire had splintered from the post and was now wrapped around a juniper tree. He sighed. Repairing fences on a good day was tough, and today, well, now that he'd gotten the call, he knew he should be building his kit. He stared at the broken fence, watching the wire bob in the wind, then spun the steering wheel.

Back at his workshop, he pulled all of the gear from the back of the truck and tossed it onto the concrete floor. He climbed into the bed with a broom and began to sweep, thinking about what he'd need. Being overprepared was better than being caught with his pants down. He'd pack the truck to the gills and have a go bag. Once the bed was clean, he went to the cab of the truck and flipped the seatback forward. A random assortment of things lay scattered behind the seat—a tattered work coat, a set of leather gloves, TP, a collapsible shovel, a screwdriver, a headlamp, a box of 12-gauge shells, a long, soft case. He grabbed the case and unzipped it.

He pulled out the Remington 870 shotgun and opened the chamber. The metal was cooler than the air. This grounded him. He shouldered the gun and peered through the ghost sight then dropped the muzzle and looked at his truck, door open, cab unorganized. He had a lot to do and probably not much time to do it.

SIX

CHEVY

Chevy stood in the hallway and watched Ugly Two file out of the briefing room where they'd slept. Her eyes swept everyone, starting at their mussed hair and moving to their boots. She knew from experience that catching problems early made the rest of the day easier. Did PFC Gandres have her glasses? She did. Did Private Tan have his coat? He seemed to lose it at every opportunity.

"TAN," Chevy barked.

The half-asleep marines startled and froze.

"Where's your coat?"

Private Tan stared at Chevy with wide eyes then dashed back into the room. He emerged seconds later, carrying his coat.

The team went into the room where they'd stored their gear. Beside everyone's kit was their breakfast, lunch, and dinner: a single drink that had enough calories for an entire day, and enough XR stimulants to make that day last twenty-four hours. The grunts called it "the smoothie." The smoothie also always caused constipation. This seemed like a shortcoming, except that no one wanted to be trapped in a drop ship with someone who had stress diarrhea.

She watched her team get ready. She was already mostly armored up, with the exception of her external plates, helmet, and rifle. Her eyes skipped over the group. Chevy had been left to make sure the platoon was ready and at the drop ship by zero four hundred hours, but once they were on the actual ship she'd only be responsible for her squad of Whitehead, Tan, Gandres, and Pendleton.

She watched Tan struggle to strip his BDUs so he could put on his Kevlar boxers and undershirt.

"Tan! Take your fucking boots off before you drop your pants!" Chevy said.

The private fell over at Chevy's words, and a host of snickers went up through the room. Tan clawed at his boots.

"Tan, drink your smoothie." Chevy's voice was less harsh this time.

The kid was a mess, but Chevy didn't have time to hold his hand until his body magically decided it was ready for the day. Her eyes fell on Private Whitehead. He had on his BDUs, and he was finishing putting on his mid-layer pieces—the armor sleeves for his legs and arms. He was way ahead of the other marines. Chevy swallowed the yell that almost escaped her. Instead, she took a breath, remembered that Winnipeg sunset, and walked to Whitehead.

She planted herself firmly before the private, and the movement in the room stilled. Private Whitehead looked up at Chevy.

"Hey, corporal . . . ma'am," Whitehead said.

"Private, where are your Kevlar chonies?" Chevy's voice was low, but it carried. She knew everyone was listening.

"I . . ."

"You what? You were looking forward to getting your nuts blown off and losing your retirement package?" Chevy's voice was ice.

"I—"

"Remember that presentation they made you watch in boot? The one with all the blown-up dicks? Remember that one? The slide where the one nut is hanging by a thread of skin? DO YOU REMEMBER THAT?"

Chevy knew she had to reel this in, or she would wig out the entire platoon before the op. Particularly the men. That wasn't what she wanted, but private Whitehead had caused her a headache over the past few hours, and the headache was only getting worse. Chevy was going to put a hard stop to it. She glanced at the watching marines then focused again on Whitehead. Chevy wasn't convinced that the Kevlar undergarments L Tech required them to wear for risk mitigation purposes actually did shit against projectiles. But she needed to remember that she was a corporal and her opinion didn't matter.

"This shit isn't perfect, but if you don't wear the gear, you break your contract, and that means you compromise your ability to get to Valhalla. So, if you don't care about the physical security of your nuts, which is odd, but you do you; remember why you're here in the first place. We all signed up to escape whatever shithole we grew up in. We all want to make it through this alive, and with a working set of junk so we can spend our golden years fucking on a beach in Valhalla. You don't wear your chonies, you lose your dick and your ticket out."

Whitehead swallowed. "Yes, ma'am."

"Get to it!" Chevy snapped. "We load at zero four, and you're making us late."

The rest of the marines sprang to life, and Chevy stomped to her place at the front of the room. She watched Whitehead manically shuck his arm and leg armor and then rip off his blouse.

Chevy inhaled and counted to four. Private Whitehead wasn't a bad kid. He was just young, dumb, and from some no-name town in one of those mid-country, rectangle states where not wearing underwear was standard procedure. He didn't know how fast things could turn bad.

No one talked while they readied themselves. The loudest noise was Whitehead's breathing while he worked to re-dress. Chevy looked at her phone. Zero three twenty-three. They were doing all right.

"If you haven't started your smoothie, do so now," Chevy ordered.

Everyone grabbed their bottle and took a swig. The newbies cringed, but most everyone else took the sludge in stride. Chevy heard the slow creaking of an armory cart coming down the hall.

"Armory on deck!" Chevy yelled.

The marines snapped to and stood at attention. The cart trundled into view, pushed by a diminutive, at least on this station, man of about one hundred and eighty pounds.

"At ease." He glared at Chevy. "I work for a living."

The chief warrant officer first doled out the M-4s. When Chevy's name was called, she stepped to the cart and took back her weapon, double-checking it was clear. Then the XM90s were passed out, followed by the P90s, the M320D grenade launcher, and finally the ammo. By twenty minutes to zero four hundred hours everyone had their weapons and ammo, and the armory cart and chief warrant officer were gone.

"Get your shit together and finish your smoothies!" Chevy said. She checked her own gear, then did a close inspection of each platoon member. "Let's move."

They went through the station without speaking, but it was still a loud, banging affair. They all weighed easily one hundred and thirty extra pounds in full kit with gear and their weapons, and with the gravity gradient in play it was like watching a bunch of monkeys fuck a doorknob. Each step they took toward the drop ship bay eased as gravity lessened its hold, and by the time they reached the bay they were in zero G and not stepping at all. The marines pulled themselves along the guide rails that lined the edge of the bay until the last man was inside. Then they waited, one hand on the rail, one on their weapon, their bodies floating. Chevy kicked herself to one of the suspended hand lines and scanned the marines, seeing that everyone, well almost everyone, still had their gear attached to them. PFC Tan's helmet was rapidly moving away from his head.

"TAN," Chevy said. "Grab your helmet. Everyone else, double-check your shit is secure."

The marines began to check their gear. Tan's eyes went wide, and Gandres offered up her knees so that Tan could launch after his helmet. He put way too much mustard into his jump, and he crashed into the bay's roof. A round of snickers went up through the marines.

"You never been in zero G before, Beige?" Whitehead called. "Should we request some mitten minders for your helmet?"

But they knew the drill. The marines, still ribbing Tan, assembled a human chain to collect him.

Corporals Rojas and Sani drifted up to Chevy. Sergeant Blue was with the lieutenant at the far end of the first ship, their heads huddled together, talking softly. Three ships occupied the bay, but Ugly platoon would only fill one of them. The other ships would drop with different platoons to different mines. Mechanics and engineers kicked past, doing what, Chevy didn't know, but she was glad they were.

"Cole." Rebeka Sani nodded at her.

"Rebeka."

"Any issues?" Pepe Rojas asked.

"Nothing worth reporting," Chevy said. "Anything in the brief I should know?"

Rebeka shook her head. "They thought they had new intel for us, but in the end, we just sat there for an hour. Finally, they dismissed us saying nothing had changed."

Chevy snorted a laugh. Rebeka was corporal of Ugly Three, and Chevy knew she both terrified and enthralled all of the straight men, and most of the queer women. Rebeka was simultaneously batshit crazy and incredibly squared away. The juxtaposition made her both a disaster and an amazing marine.

Rebeka shook her head and turned to the waiting marines. Tan was back in line, helmet strapped crookedly to his head. She stared at him for several long seconds, then screamed, "Load for drop! MOVE!"

The marines heaved themselves along the guide rails with alacrity. When they reached the ship, they pulled themselves up the loading ramp and into the passenger compartment. Chevy, Sani, Rojas, and Sergeant Blue followed a few minutes later, along with Lieutenant Quinn. The inside of the ship was cramped and hot. The actual ride was scary as fuck, but for the next four hours all they were supposed to do was sit in their seats and let the geeks do their final math.

Chevy checked her squad. They were in their seats with their gear. Even Whitehead was properly strapped in, and his new optic shined. Chevy sat in her seat, and the anxiety she'd been carrying melted away.

The last thing she heard before drifting to sleep was Rebeka saying she'd consider eating human flesh, if it were properly seasoned.

"LAUNCH IN FIVE MINUTES!"

The automated voice cut into Chevy's dream. She jolted awake and looked around. She was still strapped into the drop ship, her platoon with her. A few of the marines had startled awake with the noise, but most still slept, their heads resting against their harness anchor points or their neighbor's shoulder.

Chevy's mind immediately went to her final checklists, a habit she hated. There was absolutely nothing she could do to fix *anything* while strapped in, five minutes from a drop, but her brain did the same thing every time. It didn't matter that she was functionally powerless, her brain always conjured up something to be anxious about.

"FOUR MINUTES."

Chevy took a breath. The whole countdown thing. It seemed so unnecessary and antiquated, but here they were, still proving people could count backward out loud. And, the voice was automated, so it made their situation into an old action movie.

A drop ship had no pilot. It was designed to fall to Earth without any human input beyond the launch, so letting the people in the ship know the ride had started wasn't a horrible idea. Once the ship landed on Earth—a nice way to say crashed on Earth—parts of it would be salvaged by L Tech, but it was a one-use vehicle in its current form.

"Hey, Corporal."

Chevy turned to see Gandres staring at her.

"Yes, Gandres?"

"Is it true that in Valhalla they let you eat whatever you want? Like actual, real food?"

"What?"

"Like, my dad was always going on about this fruit, it was called a pine orange . . . no, apple. A pineapple. Do you think I can eat one when I go to Valhalla?"

"What?"

"THREE MINUTES."

Gandres looked at Chevy expectantly.

"Most of the food in Valhalla is real. Depends how distinguished you are when you retire. Which Valhalla you go to, how nice it is, all that. You know that."

"Yeah, but even if I go to the worst one, you think they'll have pineapples?"

"Pineapples . . . The yellow stuff in a can."

"Yeah!"

"I don't know, Gandres. I've never seen a real one."

"Well, Corporal, I want some pineapples. That's why I'm gonna fight harder than anyone today."

"TWO MINUTES."

Chevy opened her mouth, shut it, then finally said, "That's good by me."

Gandres kicked Whitehead, who was drooling on her shoulder.

"WHITEHEAD," she yelled. "YOU'RE DROOLING ON ME."

Whitehead stuttered awake.

"I'm hot," he mumbled. "My balls are sweating. These chonies are giving me a rash."

Chevy took a deep breath. Fucking Whitehead.

"You know about pineapples?" Gandres asked.

"I know you're loud as fuck." Whitehead rolled away from her, not opening his eyes.

"ONE MINUTE."

Chevy let her eyes roam over the squad. Those who were awake were pale. They were either completely silent or excessively, frenziedly talking, like Gandres. Two of the marines, one female and one male, were using the hosed funnels that ran from the bulkheads to each seat. The rule was you just had to piss before the end of the countdown, so the liquid could drain from the ship to the bay and not fuck up the math of dropping. Thanks to the smoothies, no one ever had to shit. Chevy felt her heart rate rise. This was it. They were about to drop, and when they hit the ground, they would immediately be thrust into an assault.

". . . THREE . . . TWO . . . ONE . . ."

For a second there was a silent weightlessness, and then the ship left the station. The thrusters sounded, quick loud hisses at irregular intervals, as the ship maneuvered a safe distance so it could start its deceleration burn.

Drop ships were no easy ride. Back in the early days of space travel, astronauts described the reentry into Earth's atmosphere as colorful but not particularly violent. They talked of how the sky outside the windows changed from a light pink to a molten red, then they would gently feel the deceleration of the craft, a signal that they were no longer in orbit and were instead being ever so gently pulled to Earth.

Drop ships by comparison were brutal. With advancements in heat shielding technology, and the tactical need for a quick reentry, drop ships entered Earth's atmosphere at a steeper angle than did the ships of old-school, government astronauts. As a result, the entire drop ship ride was a shaky, frightening, loud as fuck ordeal, that ended not in a gradual re-acclimation to Earth's gravity, but as a gut-punching wallop when the Gs of Earth assaulted them in full force.

Drop ships had no windows in the troop compartment either, so all the colors the old-timers talked about were never visible. She figured this was probably a good thing. Chevy didn't imagine it would do her men well to watch the world around them turn to slag before a battle.

Chevy became overly aware of the silent stillness of the ship. This meant they were in position to start reentry. She held her breath, and the Neil boosters, reusable engines specifically designed for drop ships, ignited. Chevy and the rest of the marines were slammed into their seats. She did her best to look bored, her eyes roaming over the marines while she told herself to relax her jaw. Gandres and Whitehead sat rigid, their eyes squeezed tight, their heads thrust back against the seat rests. A few of the marines were actually asleep. She could tell by the way their features were slack and their eyes weren't scrunched. Chevy's eyes found Rebeka's. She smiled and cocked an eyebrow. Chevy didn't have the gumption to smile back.

Sweat rolled off Chevy's nose, and she tried to steel herself for what was about to happen. At any second the Neils would shut off—

When they finally went silent, someone let out a small squeak of fear. The sound was so high and feral, Chevy didn't know if it had come from a man or a woman, but she agreed with the sentiment. They were once again floating, their boot laces dancing midway up their shins. The Neils would detach at any moment . . . The ship shuttered and clunked. The boosters were away, hopefully. Within moments, EXO would see them on their radars. There was no going back now.

Then the quaking started, and the g-forces pinned her back into her seat. Chevy's stomach roiled in anticipation. She could feel her heartbeat in her forehead. With each second that passed, the bone-shattering, rattling increased in intensity. Pendleton, who had been sleeping during the deceleration burn, now had his jaw clamped tight, the lines at the corners of his mouth vivid to Chevy's pounding eyes.

This was the part Chevy always hated the most. They were fighting the atmosphere. The noise grew exponentially. The ship shook with the manic, off-kilter energy of a misaligned carnival ride. She watched the marines' legs and chins jerk without rhythm. No matter how many times she did this, she could never get used to the viciousness of dropping. It always seemed like they were seconds away from being torn apart, the ship screeching, and the kicking, vicious, vibrations—it caused her pelvic floor to turn to jelly no matter how many times she heard it all and lived to hear it again.

The G's they were pulling now hit her with the intensity of a thousand crashing trucks. Her organs felt like they were being squeezed to the point of popping. She didn't dare open her eyes for fear they might erupt from her head. Her toenails were crawling off her feet. Her tongue was being torn from the bottom of her mouth. The orientation of the seats was designed to help keep them alive during the pull of these forces. She always hoped they did.

Then, just when she thought she couldn't take any more, the pressure in her skull lessened, the needles under her skin diminished, the searing fire where her hair met her scalp faded until they were once again floating, and Gandres threw up. A collective groan went through the ship, followed by several more bursts of vomit.

Chevy knew, from boot, that this was the point in the drop where they were at terminal velocity. This made it feel like they were again in zero-g, but actually they were just free-falling to Earth. The drop ship had successfully clawed through Earth's atmosphere. Its hull had absorbed three thousand degrees, keeping Chevy and her men alive. And while Chevy was more than happy to still be breathing, the price of her continued life was a fresh lather of sweat coating her from head to toe. And without the heat of the atmosphere, she was now not only soaking wet but also freezing cold.

The landing thrusters ignited, and a spray of vomit spackled itself to Chevy's face, some of it plastering to the back of her throat. She wanted to puke, but the Gs pinned her to her seat, and it was all she could do to keep her diaphragm functioning. Despite the flames of pain in her brain, she wondered if food service was hiring.

"TWO MINUTES."

Someone puked again, and this time someone shouted, which was a good sign. It meant people could breathe without too much effort. If someone was yelling, they were breathing. The Gs were lessening. They were slowing down . . .

"ONE MINUTE."

Chevy braced herself for the impact. Landing was like wrecking a car. Hopefully the only fallout would be a sore neck.

WHAM!

They'd found Earth.

Chevy pitched forward, one of her ribs popping as she slammed into her harness. A collective *umf* pushed from the marines. Chevy's side of the ship was hanging upside down. Gandres dangled, vomit dripping from her chin, her limbs twisting from the confines of her harness.

Then the sergeant's voice cut through the ship.

"Sarge up! L.T., you there?"

"Lieutenant up," came Lieutenant Quinn's wobbly voice.

"Ugly One, report!" Sarge screamed.

Chevy listened to the groggy voices of Ugly One sound off. When the Sarge called Ugly Two, Chevy relayed that she was conscious, and her team followed suit. Whitehead sounded the worse for wear, even worse than Gandres, who still looked dead, but it was possible Whitehead just had a mouth full of vomit.

When everyone confirmed they were conscious, the cabin's yellow lights shut off, replaced by the reds.

"Prepare to dismount!" the sergeant yelled.

Chevy hit her safety harness and did her best to slide down the side of the ship rather than just plummet onto the marine below her. She achieved a combination of both. The marine she hit, PFC Kim, let out a howl, but reeled it in when he saw it was a corporal who had landed on him. Chevy reached up and grabbed her rifle from the rack next to her seat, and the sergeant yelled, "CHARGE 'EM."

A cascade of racking bolts filled the pod. The red light went off, and the hatch hissed. It was go time.

The first few steps on land were always dizzying for Chevy. She knew she was lucky. Some people stayed dizzy for hours upon reentry, though they usually washed out in training. Even so, as Chevy stood, moved to the hatch, and stepped onto Earth, she resisted the urge to bend over and puke. She had to set a good example.

The sky was black and dotted with stars. The ship had set down only a quarter of a mile from the mine, which was lit up like a Christmas tree. Chevy jerked her eyes from it, hoping to retain some of her natural night vision. She knew the mine security knew they were there. How could they not?

"Ugly, Stef," came the soft hiss over Chevy's helmet radio. She breathed a sigh of relief, the gunship Stefanovich was there.

As grunts, L Tech didn't provide them with implants. The elite teams, depending on their duty stations, might get body tech, but the lowly grunts relied on early gen helmet mics that crapped out on every day that ended in a *y*.

"Ugly," came the lieutenant's voice, the shitty mic cracking

"We count five guards, all massed on the northern wall, spaced several yards apart."

"Copy," the lieutenant said.

Chevy exhaled. Five guards. They knew they were here. The northern wall was the wall closest to where they landed.

"Alright." Lieutenant Quinn's steady voice filled Chevy's ear. "We'll try it nicely first. Ugly One, you're launching gas. Ugly Two, you've got lethal cover. Ugly Three, you're the contact team. Stef, tell us if something changes."

A round of copies sounded, and then they were running. Well, tripping, stumbling, moving as best they could after crash-landing on Earth.

The high-powered mining lights blinded them, and Chevy felt the same thing she felt every time she ran at someone with guns: both more alive than she'd ever been, and fucking terrified that a hail of bullets would pop her skull like a watermelon.

They reached the cover closest to the northern wall. Chevy crouched behind an outcropping of rocks, Pendleton behind her.

"Ugly . . . Five, still there. Weapons in hand, but they don't seem to see you," the Stef purred in Chevy's ear.

"Masks on," Lieutenant Quinn said, the helmet radio crackling so loudly Chevy flinched.

They'd drilled this so many times it took only seconds for them to rip the masks from their leg pouches, remove their helmets, slip the masks on, and replace the helmets.

"Ugly One, prepare to fire gas. On my mark, fire," the lieutenant ordered, her voice muffled by her mask.

The XM90s could take gas or grenades, a thing of constant contention. In the heat of the moment, it was a common occurrence to mix up the rounds, but L Tech had yet to find a more practical solution for carrying lethal and nonlethal ammo.

A volley of gas rounds popped into the air. Chevy let out a breath. Gas rounds made a distinct hollow noise when they launched. No one had fired a live round.

"Ugly, all five are down. Weapons near them. I'd move now," the Stef relayed.

"Ugly Three, Ugly One, go," the lieutenant barked. "Ugly Two, you're still on lethal cover."

Chevy counted to four. She held her breath. She counted to four again. It was all happening. Everything they'd been planning for. It was happening now.

Ugly One and Three ran at the wall, which they easily climbed by using one marine as a base from which to launch to the top. Within minutes they were at the guards. Seven minutes from when they launched the gas, all five guards were restrained, and their weapons confiscated.

Chevy leaned back on her heels. It was done.

Was that really it? Had L Tech ordered more marines and Earth-based resources than she'd ever seen for *this*? Maybe the other mines were more heavily guarded?

"Ugly Two, come on up, there's a door to the eastern end of the wall. We'll unlock it now. Time to start the conversion process," Lieutenant Quinn said.

"Ugly, you have ground resources coming in. They should reach you within the next ten minutes or so," the Stef whispered into

Chevy's ear. "We'll be moving off station in two mikes. Behind us is the gunship Yosemite."

"Copy," Lieutenant Quinn replied.

Chevy looked up at the mine, its lights bright against navy-colored night.

What were they missing?

SEVEN

THE CRANE

The Crane and the Banker sat in an office in an unremarkable building in a seemingly normal strip mall. But just like the Crane's quarters, the office was equipped with state-of-the-art surveillance, weaponry, and technology capable of shifting the political infrastructure of an entire nation with the click of a mouse.

The Crane *knew* Launch Tech had found out about the fusion device before anyone else. He scanned the intel report running across a bank of monitors, the raw reportage augmented by contextual details from his retinal feed. The unprecedented influx of marines that Launch Tech had been sending into space had abruptly halted roughly twelve hours ago. Now, the marines were all just up there, sitting, and that made the Crane nervous. Launch Tech was readying, and Exoterra had no clue what they'd do. His moment was coming.

The Banker sat next to him, eyes wide and staring at the drop ceiling, the kind typically marked by stained tiles hovering above disillusioned workers in clip-on ties. This ceiling was pristine and white, comprised of an interlocking web of proprietary, sound-dampening hexagons unique to Exoterra. Unlike the Crane, the Banker didn't mind having large amounts of data play across the insides of his eyes.

The Banker was a tech guru. He could do things that most computer geeks didn't think were possible, and he didn't limit his battles to a screen. As a teen he'd been a star wrestler, which resulted in his ears blooming into full cauliflowers. He had become a tattoo connoisseur as a young adult, and they crawled out of his neckline and toward the Banker's crooked jaw, a result of not tapping to an improperly applied choke hold. He was also an expert marksman, the son of snipers raised in a notably unstable region. One of his ring fingers was missing, a parting gift from a man whose wife he'd wronged. When the man did donate his organs, the Banker sold every profitable piece of him, except for one ring finger, which he sent to said wife, artfully wrapped in a blue ribbon.

A message pinged on the Crane's monitors. The Banker blinked and sat forward, his attention on the screen. The Crane accepted the call.

"Head toward Southern Nevada," the mostly robotic Voice said. "Launch Tech is assaulting several mines across the southern half of the state. We still hold the device, but we expect their intent is to somehow drop it in that area, although the odds of them succeeding are so low, they are almost nonexistent."

The Crane, unfortunately, agreed. Now armed with all the available facts of the situation, he saw no way for Launch Tech to get the device to Earth without Exoterra scuttling it. But he said, "Copy," anyway.

"We have gunships on standby, ready to retaliate. Know we are prepared to take out their network."

"To which they will respond in kind," the Crane said, almost bored. This was going to be a dud of an assignment.

"Yes. Be prepared for no network. You are not to use a competitor network. If the device makes it to Earth, you will secure it and bring it to the prearranged safe house."

The Crane clicked to enlarge the lab feed of EX-10. Three of the five scientists were on camera. Two stared at computer monitors, and one floated over a table, foot hooked on the bar at the floor, hunched over something the Crane couldn't see. Their movements were rushed, their faces sagged, their clothes were dirty. They were obviously running on amphetamines alone at this point.

Then all the scientists on screen simultaneously turned and looked at something off camera. The Crane cycled through the different camera views until he found the one from the hallway that contained the trash hatch. He watched as sparks flew from the wall.

The Crane blinked rapidly, trying to focus the image into something that made sense.

Someone was cutting through the station's external wall.

"What . . ." The Banker's entire focus was on the monitor.

The Crane felt that same morbid fascination one experienced when driving past a car crash on a highway. He watched, knowing something irreversible was happening. A roughly cut doorway appeared in the station wall. Four small figures floated in, Tasers in hand. Aces. They were small, compact, clearly accustomed to operating in zero-g, and they moved with lethal intention. He couldn't see any insignia on their dark fatigues, but a flash of blond poked out from one's beanie. Other than that, they were interchangeable.

"Can you see whose Aces those are?" the Crane asked.

"Working on it," the robotic Voice said.

"Oh wow." The Banker had another window open—the outside of the station. Secured to the outer wall of the station was a trash truck. "They cut through a trash truck."

Trash trucks had five external docks. They could carry four containers, and the final dock was used to switch out full and empty containers. Somehow a competitor had gotten four Aces inside one of the trucks.

"We believe they are with Launch Tech . . ."

The Voice did not sound certain of what it was saying, but the Crane agreed. With all the movement Launch Tech had been making, that was the most likely scenario. The Crane knew, Exoterra would turn them into dog food before they let a *trash truck* hijack the device. And he knew Launch Tech knew that too. Unease flooded his body. What wasn't he seeing?

The Crane and Banker watched one of the scientists barreled around the corner. He held a pipe. The first Ace fired a Taser dart at him, but it went wide. The scientist was close enough to swing the pipe, but he was untrained for zero-g combat, and it showed. The Ace easily dodged the pipe, tapping her foot off one wall and countering with a knife to his throat with surgical efficiency.

"Shit," the Banker said.

The blood bulbed out of the man's neck, in sync with beats from his failing heart. The Aces pushed past him, leaving him to die in the hallway.

They watched the feed from the lab now. The remaining scientists floated, huddled together, clearly tweaking.

"Why is there no sound?" the Banker asked.

"Working on it," the Voice said.

The Aces had rearranged their order, advancing forward like they were trained to do. They entered the lab and spread out, silently yelling at the scientists. They tossed the lab, wrenching the scientists' tools and tablets free from their Velcro.

"Well fuck," the Banker said.

One Ace now held a glowing cylindrical tube. The scientists were saying something, then the Ace with the blond hair pulled out a small piece of metal. She waved it before the cylinder and nodded. The Ace holding the tube slipped it into a bag.

"They have a Conlow bag," the Banker said.

The Crane felt the pieces rearranging in his head. That was it. The NRG, the fucking fusion device. A Conlow bag would shield the device from detection, but they still had to get the device and the bag out of the station, and the Crane did not see how they were going to do that.

The Aces left the lab, pushed past the now dead scientist, and reboarded the trash truck.

"What the hell is their plan?" The Banker tapped his thumb to his fingers, skipping the space his missing finger left like he'd never had a digit there in the first place.

The Crane wondered that too. Exoterra would blow that trash truck out of the galaxy before they let it get away.

Two feeds showed the trash truck's exterior. It sat without fanfare, still connected to the station, and then . . .

"Holy fuck . . ." the Banker breathed.

Four lifeboats, the escape pods mandated to be on every ship and station, launched from the trash truck.

"TARGET THE LIFEBOATS," the Voice screamed.

But the Voice wasn't talking to the Crane or the Banker. The channel had just been left open in this moment of world-altering madness. The Crane watched the only feed that still showed the lifeboats, the tiny pods becoming smaller and smaller until they were indistinguishable from space itself. Whatever shots Exoterra had attempted to take clearly hadn't found purchase.

Those lifeboats were on their way to Earth. Only there was no scientific data to suggest lifeboats would allow someone to reach Earth alive. Every ship was mandated to have lifeboats, but the Crane knew they were nothing more than snake oil for space workers. Reentry to Earth required math so complex it could not be compiled on the fly. When an actual ship reentered Earth's atmosphere, it did so from a predetermined location at a predetermined angle. Lifeboats were meant to simply "drop" from wherever into the atmosphere, reducing the odds of an intact Earthside landing to a very narrow margin. Lifeboats were there to make people feel good, not to actually save anyone.

Never had he seen anything so ballsy. This was pure, unpredictable insanity. And while the chances of the lifeboats reaching Earth were slim, they weren't nonexistent. And the fusion device could survive even if the organic flesh sack accompanying it didn't.

"GET TO NEVADA." The Voice cut through his thoughts.

The Crane's heart fluttered. *If* those pods reached Earth, they would land in Southern Nevada. Launch Tech's plan actually had legs. The device would land on a battlefield, and the fog of war would only further Launch Tech's objective of disappearing the device.

Warmth bloomed in his chest.

Exoterra had just lost their most precious possession.

He would bring it back.

EIGHT

DOLON

Dolon was in bed but unfortunately awake when the phone clanged. He glanced at the clock and cringed. One A.M. was disgusting. The phone sounded again. He bit his lip and opened the screen.

Go to the Zola mine as soon as you read this.

One to four lifeboats may or may not be at the Zola mine.

One will have a Conlow bag onboard.

It's silver, hefty, and should fit into a cargo pocket.

If the network goes out, a set of coordinates will appear on this phone before it bricks.

If the bag is at the Zola mine, collect it and go to the coordinates.

They will bring you to east of Driggs, Idaho.

There is a defunct Sinclair gas station on the state line.

Go to the gas station and get to the dinosaur.

Dolon realized he was sighing. Without grace he messaged, Just the bag?

The phone responded.

The marines will be there.

Leave the people management to them.

If the network goes out, take the bag to the Sinclair station.

END COMMUNICATION

Dolon sighed again then turned on the light next to his bed. Once he was standing, he went to his desk and pulled out his quad maps and road atlas. He located the Zola mine and the Sinclair station east of Driggs. When that was done, he dressed in the clothes he'd laid out the night before. Three minutes later, he shifted into fourth gear, his truck running smooth in the predawn dark.

A thermos of still warm coffee and a breakfast sandwich sat on the passenger seat, both made before he'd gone to bed. Dolon looked back at the house one last time. He'd dropped Captain Picard off with his neighbor, Ms. Daisy, last night. He would miss that cat, but Ms. Daisy would spoil him rotten.

Dolon turned onto the road that would bring him to Dyer and past a fire that burned brightly in the early morning darkness. Old man Jim was slash burning again.

He switched on the radio, which was tuned to the only station that reached his little slice of Earth. Eric Church's "Knives of New Orleans" filled the cab.

Church's voice rang clear, but even it couldn't distract Dolon. He was headed into the unknown, and he knew he might not survive it.

NINE

CHEVY

Chevy stood outside of the mine's main wall, staring alternately at the stars and then at the approaching headlights of the inbound trucks. She had been assigned to rendezvous with the ground units. She watched the first vehicle's headlights bounce with an unseen bump. The two yellow orbs arced before jolting back toward the ground. The lights leveled out and a series of explosions ripped through the desert night.

"EXO gunship Philipito is opening fire!" the Stef's transmission was tinny, meaning the Stef was almost out of range.

"Get out of the mine!" Lieutenant Quinn yelled.

Several balls of fire arched through the air and into the mine's inner perimeter. Screams rose from the now smoky air, and Chevy heard a violent boom from behind her. She turned, expecting to see the convoy, but now only a crater existed where the front of the line had been.

This was a bad situation. Defending oneself from an orbiting gunship was nearly impossible from Chevy's end. She knew that L Tech would be scrambling to fire at the gunships, but EXO's maze of defense satellites would work to defend it. The most Chevy's platoon could hope for was that L Tech would amass enough of a space-based attack to distract EXO from raining death on them from above.

Chevy clawed at her radio volume knob. Someone was shrieking so loudly her ears rang. A marine came staggering from the mine.

"TAN," Chevy cried, catching the kid by his arm.

Tan shook, and Chevy realized his left side was black and charred. Chevy looked back at the convoyed ground units. Those that hadn't been vaporized had spread out and gone dark. This would cool them off and make them less visible from space. Chevy knew a medic was somewhere out there.

"You'll be okay." She jerked Tan's face, so he looked into her eyes. "We're going to get you to a medic. You have to hold on though. You hear me? You need to keep fighting."

Tan didn't seem to understand, then he nodded, his eyes focusing.

"Okay. I'm not leaving you." Chevy tossed Tan's good arm over her shoulders. Explosions continued to rip at the Earth around them. "Let's go, marine."

Chevy hurried Tan toward the darkened convoy screaming for a medic. The undamaged vehicles had stopped closer than their drop ship had landed. Tan stumbled for a while and then went limp. Chevy dragged him toward the nearest truck. A lone figure came out to intercept them.

"MEDIC!" Chevy yelled.

"Here," a woman's voice answered.

The figure stopped at Chevy, and she lowered Tan to the ground. The medic knelt over him and quickly inspected his wounds.

"I've got one with second degree burns and possible penetration injuries. Maybe concussive injuries as well," the woman said into her radio. "Send me a stretcher. He's a big boy, so we're going to need several people."

"I can help," Chevy said.

"And you will, but you'll do it when I tell you, and how I tell you. Step back. You're crowding me."

Chevy did as she was told and watched the woman shuck Tan's mid-layer armor and cut through his BDUs. Chevy was weirded out to be stopped out in the open. Several people arrived with a backboard, and the medic ordered them to load Tan and bring him to one of the waiting vehicles. Chevy grabbed one of the backboard handles, and the group lugged Tan to a transport vehicle.

Chevy passed the stretcher inside and a white light engulfed the night, blinding her. At first Chevy thought she'd been hit. Was this *the* white light? Was she dead? She felt her feet leave the ground, her body weightless. Then her body cratered into something, hard.

When she opened her eyes, her head ringing, she saw she was still in the flaming desert, the mine lights less bright now that several had been destroyed. Screams still surrounded her, and Chevy realized she was tangled on the ground with the medic.

"What in the living fuck was that?" someone yelled.

"Get off of me!" One of the medic's flailing hands connected with Chevy's nose.

Chevy pushed herself to her feet, dragging the medic up with her. The medic scrambled into the transport truck with Tan. Chevy hesitated, touching her nose, still not sure what was going on. She felt sick and kind of dizzy. What had that light been?

"Get in the fucking Humvee!"

Chevy turned to see a major, of all things, yelling at her.

"Sir? My platoon's in the mine. I'm with the marines that dropped in."

"I don't give a fuck if you're with invading aliens. You're wearing the Launch Tech uniform, and I'm ordering you to get in the goddamn vehicle. GET IN."

Chevy hesitated, and the major reached out and pushed her toward a Humvee. He was successful only because of his rank. Chevy climbed in, ending up next to two marines, a man and woman, who were already inside.

The radio was still a mess of garbled voices. Chevy knew she couldn't get through, so she sat in silence and the major climbed into the passenger seat and screamed at the driver to get to the impact site.

Chevy had questions, but she kept her mouth shut. The fact that the Humvee was driving meant the enemy gunships would be trained on it, but no enemy fire came. She silently thanked the Stef and TGSY. They must have been causing enough damage to the EXO stations that they had to defend themselves rather than continue their attack. Chevy held her breath and silently waited for whatever was about to happen.

After about ten minutes of way-too-fast driving, the Humvee screeched to a halt. Chevy was far enough away from her team that her radio was out of reach. Silence filled her helmet.

"OUT," the major ordered.

Chevy and the other L Tech marines scrambled out of the Humvee, but she didn't understand what she was looking at. The ground before her was scooped into a ragged, smoking crater. The smell of burning filled her nose. She looked into the pit and saw its center . . . Was that a fucking lifeboat?

"Get down there and open that thing!" the major yelled.

Chevy and the other marines slid down the edges of the still hot impact sight. Even with her gloves on, Chevy could only keep her hand on the Earth for a few seconds. The three of them tumbled to the crater's bottom, doing their best not to get burned.

Chevy made it to the pod first, but she didn't know what to do. It was still glowing it was so hot.

"Sir!" Chevy called. "It's too hot!"

The major let loose a string of incomprehensible curses, and then two thumps sounded next to Chevy. The major had thrown two fire extinguishers at them.

Chevy picked one up, and the female marine picked up the other. They sprayed the lifeboat. The foam seemed to melt before it even touched the pod's surface, but the glow faded.

"Open it!" the major screamed.

"It's still too hot, sir!" the female marine said.

"JUST DO IT."

Another thump sounded next to Chevy. This time the major had thrown what appeared to be a tire iron at them.

"Break it open!"

Chevy looked up at the major. Fire dotted the area in and around the crater, desert bushes burning brightly against the night air. In those dancing, arcing flames, the major looked possessed. With a surge of primal fear, Chevy grabbed the tire iron and jammed it into the gap between the hatch and the pod. The other marines joined her. They cranked on it with all of their might.

"What in the literal . . ." the woman next to Chevy said.

Chevy stared into the pod, but her brain kept hiccupping.

A tiny, delicate form lay curled in the seat. The person was so fragile looking, there was no way they could have survived crashing to Earth in a lifeboat.

"Is that . . . Is that an Ace?" The male marine's jaw hung so low it looked unhinged.

Chevy looked back at the person in the pod. That was an Ace. The nametape read *Owl*, which was normal for Aces. They never had their real name on anything. Below the letters, in a shade different from the black of the shirt, the Launch Tech Ace insignia shined.

"Wait. Is that? That's a dude. What the fuck?" the female marine said.

Chevy blinked. She was right. That was no lady. She was looking at a man. A man Ace.

"GET HER OUT OF THERE! NOW," the major screamed.

Chevy, startled into action, grabbed the Ace and tossed him over her shoulder.

"There should be something with her! A device!" the major screamed again. "Look in the pod! Is there anything in there? Get her up here. Go through her pockets!"

"IT'S A MALE, SIR," the female marine called.

"I don't give a shit if it's Jesus Christ himself! GO THROUGH HIS POCKETS!"

"Fuck! He's puking."

Chevy heard the male marine say that just when she felt the vomit go down the back of her collar. Gross. She tipped the Ace off of her and onto the dirt, tilting him sideways.

"Get him to the rig! And check his pockets!" the major screamed.

Chevy waited until the Ace appeared to be done puking then hefted him back onto her shoulder. She took a step and an explosion ripped past her.

TEN

DOLON

Dolon hit Highway 6 and spun the radio dial to NPR, which was playing the BBC news hour.

"And Yaz Redderson, retired Lua Um Ace, broke the world's free diving record yesterday . . ." the no-nonsense reporter said.

The Zola mine road was between Tonopah and Warm Springs. It would take Dolon about another half an hour to get to the turn-off for the mine. He hoped what he needed to do would be obvious by then, if he actually had to do something. Maybe he could still be home by dawn. He had a hard time conceding that a corporation as risk averse as Launch Tech would rely on Dolon as their sole hope. They probably had dozens of phantoms out there, meaning *if* he was actually needed, he had a low chance of success. And success and survival were interchangeable here. He didn't like that math.

"She took her record-breaking dive just off the coast of a little Australian town . . ."

Now Dolon held on to every word coming out of the radio, pushing his internal monologue away. The truck's clock hit two A.M. He turned off Highway 6 and started down the desolate road that led to the Zola mine. He could see its lights even from the highway. He was in the right place.

His vehicle neared the mine, and he realized he was not the only person driving toward it. He shut off the radio. A convoy of some mega corps' vehicles snaked down the road several miles in front of him.

Then the space fire started. Explosions ripped through the horizon line, vaporizing part of the convoy he'd been gaining on. He watched the mine begin to smoke, fire spewing into the air, and for a moment, he felt tired. Then the space fire stopped as suddenly as it started. He pressed his foot to the floor and drove toward the disaster.

The sky went white. He couldn't see. He hit the brakes. The truck skittered across the pavement. Something had hit Earth. Or multiple somethings. He had been told to expect up to four lifeboats.

The white faded, and Dolon could see fire about a mile out from the mine, just to the west. He switched the truck into four-wheel drive and jerked the wheel, aiming for the flaming creosote bushes, his shoulders sagging.

The odds of going home weren't looking good.

ELEVEN

CHEVY

The pressure in her skull woke Chevy. Her brain seemed to be swelling, and her chest felt too heavy. Her eyes now open, she realized she was on her back in a crater with her feet at the top of its slope. She moved to sit and found the second source of pressure: The Ace laid limp on her chest.

She pushed him off of her, his body collapsing in an all-too-telling way. Chevy scrambled to her feet. She left the Ace there, assuming he was dead, and struggled up the still hot wall of dirt toward the Humvee. When she crested the rim, her stomach dropped.

Another crater spanned before her. The Humvee, the major, and the other marines were gone. They'd made it to the top of the crater before her, and it had killed them all.

"Fuck," Chevy said.

She wheeled around, looking for cover, and spotted it in a mass of bushes engulfed in flame. Hopefully, she could blend into that heat signature. She took a step toward the fire then looked back at the Ace.

Finding an Ace in a lifeboat had been weird enough, but a *male* Ace? Chevy figured those were only made up for diversity initiatives.

She wasn't sure the Ace was dead, although after whatever had just happened, she wasn't sure he was alive either, but whatever was going on had to do with him. The major had been shitting a brick, yelling that he had something he wanted, to check his pockets. Chevy took a few leaping, sliding bounds, and skidded to a stop beside the Ace.

She began to pad his pockets and jerked her hands away. He'd breathed. *He was alive.* This froze Chevy. Then she realized rifling his gear away from the fire was dumb, so she grabbed him—he was light, too light to seemingly exist—and threw him over her shoulder. She scrambled toward the growing fire, balancing the Ace with one hand and keeping her rifle at low ready with the other.

When she got as close as she dared, she set the Ace down, doing her best to be gentle. He breathed, but they were very shallow breaths. She'd never been so close to an Ace before, male or female. He seemed so slight, so small he could have been a sick child. Yet he was one of the most fearsome of I. Tech warriors. His eyes were closed, he was covered in soot, but there was a magnetic pull about him. She felt herself drawn to his details—the delicate lines of his cheeks, the way his uniform clung to his arms. In a half-dead state, he radiated grace in a way she never did, even when she was scrubbed and shining. He was, despite the circumstances, beautiful.

The fire beside her let out a loud *pop.* Chevy jerked her attention back to her surroundings.

"What the fuck," Chevy muttered.

Everyone knew lifeboats were only on ships to make people think they had a chance if a station ruptured. How was he here? And alive? Chevy needed to get a hold of herself. She needed to realign her priorities based on her new circumstance.

The major's screams came back to her. The Ace had something important. She would start there. She padded his pockets. When she reached the left cargo, she found it. A strangely heavy metal bag. She opened it and saw a glowing tube. She pulled it out and immediately felt stomach-dropping dread. The thing radiated power. This was . . . She would have bet her life on it, that she was holding humanity's first and only working fusion device.

She jammed it back in the bag, hoping the bag was some sort of shield. The device had to be dangerous, but it seemed so benign. Like a glowing toilet paper tube. She took a breath and counted to four. What the fuck was she supposed to do now?

"Fuck." Chevy abandoned the box breathing and ripped off her helmet. She rubbed her eyes. "Oh, fuckity fuck. Shit."

The Ace lay in a heap beside her, the silver bag sat beside him. This was like sitting next to a live grenade. She needed a plan. The wind changed, and the smoke from the fire blew over her. She coughed. Then someone else did.

Chevy jumped, grabbing her rifle and spinning, looking for the source of the noise. The cough—a weak, small noise—sounded again. It came from the Ace. She lowered the rifle and sunk to a crouch, watching him.

He gave a sickly wheeze and opened his eyes. She couldn't tell their color in the flickering firelight, but their intensity stilled her. This man: he commanded attention, respect, and she could not look away.

"You're awake."

His eyes flicked at her voice, and Chevy realized, while he was staring with enough force to light the rest of the desert on fire, she wasn't sure he could actually see. He stared at her with a scary, blank expression.

"Can you talk?"

He didn't move.

"Blink once if you can't talk."

Slowly, with effort, he blinked. Chevy felt herself relax slightly.

"Shit . . . How long have you been in space?"

The Ace blinked ten slow times.

"Does that mean ten years?"

He blinked once. She felt that like a punch to the face. She let her ass hit the ground.

"Jesus. What happens when someone who's been in space ten years takes a fucking lifeboat out of orbit?"

He just stared at her.

"I guess I'm looking at it."

She opened her mouth to say more, then stopped. The Ace took a sharp breath. He looked . . . scared? No wonder he couldn't talk or move. The gravity was actively killing him.

She ran her hand over her shorn skull. "This is crazy."

The Ace stared in her direction like she might attack him. Wait, if he couldn't see, then he wouldn't know they were wearing the same uniform . . .

"Where are my manners? Sorry. I'm Chevy Cole. Corporal of Ugly Two, Launch Tech marine."

She smiled, and despite the fact he was probably dying, the Ace's face softened. He hadn't known. Jesus. This man was stoic.

"Well, it seems you can't talk, but I guess I'll just call you Owl, seeing as that's what your shirt says."

He blinked at her. She nodded back, feeling encouraged.

"Alright then, Owl, did they give you anything? Anything to help with the space sickness?"

He blinked rapidly.

"That mean yes?"

He blinked again.

"In your pockets?"

He blinked, and she began to turn out his pockets. Then she found his IFAK strapped to his waist.

She tore the kit from his gear and pulled it open. All the normal stuff was in there, occlusive dressings, needles for collapsed lungs, and . . . a syringe with white tape. That was not standard.

"Is it this syringe?"

He blinked again.

"Shit. I hate needles. I'm assuming this goes in your ass? I've been jabbed by enough L Tech docs to know."

He blinked, and she sighed. She undid his belt and eased his pants past his butt. For a second, she felt like she was transgressing, but she locked it up. His star power was fogging her vision.

"Sorry." She slammed it into his butt cheek.

He took a series of ragged breaths, and Chevy gently pulled his pants back up and refastened his belt.

"Shit. You look like you're going to puke. At least you're already on your side. Learned that one from my time in too. Put the drunk on their side." She laughed. "Sorry. Not funny," she mumbled. She felt like a clown around this man, this *Ace.*

He heaved and bile flowed out of him. Chevy watched him and remembered that he had puked down her neck. She reached to her collar. It was sticky. She wiped her fingers in the dirt. When he stopped vomiting, he looked at her, sand stuck to his face.

"Tom . . ." he whispered.

TWELVE

DOLON

Dolon wasn't going to be the first to the crash site. The thing, whatever it had been, had hit Earth in a pile of flames. Now, several vehicles were en route to the crash zone. Dolon couldn't push the Ranger too hard; it was old. At first, he thought this would be an issue, then space fire hit all of the vehicles at the site. The impact caused him to stop the truck.

He killed the engine and pulled two black spray-painted survival blankets from the side seat. They would chip, but hopefully the paint would hold up long enough to get him in and out of there in one piece.

He tossed one blanket over the hood of the Ranger and weighed it down with rocks. He got back in the truck, and the phone made a klaxon sound. He checked it.

NO NETWORK

Damn. Dolon didn't like that.

A series of coordinates appeared. Dolon scratched them down on the notebook he kept in his shirt, and the phone went dead.

He stared out across the burning desert, the sounds of gunfire breaking the night air. Fuck. This was really happening. For the first time since Flora had died, he felt fear.

Dolon looked up at the sky. The stars twinkled, and he wondered if a burst of light would erupt and vaporize him and his truck right then and there. Now, duly motivated, he jerked open the passenger door and grabbed his Model 77 Frontier.

He slung the rifle and wrapped a shemagh around his head, then pulled the second survival blanket over his shoulders. The impact site was several hundred yards away. He took off running, aiming for the lines of fire that streaked out from the new crater.

When he got to the edge of the first impact zone, he found slag but no people or vehicles. He ran to the next edge and dropped to his stomach. This crater was deeper than the first. At its center sat what looked to be a charred and mangled space lifeboat.

Then he saw them: two figures, huddled near a wall of burning bushes on the other side of the crater. He figured they were Launch Tech, since the voice on the phone told him to expect Launch Tech marines, although obviously whatever was happening here wasn't going according to plan.

He glanced at the lifeboat. Apparently at least one of them had landed here. His hopes of quickly getting back home evaporated. He focused. He had a twenty-five percent chance that what Launch Tech wanted had been in that pod, and then an even smaller chance that it was still in the pod.

He needed to deal with the immediate threat first. He lifted the rifle and peered through the scope at the two silhouetted figures. One lay on the ground, unmoving. Dolon couldn't tell if he were alive or dead. The other was obviously a space marine, a hulking mountain of a man. The man appeared to be talking to the collapsed figure. He wore a Launch Tech uniform.

Dolon glassed the mine, which was about a mile and a half away from the crash site. Vehicles were inbound. He had to figure this out, fast. He looked back at the figures. They still hadn't moved.

Then the light of the flames glinted off of something shiny.

A Conlow bag, resting on the ground by the marine's knee.

Dolon felt his stomach sink. There was certainly no going home now.

THIRTEEN

CHEVY

The Ace was attempting to speak.

"What?" Chevy tried to understand what he was saying.

"Yesh . . ." His voice was a whisper.

Chevy realized she was having trouble hearing. It was possible she blew out her ears during that last round of space fire. She felt her ass pucker. She wasn't paying attention to her surroundings. How long had she been unable to hear? She looked up and scanned the area around her.

"We have to move. We have to get back to the vehicles."

". . . tom."

"Tom? Your name is Tom?"

"Phantom."

"What?"

The fire had destroyed her night vision. Chevy grabbed the fusion device, tucked safely back inside its metal bag, and jammed it into her cargo pocket. She stood and grabbed Owl, and as nicely as she could, swung him over her shoulder. She adjusted him, got a good hold on her rifle, and began to walk along the spreading line of fire, hoping that its heat signature would obscure her and Owl until she could get back to the heat-shielded vehicles.

Owl wasn't that heavy but carrying him was awkward. The wind had begun to pick up and the fire started to swirl, making it more of a threat than she'd like. It also played with her senses. She swore she heard someone running and whipped toward the noise, only to be greeted by swirling embers.

The wind began to push the fire west, forcing her with it, but she needed to go north to get back to the mine. Chevy walked, the heat of the flames making her sweat. She looked for a gap in the growing fire when a glint caught her eye. Turning, she saw a dented Ford Ranger parked not twenty feet from them.

"Well, shit," she said to herself.

Someone stepped out from behind the car. Chevy raised the rifle and the man put up his hands.

"Come out here!" Chevy yelled.

The man stepped around the vehicle, his hands still up, and moved into the firelight. Chevy didn't know who he was, but something was off. The man's mouth was moving. Chevy couldn't hear him.

The man took a step closer, and Chevy caught a few of his words.

". . . phantom."

"What?"

". . . Conlow bag."

Chevy ordered him to stop, and he did, seemingly unconcerned Chevy had a gun pointed at him. Chevy kept the muzzle on the man and put the Ace down, spinning him so he could see the man.

"Launch Tech sent me. I'm supposed to take the Conlow bag. I know where it needs to go. I'm the phantom."

"You're supposed . . . to get me . . . out," Owl breathed, his voice weak.

The phantom cocked his head.

"What did you . . . No. They said the marines would take care of any people."

"No," Owl managed. "You're . . . supposed . . . to get me home."

Chevy stared at the man and then at the Ace. She could feel the fire creeping toward them, and she knew they were running out of time. Soon flames would box in the Ranger. She could shoot the old coot and steal the truck, but the fact the Ace had been expecting a phantom, and then one had seemingly appeared, meant things were definitely fucked up. Phantoms were a myth. A corporate boogeyman. Yet, here she was, in a totally FUBAR'd situation, apparently staring at one. While Chevy had a lot of thoughts about this, right now, she only had time for the bottom line. If phantoms were real, and one was here, it meant skills beyond her own were needed to survive. That meant shooting the guy was bad math.

"Drive us out of here," Chevy ordered.

The man looked at Owl and then at Chevy.

"You have the Conlow bag?"

Chevy waited a beat then pulled what she now knew was called a Conlow bag from her pocket. The phantom's eyes settled on it. An emotion Chevy couldn't identify flashed across the man's face, then he barked, "Strip."

FOURTEEN

DOLON

"What?" the marine said.

The whipping fire made it hard to hear. The marine's voice bubbled and whirled, like Dolon was listening to it through swirling molasses.

"You both gotta strip. If your drawers are natural, no smart fabric, you can keep 'em. Everything else stays. No tech," Dolon said.

He had followed the marine once he started walking, and Dolon was happy they'd confronted each other near his truck. He could make a dash for the engine block if the marine decided to shoot at him. Dolon probably wouldn't make it, but the thought made him feel better.

"I'm not getting in your car unarmed." The marine held the rifle at low ready.

"Is it smart?"

"No."

Dolon decided to roll the metaphorical dice. "'K. Keep it."

"I . . . need heeelthp."

The guy on the ground was trying to talk again. Dolon was trying to figure out what had happened, but the monster of a marine in front of him was preventing him from applying all his brain power to that question. Dolon was mostly concerned the grunt would kill him. He was told the marines would take care of the people part of this, not get in the way of his part of it.

"He's space sick. He's been up there ten years. You strip him. I'll work on me," the marine finally said.

Dolon hesitated then decided to go with it. He went to the little guy and pulled off his gear and clothing, tossing the Taser into the approaching fire. Dolon saved the knives; he wasn't so out of touch with the world to not respect another person's weapons when he could. He dragged the limp man to the passenger side of the truck, swept the stuff on the seat onto the floor, and set him down. He covered him in a wool blanket and dropped the knives on the floorboard.

"Who is he?" Dolon looked at the grunt. He wore combat boots, a set of boxers, and . . . a sports bra. She? She. That explained the strange pitch of her voice. She held her rifle and the Conlow bag. Everything about her was distracting.

She shrugged. "He's an Ace. A male Ace. Dropped in a fucking lifeboat. Insanity."

Dolon dropped his eyes from her abs to the apparent Ace.

"You think he has any implants?"

"Dunno. They don't tell grunts much about Aces, but he might have smart lenses. No way he's got a retinal display. Maybe he has some sort of com link, though. Check his eyes and behind the ears."

Dolon leaned over and pulled the Ace's eyelids apart.

"Yup, lenses."

Dolon fished the contacts out and tossed them into the desert. He then swept his fingers behind the Ace's ears. He felt a bump behind each ear.

"Looks like you're right. You know how to safely remove a com link?"

The marine stepped to Dolon. Her size belied her femininity, and now he could feel both as if she'd slapped him. He took an involuntary step back, but she didn't seem to notice.

"You just pull 'em out. Hurts like a mother fucker, but beyond the hole they leave, they don't do any real damage." She dug her fingers behind the Ace's ears.

The Ace gasped, his eyes flying open. The marine threw the bloody com links into the darkness. Dolon was unsettled.

"You're in back," he managed.

Dolon pulled another wool blanket from the cab and tossed it at the marine. She caught it but didn't move.

"Wrap yourself in this too." Dolon removed the mylar blanket from the truck's hood.

The marine took the survival blanket, stared at Dolon, seemed to decide something, then walked to the bed of the truck. Dolon watched the truck sink with her weight. Dolon got into the cab.

"Moving!" he called.

The acceleration pushed the Ace against the door of the vehicle. Dolon felt a little bad about how the poor kid was getting tossed around, but he needed to get them out of here.

"I'll get you situated better once we hit the highway."

The Ace muttered something, but Dolon focused on navigating through the burning desert. Then he saw lights in the sky from his rearview. He turned and saw what he knew were helicopters approaching the mines. He pushed the Ranger harder.

After several minutes, they hit the highway. It was paved, and the tires sounded good on the hardtop. Dolon felt his shoulders relax. The helicopters hadn't gunned them down.

He risked a glance at the Ace, the improbable male Ace. He'd fallen asleep. Dolon was worried. The kid looked bad. Blood seeped from behind his ears, his skin was a waxy gray, and he was covered in a lot of sweaty dirt. Dolon didn't know all that much about space travel, but he was pretty sure that you couldn't just drop to Earth after a life in orbit. He wasn't convinced the Ace would survive.

He didn't want to make it to Launch Tech only for them to say his debt was still standing because he'd brought them a dead super soldier, and a dead male one at that. The voice on the phone had said he wouldn't need to move anyone. They just wanted the Conlow bag, or more pointedly, whatever was in it.

Yet, this Ace had been convinced Dolon was there to move him, too, which in some realm of logic, made sense. After all, whatever harebrained scheme brought him to Earth in a lifeboat had to have included the knowledge that he would be a potato once he landed. A quick, sick thought jolted through him.

Launch Tech had obviously not expected the Ace to survive, or worse, they hadn't wanted him to. If they had, they wouldn't have specifically told Dolon not to worry about him. Or there had been a snafu with the marines. It seemed strange that only one of them was actually at the crash site. Obviously there had been more, but he'd only encountered the big gal who was now in the back of his truck. It was one thing to have a ninety-pound quadriplegic in his care. It was another to deal with a 230-pound monster marine. Dolon was smart, and he had to have at least forty years on her. But she had at least fifty pounds on him, as well as youth and a career of lethal training.

Dolon snorted. He knew how to get himself to the Driggs Sinclair, and he could conceive of how to possibly get the Ace there, too, but what if ol' jarhead decided not to go with the program? They could all die.

He looked at the speedometer. He was going a hundred. The truck couldn't keep that up, and he didn't want to get stopped by some corrupt cop. The federal government didn't have a good reputation when it came to justice. Neither did state or local of anywhere he'd ever been. And Dolon knew the contents of his truck would attract attention.

He slowed to ninety miles an hour, five over the speed limit, and continued on Highway 6 past Warm Springs, or whatever was left of it. The junction hadn't had a real occupant since Dolon had lived in Nevada, and he'd been here over forty years.

Dolon had been prepared to disappear into the desert. Blend into the land and make his way to the Sinclair. Now it would be more complicated. While it appeared Launch Tech didn't care what happened to their super soldier—it struck him that there were probably three other Aces who were dead, one to each of the four pods—he wasn't Launch Tech. He couldn't just leave this paralyzed man to die, and he knew the Ace would if he abandoned him. Also, depending on who reached the Ace first, his death could play out in a myriad of horrible ways.

Then there was the grunt. Dolon was now pretty sure she had only been in the wrong place at the wrong time. She made this whole shit show even more fucked. But he had a code and he couldn't, wouldn't, abandon that part of himself in the eleventh hour.

No, he was going to do everything in his power to get the bag, the Ace, and the giant marine to safety. So fading into the desert was no longer an option, especially since two out of the three of them didn't even have clothes.

He sighed. It looked like they were stopping in Ely.

FIFTEEN

CHEVY

Chevy wrapped the blankets around herself like a burrito. It was cold in the back of the truck, even if the old man had strung a tarp over the bed. They had to be moving at close to one hundred miles an hour, not that Chevy knew where they were going. That was only one of the many things adding to her anxiety.

The last several hours had proven to be completely and totally fucked and now she was mostly naked in the back of an apparent phantom's truck, going who knew where. What had happened to her men? She inhaled and counted to four. Battles were dynamic. Things changed. Her men were with the rest of the platoon. She was on her own. They had each other. They were stronger for that. They could count on each other. She could count on nothing.

She slowly counted to four, letting the air out of her lungs.

No. She could count on herself.

Maybe she had made a tactical error and should have killed the phantom. What could he possibly offer, a husk of an old man, that Chevy couldn't provide? He hadn't tried to take Chevy's gun, which was a point in his favor. But they could be headed to some sort of compound with a hundred of this guy's most heavily armed friends.

She needed to get in touch with her platoon, but the man hadn't even let Chevy keep her fucking boots. There was no way the guy would be okay with Chevy calling her unit to tell them where she was. But she needed to know what had happened to them . . . They were her responsibility.

They'd been driving like bats out of hell for over an hour without passing any towns, or even a single building. Chevy hadn't known that places like this still existed in the States. She tried to get comfortable. She was crashing. The adrenaline from the past few hours was wearing off and the smoothie stimulants were mostly out of her system by now. But she couldn't afford to sleep. She didn't have much control over her current trajectory, but she could stay vigilant.

Through a gap in the tarp, she watched the sky turn from black to gray to a blinding splatter of reds and pinks. Finally, a glowing yellow effused the sky, and the sun was up. She'd lived to see another day, somehow. The jury was still out on whether she would live through this one.

Then a car zoomed past them in the opposite direction. They had passed a few speeding semis while driving, but otherwise Chevy hadn't seen any cars in the last two hours. Then another car appeared. She turned, pushed up the tarp, and looked in the direction they were traveling. A smudge of buildings dotted the horizon.

A town.

Chevy settled back onto her stomach and considered her next move.

She knew the Ace was one of her own, and L Tech had captured EXO's fusion device. She had obviously been sent to the Zola mine to ensure L Tech successfully kept the device. War confused things, but her principles remained the same. She was an L Tech marine. The Ace was an L Tech soldier, and they had the device L Tech needed. Chevy had lost her squad but not her objective. The Ace was now her squad, and Chevy would ensure the Ace and the device made it to L Tech.

She had found her new squad.

The phantom, though, he could be anyone . . .

Chevy hadn't existed outside of the L Tech marines since she'd left her parents' home as a teen. As much as she wanted to pretend otherwise, she didn't know how to blend into the "real" world. She didn't even know you could drive for hours in America and not see a single electric light. And speaking of cars, it appeared that the phantom's truck was so old it wasn't self-driving. Chevy couldn't remember the last time she'd seen a human-driven car that wasn't a military vehicle. This only put a point in the guy's column for actually being a phantom.

It was probably good she hadn't killed him back at the mine. She didn't really know how to drive. And while she'd had a few nights of survival training in boot, she really didn't know how to walk out into the land and survive. So it was possible, if the phantom was what he said he was, he was their best chance at succeeding, and ultimately, living. That is, if he in fact knew how to walk through the modern world unseen by the algorithms, unnoticed by the ads, unaffected by newsfeeds, the updates, the status changes . . .

The truck's engine sound changed. They were slowing. She turned to see an approaching exit ramp. The truck veered right, and they were off the highway. Chevy worked to better arrange herself among the contents in the truck bed, which she'd checked out immediately upon it being light enough to see. The phantom had a lot of survival gear and a significant amount of ammo. She gave him points for that.

If they were about to stop, she wanted to be able to see through the gap at the tarp's edge without pressing up on the tarp, so she settled herself accordingly. The truck turned off the ramp and rumbled to a service station. It stopped at an actual gas pump in a bay filled with charging ports for electric vehicles. The phantom's door opened. Chevy couldn't see him, but she heard the news playing from inside the truck.

"*Retired Jinzhan Ace, Lieutenant Colonel Huang, speaks on her singing career and how she captivated the world's stage . . . But first, her new hit single, 'Fire' . . .*"

"I'm going inside to pay. I'll be back," the phantom whispered. The music made it hard to hear him, but Chevy guessed that was the point.

Then he walked away. Chevy was confused as to why they were at a gas pump, until she finally realized the car was so old it took gas, and the phantom must have been paying with cash. Cash? Chevy couldn't remember the last time she'd even seen cash. Something collapsed in her chest. She needed the phantom. How was she this incapable outside of L Tech's world?

A minute or so later, she heard steps. She tensed.

"It's me," the phantom breathed. "Your buddy's sick. I don't know anything about space sickness, and I'm afraid he might die."

"What's he doing?" Chevy asked.

A woman's voice belted from the truck's radio. "*Your love . . . It's fiiiiire.*"

"He's not conscious. He's sweating. His breathing is irregular."

"There's a gradual process to bringing Aces home. Dropping them in a lifeboat isn't fucking it. He's been up there ten years. His heart's fighting gravity," Chevy hissed.

The phantom made an *mm-hmm* noise and a whoosh of a passing truck drowned out the music. "Can we do anything?"

"Beside get him to an actual doctor?"

"Yeah," the phantom said.

"I don't think so."

"Well, I guess we'll go back to the basics then."

"What?"

"I have to alter my plan. The two of you weren't in the original version. Now that you're here, though, I guess we'll lie low for the day."

Chevy heard the nozzle thunk back into the pump. The click of what she knew to be the gas cap sounded, and then the door of the truck whumped shut.

Chevy felt the slam of the door in her gut.

She was, like it or not, on a path she had no roadmap for. The truck accelerated.

There was no going back now.

SIXTEEN

THE CRANE

The Crane and Banker lay on a ridge several hundred yards from the skirmish, the Crane's wiry, compact frame easily hidden by the land's edge. Exoterra marines surrounded him and the Banker, providing security. They watched Exoterra marines and Launch Tech marines fire at each other across the various craters. Bullets and grenades were a very real hazard for the Crane's tech, but he focused on piloting a microdrone over the ongoing battle.

As predicted, when Exoterra took out Launch Tech's network, they had responded in kind. So the Crane and Banker had forgone GPS and navigated to this site from Reno via pre-downloaded maps. But that was why the Crane had been called. He was able to operate without the internet, and while Jinzhan, Tsiolkovsky, Lua Um, and Alpha Orbital all still had working networks, the Crane and the Banker were on their own until Exoterra repaired theirs.

While the Crane could go completely analog, he didn't *need* to do that. He and the Banker had an impromptu mesh network set up between their devices, with terabytes of reference materials on hand. The network being down would make finding their prey more challenging, but he embraced that. Hunting was his favorite sport.

A burst of gunfire caught his attention, and he saw a marine faceplant into the dirt. He knew most of the poor bastards shooting and dying in those craters had no idea what they were fighting for. No doubt they had been told to hold the line as long as possible, and they were doing it without question.

The drone's scans played out in real time into his retinal implant. According to his scans, this lifeboat held residual traces of fusion atoms, although their configuration wasn't what he'd been briefed to expect. Still the traces were close enough, and he was confident that this lifeboat had contained the fusion device. *Had* being the key word. This was already more information than the Crane had expected. He'd been concerned the device had been disintegrated when Exoterra's gunships had opened fire, but his drone would have picked up traces of the splattered fusion atoms if that had happened. And it hadn't. The device had, at one point, been in that crater, and then it had left the crater.

This excited the Crane.

So now he piloted the microdrone, looking for more clues. He needed to see who had taken it.

He would find them. He just had to remain steadfast.

SEVENTEEN

DOLON

Dolon pulled into the Hotel Nevada parking lot. It was nearing seven A.M. Not a busy time on the casino floor so a good time to check in. He also knew that Hotel Nevada prided itself on its old west history. It had advertisements throughout the state. Their rooms opened with actual brass keys, not apps on your phone or implants. Like the good old days.

He parked the truck and looked over at the Ace. He lay slumped in the corner of the vehicle, his breathing a weird, fluttery mess. If he died, Dolon was going to have a hell of a problem. Despite his sorry state, Dolon could see that he was a good-looking guy. Now, though, he looked bad, deathly bad. Dolon's thoughts flicked briefly to Flora in her last days. It had been a while since he'd seen someone so close to a slow death. He got out of the truck and slammed the door harder than he meant to.

He went to the bed and poked at the tarp, attempting to look busy.

"I'm checking us into this hotel," Dolon whispered.

"How are we supposed to get in there without being noticed?" the marine asked.

"One thing at a time. I'll be back."

He walked through the parking lot and into the hotel's side door. The sounds of the casino hit him before his eyes adjusted to the dim light. He stepped onto the dark patterned carpet and wound his way through the blinking machines, taking note of the casino's few patrons—all dedicated, down on their luck types—and made it to the front desk. A fresh-faced girl no more than twenty stood behind the desk, her hair clean, her makeup bright. Dolon felt a pang of sorrow. To be trapped in this place so young. She was probably at her peak.

"I'd like a room please," Dolon said.

"Of course, sir. One bed or two?"

"Two please."

"Alright." She pulled a logbook from the desk drawer. "You'll have to excuse us, it seems our network is down." She looked concerned for a moment before her face brightened. "But the gaming floor is operational! How many nights will you be staying?'

"I'm not sure?"

"No problem. I can book you for tonight." She typed quickly on the keyboard. "We have plenty of room, so as your plans change, you just let us know."

"Thanks."

She smiled nervously. "Technically we can't release a room for tonight until eleven. So, if you want the room now, you have to pay for last night and today."

"That's fine. Can I pay in cash?"

"Of course, sir. This is Nevada." Her voice was confident again.

He smiled and pushed a stack of bills at her, and she gave him two metal keys. He headed up the stairs to the room, which he'd asked to be near the stairwell.

He reached it and went inside. Two beds filled the somewhat dingy space. A window looked out at the old downtown of Ely, the barred storefront of the pawn shop across the street a scenic sight.

The bathroom was clean, and behind the door he found a cheap, terry cloth robe. He grabbed it and headed back downstairs.

He went outside and to the truck. Through the window he could see the Ace, his chest heaving. He was still alive, if barely. Dolon opened the passenger side door and pulled the wool blanket from the Ace. The kid was burning up. He had a fever. Quickly, Dolon dressed him in the robe then shut the door. He walked to the bed.

"I got the Ace in a robe. You can wear your blanket. I think we just gotta do this, get you inside as fast as we can. This place isn't real busy at this hour. We get the two of you inside, and we can work on what comes next."

The marine pushed her head out from the tarp, her half-shaved skull grotesque in the morning light. A second later, she opened the tailgate and snaked out. She stood on the tailgate, the wool blanket draped over her shoulders, towering over Dolon. In the daylight, she was even more terrifying. Dolon took a step back.

"Could you be a little more conspicuous?" Dolon said, feigning confidence he did not feel around her. "And careful with the gap." He could see the rifle barrel hanging in the blanket's shadows.

The marine glared at Dolon but tightened her grip inside the blanket. The rifle disappeared. She stepped to the pavement.

"You got that bag?"

The marine nodded.

"'K. I'll carry the Ace," Dolon replied. "Anyone asks, you guys tied one on a little too hard last night. Lost your clothes in the desert."

"Ha," the marine laughed. "I can act like I've got a hangover."

"Great. Shut the tailgate."

The marine did so, and Dolon opened the passenger door.

The Ace slipped out like a bag of rocks. Dolon caught him, but he was dead weight. Dolon hefted him into a standing position then realized he was going to have to completely carry him. There was no subtle way to do this, and it wasn't going to look good from any angle. Two people with a totally unconscious, very petite human—not on the level.

"Best to get this over now," Dolon said.

The marine shook her head and the two of them started across the parking lot. They got in the casino and hurried between the machines. Most of the people gambling didn't look up as they passed. One woman caught Dolon's eye, but she clearly wasn't sober.

"Get between me and the desk," Dolon said when they neared the front desk.

"Copy."

The marine moved her hulking mass to block Dolon from the fresh-faced girl, and they mounted the steps.

When they reached their room, Dolon leaned the Ace against the wall, fished one of the keys from his pocket, and let them into the room. Once inside, the marine bolted the door, and Dolon put the Ace on the bed.

Dolon looked down at him, sweating, pale, and breathing quickly. For a second, Dolon froze. This seemed all too familiar. Recovering himself, he adjusted the Ace so his head was on a pillow and cinched the robe closed.

"Alright, Pops, we got some stuff to talk about."

Dolon turned to the marine, who had discarded the green wool blanket. She stood in her underwear, rifle in one hand, Conlow bag in the other, staring at Dolon with the gaze of a predator. Dolon couldn't help but notice the way her abs formed a V that led to her boxers. The veins on her biceps stood out proudly, and Dolon was unsettled in so many ways.

"First," Dolon said. "I'm not your Pops. Second, I'm not talking to you 'til you put down the rifle. You're not going to intimidate me into anything, so we may as well just clear that up now."

The marine sized Dolon up, then put the Conlow bag under her arm. She made a show of ejecting the magazine and clearing the round from the chamber, catching it when it jumped into the air. She set the rifle, butt down, in the corner and kept hold of the ammunition.

"What's your name?" the marine demanded.

"Dolon."

"I'm Chevy."

Dolon laughed. "You're straight out of a country song."

"I'm straight out of a warzone, and I'm not sure you're on my side, *pops*."

Dolon sighed. "What do you need to know?"

"How about all of it?"

"Well, you're asking the wrong person."

"Tell me what you do know."

Dolon knew that even with Chevy not holding the loaded rifle, there was no way he would get out of this room if she decided that wasn't going to happen. He let out a tired sigh and sat on the desk chair. He had a rock in his boot.

He lifted his right foot to his left knee, when an automated voice said, "No network detected."

Chevy whipped her head at the TV.

Dolon stood and walked over to it, exhausted. Had Chevy not gone all goon on him, he would have unplugged this piece-of-shit idiot box immediately, but he was tired and now dealing with a meat wad throwing a temper tantrum. His OODA loop was all out of whack.

Dolon unplugged the TV, then popped open the backup battery compartment and removed the batteries. He went into the bathroom and came out with a smart speaker. He unplugged a second speaker from the top of the desk. He opened both and took out their batteries too. Once done with that, he stuffed them under one of the mattresses.

Dolon sat again and began to untie his laces. Finally, he said, "My wife died fifteen years ago. Cancer. It was . . . terrible." He glanced at the Ace whose irregular breathing seemed louder than it had a few seconds before. "I sold my soul to try to save her. I didn't have any real money at the time. Launch Tech offered to give her the royal treatment, on the condition I went to work for them. I said sure. In the end she died, but that didn't get me off the hook with them."

He tugged the laces harder than he needed to.

"Truth be told, I'd make the same bargain again today, even if the pieces were in the same places." He let out a soft laugh. "Hope is priceless, I guess. Anyway, after she died, Launch Tech gave me a phone and said that when it rang, I would do what they said. If I did that, my debt would be paid. Phone rang. I was told to go to the Zola mine, if the network went down, I was to get a Conlow bag and deliver it to a gas station in Idaho. The network went down, so here we are. I was told nothing beyond that, other than I wasn't supposed to deal with any people. The marines were supposed to handle that part."

He cocked an eyebrow at Chevy. She stared at him, unmoving.

"That's it?" Chevy finally said. "That's your story?"

"That's all, that's it." Dolon pulled the boot off and tipped it up. A large pebble bounced off the thin carpet.

Chevy's face screwed into a frown. "So, the Launch Tech network is down?"

"Appears so."

Chevy absorbed this. "You know what's in the bag?" She held it up.

"Nope."

"You're serious?"

"Don't know, don't want to know. Also, don't take it out. That bag is maybe shielding whatever it is from Skynet."

"Skynet? How old are you?"

"Old enough." Dolon unlaced the other boot. "So, what about you?"

"What about me what?"

"I know why I'm here. You now know why I'm here. Why are you here?"

"I'm a Launch Tech marine."

Dolon tipped his head at Chevy. "You don't say."

"Our mission was to take the Zola mine. We did, and then all hell broke loose. A bunch of fucked-up shit happened, I got hit by space fire, and when I woke up, everyone but he and I were dead. But he had it. He had the device. The *fusion* device. The *only* fusion device."

A fusion device? Fuck. Dolon did not like that. And, if he thought what that meant for him, for the world, he was going to get distracted. He did not have time to get philosophical. So he said, "The Conlow bag."

"C'mon, are you going senile?"

Dolon stared at the kid, because that's really what she was, a kid in a giant, soldier's body. "You're telling me the thing in that bag is for real?"

"Yeah. I am."

"Is it stable?"

"How the fuck should I know?"

Dolon opened his mouth to ask another question, then stopped. The repercussions of fusion's existence, good or bad, they didn't matter. He was here to settle a debt. That was it.

"I'm going out. I'll get you both some clothes. Don't use anything digital while I'm gone. Especially don't get on the internet. Launch Tech's network was killed and from what I can figure, that's why the three of us are here. There's absolutely no reason the three of us would be in this room with that thing," he pointed at the Conlow bag, "if Launch Tech was running at full power. They told me to go dark and assume I was being tracked. So we aren't using *any* form of technology as long as we're running for our lives. Because that *is* what we're doing. Any trace we leave could be the thing that kills us."

Chevy's jaw flexed. "How long will you be?"

"Dunno. My original plan was to move myself and an unspecified object to Idaho. Now I got you and him, assuming he lives, and fucking fusion. This changes shit."

"What do I do while you're gone?

"Did you bring a book?"

Chevy wasn't amused.

"Then grab some shut-eye."

Chevy glanced at the Ace. "What's the plan for him?"

"I'm not sure there's anything we can do," Dolon said. "I guess we just wait and pray. Not that that's ever worked for me before."

EIGHTEEN

CHEVY

Chevy waited for Dolon to leave before sitting on the unoccupied bed. She was exhausted, and squaring off to Dolon had been tiring. It was one thing to have the adrenaline of war rushing through her, pushing her forward, but to have to play a game of verbal judo with a possible enemy after all that had just happened? While she was in just her undies? Her actual armor lost to the desert, without any chance of backup . . . She could not let the hopelessness of her situation overwhelm her.

She fell back against the covers. Now that Dolon was gone, she could hear Owl's short, desperate breaths. She looked at him. What was she supposed to do? Just take a nap while he died slowly next to her?

Again, she was caught by his magnetism. Despite his wrecked physical state, he radiated something that made her feel insecure . . . insignificant, even. She wasn't physically intimidated by him; he was so slight. But her own misgivings about her body, her size, and her lack of beauty all hit her with full force when she looked at him. He was perfect compared to her. This only solidified why she liked being a grunt. None of that stuff mattered. Beauty, allure, sexiness . . . Just doing the work mattered in the marines, and by doing the work well she could achieve her own version of beauty. But now, outside of her L Tech world, with an actual superstar Ace . . . It made her feel alien on her home planet. Her form of grace was nothing compared to his.

Owl's breathing hit a desperate pitch. She locked up her own issues. He needed help. If only she had her phone, at least then she could do some research. Hell, she would have used the TV, if it had network, although Dolon had been clear in his orders. Not that Chevy was really on board with taking orders from him. Still, she was in a bit of a pickle. She had to tentatively trust the phantom, at least until he got her a pair of pants and some shoes. Before Dolon had left, he'd asked Chevy her sizes, his eyes growing huge when Chevy had told him. Chevy wasn't sure she'd end up with footwear from this town.

She refocused. What the phantom had said made a weird amount of sense. The world was so dependent on technology that losing the network should have been a death blow. Unless they had a Hail Mary. Like a phantom.

Chevy groaned. She did not like being a part of a Hail Mary.

She stood and began to pace, but her attention again keyed on Owl's irregular breathing. She went to him. His peach fuzz hair was slimy and damp. Dirt coated him, and he smelled. Chevy realized if he'd been in space for ten years, he also hadn't had a real shower in all that time. Sponge baths only in orbit.

She glanced at the bathroom. If this were one of her teammates, she'd strip him down and put him in the tub to cool him off and clean him up. But this was an Ace. He wasn't one of her marines. But it wasn't just that. Female Aces were a prime sexual fantasy of straight male and queer female marines. And while Chevy wasn't either, the idea she might be about to see a naked male Ace had her off balance. She felt like she'd be transgressing if she stripped off his chonies. She also realized she wanted to see what was under them, and that made her sick. He was dying.

Chevy mentally kicked herself. She'd decided in the truck. This Ace was *her* responsibility now. She would do anything and everything to protect him. She picked him up and moved into the cramped bathroom. She turned on the water, fiddled with the temperature, plugged up the tub and grabbed the hotel soaps from the sink. She unwrapped them and set them on the tub's edge, the Ace's breathing quickening.

Chevy was a professional, she could do this. When the water was full enough, she stripped the robe from the Ace. He wore the standard issue, male Launch Tech boxers and a thin piece of leather around his wrist. She left the bracelet alone and, taking a breath, she peeled off his underwear.

She got him into the tub quickly, although without the grace she would have liked. He was so slight, and without the disgusting undergarment, he initially seemed even smaller, until she clocked all of him. He wasn't entirely dainty.

Methodically, she went about washing him, just like she'd been taught to wash herself in boot. At the time, she'd found it ridiculous that she'd been drilled into bathing in a prescribed manner and order, although when she became a corporal, she realized that lesson hadn't been for someone with her hygiene habits. Now though, she was glad L Tech had made bathing rote. She started at Owl's hair and moved to his feet, doing nothing with her mind but counting to thirty each time she moved to a new body part.

When she was done, Owl's condition actually seemed to improve. His breathing seemed to have leveled out, and his skin wasn't as dull. Now that he was clean, she saw he had olive skin, and hair so black it shined in the bathroom light. She picked him out of the tub, swaddled him in a towel, and set him on the bed. Chevy left him there so she could shower. Once she was showered and wrapped in her own towel, she stepped back into the bedroom. Owl's eyes were on her.

"You're awake!"

"Yesh."

"I gave you a bath. I thought it would help. I didn't . . . Nothing happened, other than the bath. You look like you feel better?"

Chevy sat on the bed across from him. She realized his head was positioned to see up her towel. She refused to cross her legs, so she dropped her hands between her knees as nonchalantly as possible.

"I . . . feel . . . behtar."

"You aren't breathing so fast. And you're awake. That seems good."

"Yeah."

"Dolon is out getting us clothes. The Phantom."

"The . . ." His eyes swept the room.

"Oh, yeah. Your device is here." She fished it out from under the pillow on her bed.

His eyes relaxed.

"Dolon said he's supposed to get the device to a gas station in Idaho. Says he wasn't told to expect people. Says the marines were supposed to take care of any people. I'm a marine. No one told me shit, not that that's new. I'm a fucking corporal. Still, the math is bad."

He stared at her, his eyes wide and unblinking.

"Is there anything we can do to help you? I doubt old Dolon is going to want to bring you to a doctor. As much as it chafes me, I think we gotta stick with him. I don't know how to be alive and not use anything digital. All that shit's tracked, and he has *cash.* Actual cash. And I look like a fucking space marine. And you, well you can't walk, so . . ."

"We . . . need . . . him."

"I'm not even supposed to be here. I just met the wrong major at the wrong time. I don't even know what happened to my men."

"The other . . . pods . . ."

"What?"

"Where?"

She stared at him then finally realized what he was asking. "You were the only lifeboat."

He looked away from her, his eyes wet.

"I'm sorry," she said, but she knew it didn't help.

NINETEEN

THE CRANE

The Crane stared at the screen. He was parked at a service station in Tonopah, a cup of coffee in one hand, his tablet in the other. He scanned the drone's report while their rig charged, his long legs bent in the car's passenger seat. He had traces of fusion that led nowhere beyond the crash site. Not far from where they found those traces, they'd found a set of all-purpose tire treads that lead to the main mine road.

"Goodyear Wranglers, sir," the Banker said from the rig's driver's seat.

The Banker sat, his eyes open, staring at the roof of the vehicle. The Crane knew he was comparing the photos from the microdrone to the data stores they'd brought with them.

"It's a common all-purpose tire. I'd say a Jeep, maybe a truck, possibly an SUV," the Banker continued.

"Does Launch Tech use that tire? On any vehicles?" the Crane asked.

"Yes, but it's also a popular civilian model," the Banker said.

"So, they drove out of there, but they can't be far, unless they flew somewhere, which is possible, if they were operating with just instruments."

The Banker leaned back in his seat, his eyes still roving the ceiling.

"While it is in the realm of possibility," the Banker said, "the risk of landing and taking off in a warzone without a functional defense network puts the odds of success lower than I believe Launch Tech would want to accept. The numbers are telling me it's more likely they left via ground."

"And the Ace is, if she's alive, actively dying. If they want to save her, they'll probably head to a town."

The Banker blinked. The Crane could tell by the way his eyes focused that he was no longer looking at data.

"I doubt they would take her to a hospital. Not if they're trying to get the device to a safe house. Besides, the mission was a suicide run. Launch Tech probably planned on her dying. One less loose end."

"I agree, but they'll need to charge their vehicle, and they could try to medicate her. Let's look at the nearest towns with pharmacies," the Crane said.

"This place fits that bill." the Banker gestured out the window at the blinding desert peppered with washed-out buildings.

"Yes, but I doubt they're here. Too close to the mine."

The Banker's eyes swiveled upward. After a moment, they returned to the Crane's.

"Boss, I think we need to do this old school. The library in this town has computers on Alpha Orbital's network. Give me ten minutes from a public terminal, and I can pull video from the surrounding town's service stations. I can cross-reference it with medication requests from those towns."

The Crane considered it. Exoterra didn't want them on anyone's network but their own, but time was fusion, and their prey was widening the gap between them and the device. The Crane knew what Exoterra said they wanted, and what they really wanted. Recapturing the device trumped everything else.

"How traceable will it be?"

The Banker bobbed his head. "I prepped several viruses for this. I know Exoterra said we'd be without any network access, but that's stupid. Those orders would be fine if all the networks were down, but they aren't. I'm not interested in fighting honorably. I'm interested in winning, and we can get the information without leaving a trace."

He pulled a data drive from his bag.

"Alpha Orbital won't care about a slagged computer in a shithole of a town. Even if they did make the connection between it and our mission, this will corrupt everything."

"Do it," the Crane said.

The Banker smiled and tapped each hand's fingers to the corresponding hand's thumb. Four was the Banker's lucky number. Before every aggressive move he made, the Banker did a movement in quadruple. Initially, the Crane thought such behavior to be superstitious. Now he knew it simply focused the Banker's mind. It wasn't weakness, it was professionalism.

The Crane tightened his abs. It was easy to let his posture get lax with so much sitting. Drawing his shoulder blades together, he exhaled and felt a twinge at the back of his head. He was jumpy and wound tight. Running was the immediate answer. While the Banker was at the library, he'd get out and let go of some of the early hunt nerves. Before he did that though, he had one more thing to do.

He flicked his eyes and brought up a downloaded video feed to his retinal display. With the network down, he couldn't watch it live, but he'd saved some of his favorite videos for this trip. He activated one from three weeks ago.

Lucy, the desert tortoise of the San Antonio Zoo, appeared on the inside of his eyes. The Crane watched a zookeeper feed her a crisp piece of lettuce, her sharp beak snapping the leaf with a delightful intensity. The Crane let the dopamine generated from the video saturate his brain.

TWENTY

DOLON

Dolon walked to the librarian's desk. Libraries of the modern age were overwhelming to him. They were not the quiet, book-filled spaces of his youth. No, today's libraries lived in community centers. They were built into complexes that contained gyms, daycares, virtual reality decks, and library servers, which held digital media. He couldn't remember the last time he'd been in a library and seen an actual printed book. This particular library appeared sickeningly modern to him. As he expected, he didn't see a single book. The library's hand drawn signs touted a robust collection of visual and auditory media.

Behind the librarian's desk, a TV played, subtitles rolling below a newscaster. Photos of burning buildings, exploding bridges, and crying people flashed on the screen.

"*Launch Tech has launched four synchronous assaults against Jinzhan, Tsiolkovsky, Lua Um, and Alpha Orbital . . .*"

Dolon didn't want to know more. He looked away and stepped to the desk.

"Hello." The librarian was about his age, and her smile was warm. She wore a name tag that said Alex.

"Hello, ma'am." Dolon took off his hat and held it in his hands.

"Oh please, 'ma'am' is for my mother." She blushed.

"Miss."

She tittered.

"I'm driving through town, and I forgot to pack my medicines for my horse. We're headed to California for a show. Is there a vet in town who might be willing to help me?"

Dolon had figured a good place for local knowledge was the community center. He watched Alex's face change and knew he'd figured correctly.

"Well," she dropped her voice, "there is Dr. Morgan, but well, he's rather young and . . ." she sniffed, her mouth turned down. "I think you should go see Dr. Bakirtzis. She's . . . much more flexible."

"She sounds wonderful." Dolon forced a smile. "How do I reach her?"

Twenty minutes later, Dolon pulled down a dirt road near the outskirts of town. His Ranger bounced over the rutted lane until he pulled up to a sprawling ranch house, parked in the driveway, and got out.

This was a step back in time. The house didn't have any obvious smart enhancements. A human and not a machine had clearly planted the garden; the flowers were not spaced exactly the same distance from each other. The porch sloped at an angle that suggested it had been built without the aid of modern leveling technology. He took in the house, feeling better here than he had in the library. Then he noticed a hand-painted sign that said to ring the bell if looking for veterinary help. He did so.

A moment later, a middle-aged woman opened the door.

"Hello, ma'am," Dolon said, keeping his hat on due to the sun. "I'm looking for Dr. Bakirtzis."

"That's me." The woman peered past him at his truck then wrinkled her nose. "How can I help you?"

"I'm traveling and lost my horse's midodrine. I was hoping you could prescribe her a replacement."

Dr. Bakirtzis stared at him flatly. He took off his hat and clasped it in his hands.

"Your horse is prescribed midodrine?" Her voice was devoid of inflection.

"Yes, ma'am."

"And why don't you call your own vet to renew the prescription?"

"She's on vacation."

"And why doesn't whoever she left in charge do it?"

"I can't get ahold of them."

"And where is your horse?"

"She's with the trailer. A tire blew. My wife is waiting for the tow truck with her."

"Does your horse have a name?"

"Bronco."

"You named your mare Bronco?"

"Mares can be broncos."

Neither said anything for several moments, then Dr. Bakirtzis replied, "I'm not going to lie for you."

"I wouldn't expect you to."

The woman studied him and his truck before once again leveling him with her blue eyes. He did his best to look beseeching and trustworthy.

"Wait here," she finally said.

She disappeared back into the house. A moment later, she returned with a piece of paper.

"Thank you."

"You need to leave."

It wasn't until he pulled into the thrift store parking lot that he looked at the prescription slip. It was from the office of Dr. George Bakirtzis. The prescription was for ninety 10 mg tablets of midodrine, with one refill written to Bronco Mays. Dolon wondered who George was. And why the vet had chosen to give Bronco the last name of Mays.

He let out a long breath. He'd done the research in the library. He'd been forced to use the digital archives, which he didn't like, but he knew the Ace would probably die if he didn't. He'd learned that astronauts were often given midodrine to combat the hypotension that onset with reentry. He'd gambled, and Alex the librarian had sent him to the right woman. This was the first stroke of good luck he'd had since picking up the Ace and grunt.

He tucked the paper into his wallet and walked into the thrift store, even though it annoyed him completely. He wasn't supposed to be dealing with people, just the stupid Conlow bag. Yet, in addition to getting the Ace medicine, he now had to shop for him and the grunt, Chevy, like they were infants. Launch Tech had changed the rules at the last second, but Dolon's indefatigable moral compass wasn't going to allow him to do anything but try to keep the two interlopers alive, even if it killed him. It didn't matter what Launch Tech was plotting. Dolon would do what was right. He huffed, grabbed a basket, and found a set of huge boots buried under a heap of scuffed high heels. He threw them in the basket. Chevy might get usable shoes after all.

Buying clothes for both the Ace and Chevy had initially seemed doable, but upon turning to the clothing racks, Dolon was immediately overwhelmed. Chevy was big, but would a men's

3XL fit her? She wasn't a man, even though she was bigger than Dolon ever would be. Was there really a big difference between men and women's clothes? He found two T-shirts labeled unisex that seemed big enough for her. One was red, white, and blue. Across its front was a cartoon of angels flying above several fat men with beards waving assault rifles. Dolon wasn't sure if Chevy would love or hate it, but the selection was limited. She had told him her inseam, and somehow, he found two sets of work pants in her size, although if they would fit her curves, Dolon wasn't sure. He tossed a bunch of other things that seemed big into the basket too, just in case.

The Ace was even trickier. It occurred to Dolon that women's clothing might better fit him. But women's sizing was completely foreign to Dolon, especially with Flora no longer in his life. He found several T-shirts that seemed like they could possibly fit the Ace, but . . . Fuck it, the little guy wouldn't know the difference.

At the dollar store next door he picked up socks and underwear, and a large sports bra for Chevy. The image of her standing before him in just her boxers and bra popped into his head and made him uncomfortable again. In the same strip mall, he filled the prescription and grabbed four orders of Chicken Tikka from an Indian restaurant beside the pharmacy. Finally, he was done. Mission complete. This one, anyway.

In the parking lot, he saw a Ford Ranger that looked a lot like his, albeit this one was electric. It was parked behind the Indian restaurant. He went to his truck, dropped the food and pills, and pulled a multi tool from the glove box, then went around to his rear license plate. He removed the plate, then walked over to the other Ranger and switched it with his. He had the new plate on his truck in a matter of minutes, jumped in the driver's seat, and pulled out of the parking lot, pointing the truck toward the hotel.

Fifteen minutes later, he made three slow, long knocks on the room door and waited.

TWENTY-ONE

CHEVY

Chevy jerked awake. She didn't recognize the room she was in. She sat up, realized she was wearing a robe, and remembered her situation. She turned to the Ace. He was under the covers on the other bed, asleep, his breathing ragged and alarming. He was hers to protect now. This caused a mishmash of stirrings in her gut, but mostly she just felt helpless watching him.

They had talked for a few minutes after she'd bathed him, and then she'd told him his teammates were probably dead. He'd turned away from Chevy and had eventually fallen asleep. Chevy hadn't pressed him then. She'd just let him grieve because they both knew the odds of them having survived were long. When she'd heard his breathing change, she'd tucked him into the covers and removed the wet towel. It appeared she'd then fallen asleep too.

She rammed her hand under the pillow and felt the Conlow bag. Just touching the device made her blood pressure drop. That's when she realized someone was knocking on the door.

Silently, she swung her feet to the floor and grabbed the rifle from beside her bed. She crept to the door and checked the peephole. Dolon stood there, looking nervous.

Chevy unlocked the door.

"Get some shut-eye?" he asked, his voice a mixture of anxiety and annoyance.

He dropped the bags he was holding and set what was obviously takeout on the desk. Chevy shut and locked the door.

"I might have dozed off."

Dolon nodded, looking at Owl.

"How is he?"

"I gave him a bath."

Dolon gave her a flat stare. She held up her hands.

"What, you think because I'm a marine, I'm a monster? He was burning up and covered in crap. He actually did a little better for a bit after the bath. Then he fell asleep and started breathing all weird again."

Dolon rifled through the bags he'd set on the floor. He pulled out a small white bag and dumped a pill bottle into his palm.

"I did some research. We give him one of these every eight hours, and it should help."

"What is it?" Chevy asked.

"It's a med they give astronauts when they come back to Earth. It helps with low blood pressure."

"How'd you get it?"

"I got linked up with a sympathetic vet."

Chevy nodded. That was always a good bug-out plan. But it could be traced.

"You were right. I checked on the status of Exoterra's network. Both theirs and Launch Tech's are down. And your employer is starting fights with everyone."

"My employer?"

"Launch Tech attacked Alpha Orbital, Tsiolkovsky, Lua Um, and Jinzhan."

Chevy would have to think on that. “We should still leave soon.”

“The other Big Six’s networks are still intact, though, which I guess means Exoterra could be using an ally network.”

“Maybe,” Chevy said, “but I think their first plan would be to keep the fusion device for themselves and not share it with anyone.”

“Really?”

“It depends on how long it takes for one of them to fix their network. Whoever gets theirs up first forces the other into a corner.”

Dolon nodded slowly then motioned to the bags. “I got you clothes. I’m going to give him this.” He held up the pill bottle. “It’s noon now. He gets another dose at eight and we just keep it up for as long as it takes.”

“Copy.” Chevy looked into the bags. “What the fuck is this?”

She pulled out the angel shirt.

“It’s what they had in your size.”

“You should have gone to another store.”

Dolon said nothing, and Chevy looked through the rest of the bags.

“Why’d you get him so many clothes?”

“I had no idea how to shop for either of you. You’re giant, but you’re a woman. They didn’t have that section. And he’s small and a man, and I couldn’t figure out what section to shop in for him either. Women’s sizing makes no sense. I got what I thought could work. You’re lucky you gave me actual measurements, maybe something I got will work for you, but for him . . .” Dolon tossed his hands in the air.

“This is funny.”

“What is?”

“I dunno. I guess that you thought either of us would wear this?”

Chevy held up what appeared to be a giant flowered muumuu.

"This could fit me, but without pockets it's not really practical."

She pressed it to her chest and swiveled at him. Dolon, now holding a glass of water and the pill bottle, glared at her.

"And you, in your infinite wisdom, of what, nineteen years, know how to shop for someone of the opposite gender?"

"I'm twenty-four . . ."

Dolon snorted. "Excuse me."

"I can dress a man, old man. I could dress you, if I chose to."

"I didn't know you swung for men."

"Ahh, I'm not playing that bullshit game. I'm just saying, for someone as old as dirt, I figured you'd bought a lady a pair of underwear before." She held up the pack of large boxers.

"You're wearing boxers now!"

"Calm down. It's standard issue, not my choice." Chevy hefted a set of sweatpants. "I mean, what happened here? These are too small for me, and he'd have to gain a hundred pounds to wear these."

The skin above Dolon's white beard reddened, and Chevy realized she'd hit a nerve.

"Fine, figure out what will work, and we'll ditch the rest."

Chevy considered saying something else but nodded instead. She picked through the clothing while Dolon woke up Owl and convinced him to swallow the pill. He made some mumbling noises but got the pill down.

"'K, these we should keep. This stuff we can leave." Chevy pointed at the two piles she'd made. "Not all of it was trash."

Dolon nodded. "I got some food. Eat your fill."

Chevy glanced into the bag.

"I could eat all of this. You and Owl should eat first, and I'll eat everything that's left over."

Dolon looked like he might argue, then said, "Maybe you can put on some clothes while I try to get some food in him."

Chevy laughed, looking down at the gaping robe she wore. "Sure thing."

The pants Dolon bought her actually fit pretty well. The shoes were a little tight but after having worn standard issue boots forever, she was used to having footwear that was either too big or too small. They wouldn't jam her up too badly. The angel and assault weapon tee was something she'd never wear, but she was in Nevada. Here was as good of a place to wear it as anywhere.

Dolon sat on the edge of Owl's bed spooning curry into his mouth. He slowly chewed, keeping his eyes shut, and after a few minutes he turned his head away. Dolon tempted him to drink a few sips of water, then pushed the rest of the food boxes to Chevy.

"I'll eat what he left in this one." Dolon gestured to the box and took a bite of the curry.

Chevy was starving and eating actual food, not processed soy, was heavenly. She tried to slow down to taste the spices, but by the time she consciously slowed herself, she'd eaten two of the three boxes Dolon had given her.

"You were hungry," Dolon said, raising an eyebrow.

Chevy nodded and considered Dolon. Tan-faced, with a white beard and bushy white eyebrows, he wore green pants and a long-sleeve work top. His wide-brimmed hat rested next to his boots, and he looked like a guy who had worked hard most of his life.

"How old are you?" Chevy asked.

"Why do you want to know?"

"You know how old I am. I figure I can know how old you are."

"I'm sixty."

"Whoa. Yeah, you've seen some stuff."

Dolon shrugged. "Sure."

"So, what do you do? When you aren't being a phantom?"

"I stay off the grid."

"What does that mean? You live underground?"

Dolon gave Chevy a look that Chevy found insulting.

"I have some property at the base of the Whites; that's a mountain range on the Nevada/California border. I'm a handyman. I mostly keep to myself."

"Sounds lonely." Chevy spooned more food into her mouth. "I'm surrounded by people all the time. I don't think I could just *keep to myself*."

"It grows on you."

"What?"

"Solitude. I read. Build things. Spend time with my cat."

"You have a cat?"

Dolon nodded. "He's living with my neighbor, Ms. Daisy, right now. She'll spoil him while I'm gone."

It took Chevy several seconds to realize her mouth was hanging open. Was this man for real?

"You have a neighbor named Ms. Daisy?"

Dolon let out a long breath. "What about you, jarhead. What's your story?"

"Enlisted when I was eighteen. Before that I lived in bumfuck Mississippi. My family thought education meant learning to cook, so I've never looked back." Chevy downed more of the food. "I'd die for Launch Tech. Without them I'd be a sad copy of my mother."

"Not a fan of the conservative ways."

"Nope."

Dolon nodded slowly. "I can appreciate that."

Chevy nodded, licking some curry from her lips.

"Launch Tech could be just another form of that, though," Dolon continued. "They'll sell you down the river if the price is right. It may not be that expensive of a ride."

"What are you saying?"

"You know what I'm saying. They expected him to die." He gestured at Owl. "I was told to expect four pods. And by my understanding, Aces are worth more than grunts. Be wise, my young friend. You work for a monster, even if it has moments of benevolence."

Chevy felt her jaw flare. Nothing Dolon said was earth-shattering. She knew she worked for a mega corp and was only a small cog in a giant machine. Even though she knew that Launch Tech had expected Owl to die and had possibly sent three of his peers to their deaths in a crazy half-baked plan, Chevy couldn't hate them. Launch Tech was focused on the big picture. Little things were often sacrificed for the greater good. Little Chevy and little Owl knew this when they joined up. Everyone in the military did.

Life was too messy and complicated to divide into neat categories like good or evil. So as much as what Dolon said was true, so was the love she had for Launch Tech. Loving and hating the same something was possible. Chevy's life was built on that.

TWENTY-TWO

THE CRANE

The Crane ran toward their parked car, the Nevada wind pelting him with sand. He sprinted down Highway 95 as fast as his body would let him. The unfortunate state of bio-upgrades was that they had yet to invent one that increased a person's cardio or physical strength. There were beta versions of those upgrades, but none he was willing to put into his body in their current form. As such, it was on him, and only him, to be in peak physical form.

This town sucks, he thought, sprinting back to his vehicle. The people, the buildings, the land, all of it depressed him. Ramshackle trailers on tailing piles, wrinkled, hunched people, nothing but barren too-bright dirt swallowing him. He ran hard, doing his best to put distance between him and the sad state of this place. But even after having run three miles in fifteen minutes, he felt the disgusting town clawing at him.

They needed a clue so they could start their pursuit. He could not sit in town any longer. He hoped the Banker had found something.

He stopped at the SUV and took a second to settle himself. When he was breathing normally again, he pulled open the front passenger door. The Banker sat inside.

"Anything?" the Crane asked.

The Banker looked away from the ceiling and smiled, his bent jaw casting a sinister shadow.

"You were gone fifteen minutes. I told you it would take me only ten."

The Crane folded himself into the vehicle.

"Fine. You win. What did you find?"

"Well first, Launch Tech is rewriting the globe."

The Banker flicked his eyes and a series of documents appeared on the Crane's retinal display. They were news stories. Just after starting the battles across Nevada with Exoterra, Launch Tech had gone to war with Tsiolkovsky, Jinzhan, Lua Um, and Alpha Orbital. Tsiolkovsky's HQ had been overwhelmed in minutes. Alpha Orbital had surrendered. Lua Um was unreachable. Only Jinzhan was still fighting. Launch Tech had changed the balance of global power in a matter of hours. But they were doing it in a sideways fashion. They were not fighting their true enemy, Exoterra, head-on. Still, by absorbing the other Big Six, they became incredibly dangerous to Exoterra.

"This is unsettling," the Crane said.

"Agreed, but I don't believe it changes what we need to do."

"I concur. If we succeed, we will still be stronger than Launch Tech."

"Yeah. Which is why I think we should go to Ely."

"Where the hell is Ely?"

"It's northeast of here."

"Tell me," the Crane said, pulling the door shut.

"First, one of the service stations just off the highway has original version smart *gas* pumps. The tech is outdated, but they aren't so old that they don't have listening and targeted ad features. One of the pumps caught a male voice saying what sounds like *space sick*."

"I'm listening."

"In addition to that, a vet from Ely wrote a prescription to Bronco Mays for midodrine. After I found that, I checked their library search records. A guest user, no pertinent information given, made several inquiries about space sickness, including the use of midodrine."

"Explain."

"Midodrine is a drug commonly used to treat the hypotension related to reentry in astronauts. Based on my cursory research, you don't give it to animals."

The Crane smiled. He grabbed a protein packet from the center console and dumped it into a water bottle.

"The library's cameras are down, but the service station might have captured some footage at the pumps," the Banker said. "We need to go there to access it."

"Well, let's hope Ely is nicer than Tonopah," the Crane said.

TWENTY-THREE

DOLON

Dolon watched the road, but he couldn't help glancing at the Ace while he drove. The kid looked better than he had when they first pulled him out of the desert, but still. Dolon was just waiting for him to decompensate and die. He'd seen it before. And it was clear the kid wasn't firing on all cylinders. They'd been having the same conversation since the Ace had woken up and realized they were back on the road.

"Where are we going?" the Ace asked, again.

"I'm supposed to get the Conlow bag to a gas station on the Idaho border," Dolon said, again.

"But not me?"

Dolon shifted. "They said the marines were supposed to handle you."

The Ace looked at the bed of the truck. Chevy was there, back under the tarp.

"So things went sideways."

"Looks like."

Last time they got to this part of the conversation, the Ace went silent. Dolon thought that was what was happening again, but the Ace surprised him.

"You . . . Are you former military? Phantom work is . . . specialized."

Dolon licked his lips. "Not officially."

"What does that mean?"

"America is built on a long tradition of unofficial work."

The Ace stared at him. Even though he didn't want to say more, Dolon said, "I've just been around a long time. Seen a lot. Prepared for a lot."

"That's . . . not an answer."

Dolon shrugged. He wasn't going to get into his family history with this *Ace.* Chevy seemed taken with the guy, which he supposed was normal thanks to the global infatuation with Aces, but he wasn't sold on it. The man seemed a little too . . . perfect, even in his nearly dead state. He knew people loved Aces so much they planned entire vacations around the *chance* to even see one, but Dolon, he wasn't caught up in that shit. Never had been, never would be.

Dolon had been born on a compound on the Nevada/Idaho border. He had no birth certificate. He learned how to reload ammo before he learned how to write. Never even heard of the internet until he was in his teens and in town to resupply. His family lineage changed depending on who was drunk and talking. His father was a prepper and a sovereign citizen. His mother . . . Who was his mother? She'd been young when she had him, and in one of the few photos he had of her, she held him, a swaddled baby, in front of a brown building, squinting into the sun. He'd realized, after years of looking at it, that it had been taken on the Duck Valley reservation. By the time he was old enough to ask about her, his father would no longer speak on the subject.

"What do they have on you?"

The Ace's voice brought Dolon back to the truck. The Ace looked so young and earnest, the words physically hurt Dolon. But he could ask questions too.

"How 'bout we start with your name?" Dolon said.

"Izan."

"Izan, I'm Dolon."

Izan nodded. "So what do they have on you?"

Dolon sighed. He'd told Chevy. Why not tell this guy too? Yeah, he got under Dolon's skin, but it wasn't just that he seemed too polished. He also made Dolon hurt where he was most vulnerable. Flora was dead and gone, but the ghost of her could pop up anywhere, at any time.

"My wife had aggressive cancer. I told them I'd do whatever they needed if they treated her. They did. She still died. I'm just paying that balance."

"I'm sorry."

Dolon hit the radio. A staticky voice filled the small space.

The Ace took the clue and turned to look out the window. He seemed suddenly sad. Dolon asked, before he could stop himself, "What's up?"

Izan clenched his jaw. "Seems like maybe . . . They wanted . . . I wasn't supposed to make it this far."

So the kid was with it enough to figure that out. Dolon's heart tweaked. Being around this kid was a trip. Dolon was both repelled and drawn to him. He felt off balance.

"People don't always get what they want. Sometimes that's not a bad thing," Dolon managed.

Izan's eyes roamed Dolon's face. He gave a curt nod, then turned and looked back out the window. Beyond the highway, Earth stretched before them, a flat plain of golds and yellows extending to a mound of purple mountains. The mountains jutted up, their craggily tops scratching the azure sky.

"Is it weird?" Dolon asked.

"What?"

"Being back on Earth? Is it different than you remembered?"

"It's nothing like I remembered, and it's everything I remembered. It's the smells that really are strange. Space . . . It smells like ass and chemicals. Disinfectants, polymer, cold—that kind of shit. This though . . . This is nothing like I remembered. It's amazing."

Dolon sniffed the air. "Smells like the desert and my truck to me. Dry with some rot. These seats have seen better days. They have that old, sunbaked smell." He poked at the cracked leather.

"You smell like the wind."

Dolon chuckled.

"I'm glad I get to smell this all at least once more before I die."

"You're not gonna' die." Dolon said, unconvincingly. "Hell, you seem pretty hard to kill."

Izan turned away from him, his flawless body weary. Dolon's heart creaked. The slump of Izan's shoulders was telling. It was unsettling to be thrust back into the presence of a sick person. A sick person and a woman. With the exception of his occasional conversation with Ms. Daisy, Dolon was out of touch with anything female. And as alpha as Chevy was, she was still a woman. The rush of her voice, the way she flicked her eyes, even things she didn't do but just were a part of her. The blush in her skin, the arch of her neck.

Being so close to a woman made him think of, no *feel,* Flora. And then being around a dying person . . . He could feel Flora and her slow, painful crawl into death. His brain went to that final hospital room, so he kicked that memory away and instead made himself remember when Flora had fallen into his life.

He'd been in the Sierra, running mules for a company out of Bishop. In late summer his outfit was getting ready to start packing for hunting camps. The air was still warm, but the nights had the bite that precipitated fall. He'd been coming down the trail, no string that day, just him and his horse. Suddenly, there she was. Alone, vibrant, and strangely, picking red berries.

"Be careful with those," he said, stopping next to her. She was cute, beautiful even, but not because she tried. Her hair was carelessly pulled into a falling apart bun. She wore running shorts, a frayed but clean-looking T-shirt, and a trucker's cap. She held a plastic container half filled with berries. It was the way she moved, and the dimple in her cheek . . . He wasn't ready to ride past her to his bunk at the barn.

She cut her eyes at him.

"Thanks." Her voice was flat.

"I'm not kidding, you can poison yourself."

"Uh-huh." She continued to collect the berries. She didn't look at him.

Something shifted in him when she did that. He suddenly felt . . . like he'd transgressed. The horse sidestepped below him.

"Okay. Do you know what you're picking?"

She stiffened, clearly annoyed he was still talking to her.

"Currants."

"Currants?"

"Currants," she concluded.

"Why?"

"I like to bake with them."

He looked at the bush she was plucking from. It was indeed a currant bush, which he would have known had he been paying attention to anything other than her. He'd seen her legs and the flash of red berry, and he'd stepped in, hoping to be the hero.

"You know what you're doing," he said, hoping to recover.

"Shockingly, yes."

"I'm sorry if I came off as . . ."

"Mansplainy."

"What?"

She laughed. "Should I mansplain what mansplaining is to you? Is it womansplaining then?"

"No. I get it. Sorry."

He'd been dealing with tourists so long, people who had no brain about them while on vacation, he'd forgotten that not all people needed to be walked through the most basic of things. He suddenly saw himself from her point of view and cringed.

She considered him for several stretching moments then said, "Okay. Thanks."

She went back to foraging. He still didn't move. She picked several more currants then looked him in the eyes again. Something in his stomach flipped when her eyes met his.

"Why are you just sitting there?"

"I . . . Uh . . . What's your name?"

"Flora."

"I'm Dolon. I . . . I'm sorry I, uh, mansplained you."

"You said that, thanks."

"Uh . . ."

He wanted to dig deeper into this woman, Flora. She might have been mean, or she might just be doing what she wanted, and no one, not even a dusty cowboy, was going to stop her. She wasn't up here to live out a weekend-long cabin fantasy. She was so much more . . . real. He was transfixed.

"Can I buy you coffee sometime?"

"What makes you think I live here?"

"Just a hunch. You carry yourself like . . . not like a tourist."

She narrowed her eyes but didn't say anything.

"I'm not a tourist, but I don't live here. I'll be in town next Monday."

A bloom of happiness erupted in his gut, and he knew, he was going to do anything and everything to see her.

"Where are we going?"

Izan's voice cut through his reverie.

"Idaho," Dolon replied, feeling like he'd just taken a fist to the gut.

"I've never been to Idaho."

Dolon blinked away the growing moisture in his eyes. Who was he kidding? This kid was dying. Why was everyone always dying around him?

TWENTY-FOUR

CHEVY

It was just after noon, and Chevy felt herself drifting to sleep. She'd maybe gotten a few hours of shut-eye at the hotel room, but that wasn't enough after the day she'd had yesterday. Now, in the bed of Dolon's truck, wrapped in one of the wool blankets, tucked under the tarp, with the rocking of the highway . . . It'd be okay to just take a quick nap.

She opened her eyes when she felt the truck slow. It was September in Nevada and after having spent a few days riding around in the back of Dolon's truck at ninety miles an hour, she couldn't say she was mad about climate change. Had it been less than a hundred degrees out she probably would have frozen. As it was, she just felt wind whipped. The flapping of the tarp Dolon had lashed over the bed was loud, and the ever-present shrieking wind mummified her. Still, at least she wasn't cold. She peeked out from under the tarp. Buildings surrounded them. They'd made it to another town. She touched her pocket. She still had the device.

Back in Ely, Chevy had made it clear to Dolon she would carry it. He hadn't looked happy about it, but he hadn't fought her on it either. He had just dipped his head and then they'd left the hotel room. When Chevy asked Dolon about their route, Dolon refused to say.

He had implied that they could reach the Idaho gas station in less than a day if nothing bad happened. Chevy doubted they were there already. The sun was still up, the day still bright. They probably needed gas.

The truck pulled into a service station and Dolon got out. He filled the rig, again paying in cash. Chevy wondered where he'd even gotten the stuff. He didn't speak to her at this service station, and Chevy figured that was a good thing, since last time he'd told her that Owl was dying. No news was good news.

They drove through the city—it was more of a city than a town—the truck slowing about twenty minutes later. Chevy felt them turn and could hear gravel under the tires. The truck stopped, and the driver door opened.

"I have to grab some shut-eye. I'm no spring chicken. You drive for a while. We need to get to Driggs," came Dolon's voice from above the tarp.

Dolon opened the tailgate, and Chevy crawled out.

They were in an empty trailhead parking lot.

"We're in Twin Falls now. You're going to take 84 East, then get on 86 to Pocatello, at Pocatello get on 15 North. After we pass Idaho Falls, you can wake me. I'll drive from there. Wait . . . You can drive a real car, right?"

"Of course I can," Chevy snorted.

She'd done it in boot, all those years ago, but Dolon didn't need to know that.

Dolon wearily climbed into the bed.

"I bought some food at the gas station. Izan's got it. Keep it below the speed limit."

Chevy nodded, and once Dolon was situated, she shut the tailgate.

Izan. That was his name, not Owl, but she liked thinking of him as Owl. There was something familiar about it, intimate if she let her thoughts run away. But familiar in that it reminded her of her squad. Her squad that probably thought she was dead, assuming, of course, they were alive. She shook them from her mind. Izan was her squad now.

She checked the ties on the tarp then climbed into the cab. She hardly fit. The bench seat was as far back as it would go. She felt like a hippo in a sardine tin. Hardly a good look. Best not to think about it, especially while sitting next to a real-life man Ace. She slammed the door and twisted the key.

Back in the driver's seat of a truck, something deep and primal, or maybe cultural, began to hum inside of her. Feeling the sun-cracked steering wheel beneath her palms . . . Smelling the leather of the seat . . . Knowing she could drive for days, for months, and never exhaust all of the available routes in America, Canada, and then there was all of South America too . . . She felt . . . free . . . powerful . . . young . . . infinite. Even if most of her driving before this had been done in a self-driving car.

"Hi," Owl said.

Chevy glanced at him, shaken from her daydream. Owl looked markedly better. Color had returned to his cheeks, and he was sitting up, not lying against the door. He had an open bag of chips in his lap and was drinking from a bottle of Coke. For a moment she considered that they were normal people in a normal time. He was hers and she was his and nothing more complicated than a blank slate of asphalt stretched before them. She shivered. What would it be like to be with an Ace?

She reoriented herself. She had a job to do. “You look like you’re feeling better.”

“I still feel like shit, but better shit than when you found me. The meds Dolon got helped.”

His nose crinkled when he smiled, and her stomach did a flip. She groaned internally. She needed to lock it up. They weren’t on a road trip, posting filtered photos of diner food and sunburst selfies. They were soldiers fleeing a massively more powerful army.

“I’m glad.” She carefully shifted the truck into gear. “You know which way to the highway?”

Owl pointed right, and she eased back onto the main road. They drove in silence for a few minutes. She remembered how to drive. It wasn’t that hard. She found the road to 84, and within a few minutes they were on the highway.

“Thank you,” he said.

“For what?”

“Not giving up on me. Saving me.”

“We’re teammates. No ‘thank you’ required.”

And she believed that. They were teammates. And not just because they were part of Launch Tech. Had Chevy passed Izan on the street, she would have felt the pull between them. She wondered if he felt it too? Or was this just what being around an Ace was like?

He waggled his head. “I want to say, ‘Thank you’. I don’t take the danger you put yourself in lightly. I know I’m not entitled to be saved just because of my rank.”

He was also humble. Fuck. Her stomach did that thing again.

“You’re on my team. No need to think about it more than that.”

He nodded and ate a chip.

She focused on the road, but it was a straight line. The traffic was light. There was nothing but him to take her focus. She wanted to ask so many questions. She didn't want to come off as a fan girl, but she couldn't just let this opportunity go to waste.

"So, how long have you been an Ace?" She did her best to sound nonchalant.

"I was tracked into it when I joined up. The training takes a few years, so I didn't get my wings until I was twenty. I've been in space ever since."

"So, you're thirty?"

He ate another chip and nodded.

"Big three-oh this year. I thought about having an existential crisis and then decided I didn't have the time." He chuckled. "I mean, with all this dropping to Earth in a lifeboat kind of thing, I really had more to think about than the fact I don't have a wife and a passel of kids."

So, he was unmarried, straight, and only a few years older than her. Six years was nothing.

"You like being an Ace?"

He cut his eyes at her, and she realized she must have sounded ridiculous.

"Yeah, it's pretty nice, most days."

"I . . ." Chevy swallowed. The question was dumb, but she already sounded dumb. She was just going to ask it. "I thought male Aces were a myth."

Owl crunched on another chip, shrugging.

"I mean less than one percent of Aces are male. So, real *and* a myth." He smirked. Chevy couldn't help but smile back.

"Is it true you get cookies in your briefing rooms?" she blurted.

"Yeah."

"Really?"

"Yeah. They make us our favorite kind for important briefs. Lesser briefs we get whatever they made that day."

She let out a snorting laugh. "You and I live very different lives."

He replied, his voice neutral. "I'm sure we do."

They lapsed into silence. The longer it went on, the more of an idiot Chevy felt. She needed to say something, to erase the cookie comment.

"Where are you from originally?" she asked.

"All over. My parents were migrant workers. We followed the crops up and down the Pacific Coast." He took a drink. "How about you? How long have you been in?"

"Seven years. Some days seems like more, though."

"I imagine it does. You like it?"

"Yeah, for the most part. I mean, it's got its days and all, but it was a way out for me."

"I get that. I was lucky my parents insisted on putting me in school. With all the moving we did, it would have been easy for them to just," he made quotes with his fingers, "*homeschool* me. Really, I would have just been in the fields, though. I would have never made it into the Aces if I'd done that."

Chevy bobbed her head. "I was homeschooled. It did not get me close to the Aces."

"Well, that and you're a giant," he said, a sneaky smile on his face.

She couldn't look at him without getting tingles in her gut. She kept her eyes locked on the road, and before Chevy could reply, a siren split the air. She looked in the rearview mirror and saw the red and blue lights of an approaching cop car. With horror, she looked at the speedometer. In her agitation, she'd bumped the speed to ninety, five over the speed limit.

"Fuck . . ." she hissed.

She looked at Owl. The color that had so recently come back to his face was now gone.

TWENTY-FIVE

THE CRANE

The Crane stared at the small sign on the porch. He supposed he was looking for veterinary help, so he pressed the buzzer. The Banker stood behind him, looking like he'd just slithered out of hell. The Banker's compact frame had that scrappy edge the Crane had once heard compared to a cockroach. *If the world ended, that guy and the cockroaches would be the ones to survive.* Even though the average person wouldn't look at the Banker and know he'd augmented the bones in his hands with additional weight, taking a punch by the Banker felt like getting hit by a fist full of pipes. He alternately gripped and stretched the knuckles in preparation for putting them to use. The Banker was always thinking ahead, and the Crane appreciated that.

The Crane had been given his name in part due to his physical stature. Long, lanky, and lightning fast, the Crane had limbs that seemed to stretch for miles. Like a crane, he also had patience. He could wait in the most extreme of circumstances, poised and alert, and when the timing was right, strike at his quarry, catching it before it ever realized he was there. An idiot might describe him as gangly, but he radiated predator, almost alien, intelligence. A soft, past ripe, general who was an avid ocean fisherman in his increasingly abundant downtime, had once told the Crane he had the eyes of a barracuda. *Cold, dead, and calculating.* The Crane had taken the words as a compliment, although he knew the general hadn't meant it as such.

Made of sun-bleached boards, the porch under the Crane's feet kicked up splinters when he stepped forward and hit the doorbell again. Finally, the door opened a crack. Behind it appeared a middle-aged woman. She had probably been pretty once, but now with the gray at her temples, she looked used and worn-out.

"I'm looking for Dr. George Bakirtzis," the Crane said, his voice efficiently professional, but not intimidating, yet.

"Let me guess, you're here about the prescription to Bronco Mays," she replied, her eyes on the Banker.

The Crane watched her eyes rove over their fitted suits, the Banker's scarred hands, the Crane's sharp nose.

"Are you Dr. George Bakirtzis?"

"I am. Do you have a sick animal or are you just here to scare me?" She looked from him to the Banker.

The Crane felt his eyebrows rise, and a small smile slid across his face. He had not expected her to be the owner of a first name like George. He had also not expected such . . . spunk.

"May we come in? I have a few questions I'd like to ask you." The Crane shifted his weight forward.

"No, you may not." He heard her slide a foot behind the door. "I had a feeling I'd be hearing from your kind, and I've already called the locals. They're on their way, so what is it you want before the sheriff gets involved?"

"Our kind?" the Crane asked with mock offense.

"Yeah. I watch the news. Mega-corp goons. Your kind."

The Crane admired her pluck. Not that some Podunk sheriff scared him, but still. He loved a good twist of the plot. And if she did just tell him what he wanted to know, he would have been disappointed.

"Who did you prescribe the midodrine to?" He'd go along with her game, at least for the time being.

"An older gentleman. Didn't get his name."

He raised an eyebrow again. "I'm afraid you'll have to do better than that."

"Said his horse was prescribed midodrine and he'd forgotten it. He had a not so plausible story about not being able to reach his vet."

"And did you see his horse?"

"No. He said his trailer had blown a tire and his wife and family were dealing with that, so he couldn't bring the horse to me."

"And are you in the habit of prescribing strange meds to strange men with no actual animals?"

"I'm in the habit of helping people. And their animals," she said, her eyes on his. "Sometimes that isn't as clear-cut as it seems."

"Describe him, please."

"Middle-aged, sun dark, wind-wrinkled, white beard, about six feet, wearing work clothes. Had a truck; a Ranger, I think. It was tan. No one was with him."

"Did you get a plate?"

"Why would I do that?"

"You clearly had suspicions."

She shook her head.

"It was a Nevada plate. That's all I recall."

"I see. You don't seem to have any loyalty to him."

"I told him I wouldn't lie for him. He told me he didn't expect me to."

The Crane nodded and let his eyes wander over her property and its abundance of brush piles. "You're clearing a lot of brush, I see."

"Of course. It's September in the West. Now, is there anything else I can help you with?"

The Crane held her eyes. She stared back at him, defiant.

"You should be careful with who you talk to, Dr. Bakirtzis. You never know what rogues are lurking out there."

She didn't react. That tweaked something in him. He liked a good fight, but for her to have zero respect for the balance of power so clearly playing across her front lawn, well . . .

"Whom."

"Excuse me?" the Crane said.

"With whom you talk to," she corrected.

Beside the Crane was a lone piece of rebar, sticking up from the garden. He resisted the urge to split the doctor in two with it.

"We'll be going now. Remember, there are powerful people in the world, and you aren't one of them." He looked at the Banker. "I think we should help her," he said. "Burn her piles for her."

The Banker nodded and trotted off the porch, heading to the back of their SUV. He tapped his fingers as he ran. The Crane watched Dr. Bakirtzis. She looked fragile now, the color gone from her face.

The Banker pulled a gas can from the rig and began dowsing the piles, which were clearly not finished. They were way too close to her house. He moved from pile to pile, trailing gas out of the can, creating a path that connected every pile to the others. When he had emptied the can, the Crane looked at Dr. Bakirtzis.

"It's a dangerous world out there, Dr. Bakirtzis. Be careful *whom* you help."

The Banker flipped a match into the nearest burn pile, and all the piles ignited.

There was fear in her eyes, at first, but that flash of defiance returned. For a moment the Crane felt anger, then nothing but calm.

"On second thought," the Crane said, "Banker . . ."

In a flash, the Banker was at his side, his fist flying. The sound the Banker's augmented hand made when it struck the vet's head was brutal and finishing. She collapsed like a bag of rocks.

The Banker picked her up, the heft of her body insignificant to his pit bull–like strength and tossed her on the growing inferno.

She didn't react. Immediately, the air smelled like charred meat. The Crane idly wondered if the punch had killed her. They got into their SUV and pulled out of the driveway. The flames licked at the side of the vet's house. The Crane could hear distant sirens. She must really have called the sheriff before she opened the door.

"Let's go to the service station next," the Crane said.

Unhurriedly, the Banker merged onto the county road. "You got it, Boss."

TWENTY-SIX

CHEVY

Chevy's eyes did not leave the mirror. The red and blue lights grew closer. The siren grew louder.

"Fuuckkk," Chevy said. They were getting pulled over. *She* was getting them pulled over.

"We have to hide the device. They're going to detain us. We don't have ID cards. I mean, I don't have one, do you?" Izan's voice was rushed.

"Fuck no," Chevy replied. "Twenty-four hours ago, I was in space with my platoon."

"We need to hide it. Not on our person. They'll search us."

"They'll search the rig too," Chevy said.

She thought about running, but the cop was driving a vehicle decades newer than Dolon's truck. She sighed and let her foot off the accelerator.

"Hopefully there's only one of them. Whatever side the cop goes to, the other one of us gets the device. We get out of the car, that person slips it into the bed," Izan said.

"You're hoping the old man can get it out of here?"

"You want to make a stand?" he asked.

She navigated onto the shoulder. The police car pulled in behind them. "My rifle's in the bed."

"I know, but killing a cop isn't going to help us get anywhere right now."

She pulled the Conlow bag out of her pocket and set it between them. Izan tossed the blanket over it.

"Can you walk?"

"I don't know."

"Fuuuck," Chevy said again.

She looked at the side mirror. A man unfolded himself from the driver's seat of the white cruiser. He bent over and plucked a cowboy hat from his car, set it on his head, and began a leisurely walk to Chevy's side. The sun now sat lower in the sky, still hours from setting, but it was bright enough that Chevy could see the shiny gold badge on the cop's chest.

"He's going to your side," Izan whispered. "I'll put it in the bed . . . We have to be smart about this."

The cop was at the door, a thirtysomething, white guy with no facial hair. He was tall, not the same size as Chevy, but tall enough he had to lean over to see inside the car.

"License, insurance, registration please," he said.

"Uh, what seems to be the issue, officer?" Chevy asked.

"I clocked you doing eighty-nine in an eighty-five." The cop's jawbone was pronounced and unsettling.

"I see," Chevy said.

"Documents. You," the cop said, looking at Izan, "you got an ID on you?"

"I left my wallet at home," Chevy said.

"Mm-hmm. Would both of you get out of the car please?"

He stepped back to make room for Chevy's door. Chevy could probably have given the cop a run for his money, but the cop had a gun and Chevy didn't. Izan had his knives, but he was right: Killing a cop in Idaho wasn't what they wanted to do.

The cop pulled Chevy's door open.

"Ease out nice and slow, big girl. I'll have my eye on you. Don't get spunky on me."

Izan mouthed *Don't panic* at Chevy and opened his door. He grabbed the device and slid out of the car, while Chevy unpacked herself from the driver's side.

"You look like a marine," the cop was saying. "What outfit do you work for?"

Chevy didn't respond. From the corner of her eye, she saw Izan slip the device under the tarp and into the truck bed.

"Not going to talk, huh? You AWOL? Walk on over there to the grass. You and your boyfriend can stand off the road."

Chevy nodded and moved to Izan's side of the truck. Izan hadn't let go of the vehicle. She knew he might not be able to without falling.

"Let go of the truck, kid." The cop prodded Izan.

"He's sick. He can't walk. I'll help him."

"What's wrong with him?"

Chevy moved to Izan and put her arm around his torso. She picked him up and moved him to where the cop indicated. He was so light.

"I don't know. We were going to his mom's house in Idaho Falls. Sometimes that helps when he gets like this."

Chevy pulled Izan to the grass. They turned so they faced the highway again. The cop now stood between them and the truck.

"Alright, I'm gonna pat you down for weapons so let go of him and turn away from me. Hands at the center of your back, knuckles together, thumbs up."

Chevy's grip tightened on Izan's ribs. This was the time. This was the moment for her to make her stand . . .

"You hear me? I said turn away from me . . ."

And then Dolon exploded from the back of the truck. Chevy, half a second behind, lunged at the officer while letting go of Izan. The startled cop instinctually backed away from Chevy, but Dolon was out of the bed and swinging some sort of stick.

The wood connected with the cop's jaw. He crumpled.

"Grab his body camera!" Dolon said, scrambling toward the limp officer.

Chevy was already on it, and she had the black rectangle in her hand. Dolon was fussing with the cop's belt. He took out a pair of handcuffs and slapped them on the guy's wrists. Chevy took his gun.

It was a Glock 17 gen 8. Chevy did a press check. The slide gave easily; it had been recently oiled. She popped the magazine. The top bullet gleamed in the sun. She reinserted the mag but didn't rack the slide. Chevy wiggled the gun light. It didn't budge. She tapped the light's power button, and a bright burst of yellow appeared against her cupped palm. The red dot shone. This cop took care of his weapon.

"Get his radio," Izan said, half pulling himself, half crawling toward the truck.

Chevy grabbed it, then ripped open the truck door and tossed the radio and body camera inside. She jammed the gun into her belt. Dolon was already running to the driver's seat. Chevy grabbed

Izan and practically threw him into the cab. She slammed the door and jumped into the truck bed, diving under the tarp. Dolon hit the gas and they sped back onto the highway. Chevy wrestled the tarp into submission.

She had fucked up . . . Bad.

TWENTY-SEVEN

DOLON

"I told her to go the fucking speed limit!"

"That cop pegged her going four over," Izan said.

Dolon opened his mouth but found the words stuck in his throat. Was Izan defending Chevy? The two of them siding together was not ideal. Finally, he managed, "In these parts that is all the reason they need."

Dolon pulled into the left lane and the median, then merged back onto Highway 84 headed west, back to Twin Falls.

"We're going back?" Izan asked.

"We have to ditch this truck. The biggest city is behind us, and that's the best chance of finding a new ride."

They drove by the cop, who was still out cold on the side of the road. The cop's radio blared from the passenger floorboard.

"Romeo-one-two, status?"

"What did you hit him with?" Izan said, looking at the radio.

"Broke axe handle. I figured it might come in useful."

"You figured right."

"Break the body camera," Dolon said. "Smash it to pieces and then drop them out the window every few miles. There's a wrench in the glove box."

Izan pulled open the glove box and found the wrench. He set the body camera on the floorboard, lens down, and began to hit it, but his strikes were weak. Dolon watched the plastic withstand Izan's feeble blows and felt his heart sink.

"You can do this," Dolon said.

Izan sucked in a deep breath and the next strike cracked the plastic casing. Then Dolon heard the thwack of the circuit board bending. Soon, Izan was panting. He dropped the wrench, on the body camera and leaned back against the seat.

Dolon peered at his handiwork.

"Good job. When you recover, hit it a few more times and then get it out of my truck."

Izan squeezed his eyes shut and nodded. Dolon worried he might puke, but after a moment he picked up the wrench again and hit the destroyed body camera a few more times. He scooped up the pieces and cranked down the window. The wind whipped them from his fingers.

"I knew it wouldn't be that easy," Dolon mumbled. "Only a few hours away. I knew something would go sideways."

The radio sputtered to life again.

"Romeo-one-two, second attempt."

No answer.

"Romeo-one-three, dispatch."

"One-three."

"One-two has missed several status checks. He's just east of exit 188, on 86 East."

"Copy. En route."

"Our guy must be Romeo-one-two," Izan said.

"More than likely."

Izan sprinkled more pieces out of the window.

"I've got a shotgun and a rifle behind the seats," Dolon said. "Can you break them down?"

"If you tell me how."

Dolon nodded and reached behind the seat. Once he got Izan working on taking apart the guns, his mind went through the checklists of what they would take, what they would abandon, and how this would all work with a mountain of a marine and a boy who couldn't walk.

He'd removed his VINs before he went on this trip. The insurance and registration were in his wallet. Once he grabbed his go bag and the guns, there would be nothing to tie him immediately to this truck.

Izan followed instructions well and was a quick learner, even if he was so weak that he could barely even hold the guns. Dolon found it mildly amusing that a super solider didn't know how to take apart a long gun but didn't dwell on it. Soon, Izan was finished with the 870.

"There's a bag under the seat. Put the pieces in there," Dolon said.

Izan did so, and they moved onto the Ruger. Dolon wasn't thrilled about the condition of the long guns, their disassembled pieces bouncing together in a canvas sack. But it would have to do, for now.

The exit for Twin Falls was coming up. It was past five in the afternoon. They still had a few hours of daylight, which was both a blessing and a curse. It was easier to steal a car in the dark, but during the day he could see what he wanted to steal and where he could stash his truck.

A police car sped past him in the eastbound lane, and the radio belched another status check. Dolon did his best not to hit the brakes or speed up. Soon the car was gone. Izan sprinkled a few more pieces of the body camera out the window.

He turned off the highway, and in a few minutes the Perrine Bridge loomed before them. Dolon drove onto the bridge and watched a man in a helmet climb onto the bridge's railing. He stood, balancing for a moment, then stepped off.

"Holy shit," Izan said.

"BASE jumping's been legal here for ages. Let's see if we can find that guy's car," Dolon said.

He drove over the bridge, which spanned the Snake River Canyon. Below them, the green Snake River coursed through the bottom of the canyon. Dolon knew the BASE jumper had already pulled his chute. It would take him a while to get back up to the rim of the canyon, though.

Dolon turned onto the canyon rim road, which paralleled the river. Various turnouts and parking areas ballooned from the road's edges. Cars filled the spaces. The day had become a gorgeous September evening. People, dogs, and babies laughed and filled the areas that Dolon wished held nothing but a car he could easily hotwire. Finally, as the Perrine Bridge dwindled in his rearview mirror, he came across a dirt space with a blue minivan. A sticker on its back window read, BASEic Bitch. Dolon had found their next ride. He pulled in behind it.

"We're taking the minivan?" Izan asked.

"Dispatch!" the radio screamed.

"Dispatch."

"Romeo-one-three. I need medical here! And send me the world. Romeo-one-two's been attacked. I repeat, send me an ambulance and anyone in the area."

"This is as good a car as any," Dolon replied, getting out of the truck.

He scanned the area, but the van was parked near a rocky outcrop, preventing him from seeing anything to the south of it. He walked around the van, made sure no one was in it, then tested the doors. Suddenly, Chevy was next to him.

"This our new ride?"

"Might be," Dolon said. "Keep a lookout."

Chevy jogged back toward the road, while Dolon considered the van. The doors were locked, but Dolon could see that the van belonged to someone who was an outdoorsman. It wasn't made up to live in, but through the window he could see a climbing guide, an avocado, a trucker's hat, and what looked to be an incense dish sitting on the center console.

Dolon walked to the gas cap and opened it.

"Perfect." He scooped up the key that was balanced inside.

He unlocked the front door and started the minivan. Dolon's heart danced. The van was both old enough to take gas and old enough it would allow him to disable the early generation self-driver. He hit the button to do so.

"Get Izan and the bag he's holding," Dolon told Chevy.

Chevy went to the truck. Dolon pulled the tarp back on his truck bed and grabbed the two go bags he'd made, tossing them in the van. Chevy helped Izan and the bag into the van's back seat, then wrapped her rifle in a wool blanket and put it in the van. Dolon touched his pants pocket. The Conlow bag was still there. He grabbed the bag of shotgun and rifle pieces, and then the case of the final gun he'd packed, a 10/22 Takedown, and transferred them to the van.

"Dispatch Romeo-one-three." The radio squawked from the Ranger's front seat.

"Romeo-one-three."

"We're closing the road from exit 188 to exit 194."

"Copy."

Dolon sighed. Not that he was planning on trying to take 84 again. But it was good to know that even if he had been willing to risk it, it wouldn't have been worth it.

"They teach you to throw in the marines?" Dolon pointedly looked at Chevy, then at the radio, and then at the canyon edge.

"I was throwing hay barrels in diapers," Chevy said. "I got this."

She picked up the radio, twisted it so it sat nicely in her palm, then ran at the canyon edge, arm back. She let go of the radio and it arced into the air, disappearing against the lines of the far canyon wall. Dolon didn't hear it impact, but it was gone, and that was what mattered.

"You drive the van." Dolon was still mad at Chevy, even if watching that radio fly had been cool. His voice was cold. "There was a sign for a Walmart a little way from here. We're going to leave the truck there. Follow me."

"Wait, you have the device?" Chevy asked.

Dolon nodded and touched his pocket again. Chevy's jaw twitched, but she only nodded.

They got into the cars. Dolon drove back toward the Perrine Bridge, checking in his mirrors for someone running after him. His feelings dashed between anger at Chevy and, he realized, fear that Chevy and Izan were now in more danger. He wasn't sure he even liked either of them, yet he couldn't shake the fact that down, under his anger, he felt a primal need to protect them. His mind flitted to Flora. Was he turning into a dotty old man? Suddenly, upon being around two people who, in very different ways, reminded him of his dead wife, did he really have the burning desire to papa bear their enemies? Was this what happened to people in their old age? They became illogically sentimental?

He needed to focus. He turned into town and followed the signs that led him to Walmart. He drove through the massive parking lot until he found a spot near the back docks where he could back the truck in. He backed it in halfway, got out, unscrewed the plates with his Leatherman, and then backed it in all the way.

He left the door unlocked and put the key on the dashboard. Before he shut the door, he put his hand on the steering wheel.

"You've been good to me," he told the truck.

He walked to the van.

"Let's see if we can find a plate that'll match this rig," Dolon said, tossing the truck's plate onto the van floor.

They drove through the parking lot, Izan now asleep on the van's rear bench seat. Soon they came across a van of the same make and model as their new ride. It was a light green, not blue, but close enough.

"It'll do," Dolon said, getting out.

People milled through the parking lot, so Chevy stood blocking Dolon while Dolon swapped the plates. No one seemed to take notice of them. They got back into the van, and Dolon felt a slight weight rise off his shoulders.

He glanced at Izan, his heart doing something soft and painful he did not like.

"Did he take his pill at four?"

"I dunno," Chevy said. "I didn't see him take it."

"Shit. I have them," Dolon realized, fishing the bottle out of his pocket. "Give him one."

Chevy took a bottle of water from the gas station food bag and awkwardly climbed into the rear of the vehicle.

He pulled out of the lot and pointed the car back toward Ely.

A few moments later, Chevy climbed forward.

"Stay back there," Dolon said. "They don't know who they're looking for, but an old guy driving a minivan probably isn't it."

"Got it." Chevy strapped herself into one of the middle seats. "I got a pill in him. What's the plan now?"

"We're going back toward Ely."

"We're back tracking?"

"I doubt they expect that."

Chevy paused before saying, "No, probably not."

They traveled in silence for a while before Chevy asked, "You want me to drive?"

"You didn't do so hot last time."

"I was going four over."

"Maybe later," Dolon said, his voice softer.

Is this what having a kid would have been like? Holding the line but wanting nothing more than to just make everything okay?

Chevy let out a sigh, and Dolon could hear her settling into the chair.

"Okay," she said. "You just let me know when I'm out of the penalty box."

"Will do," he said, blinking rapidly because if he didn't his old man, runaway emotions would undermine what he was doing here.

He was here to pay his debts. Simple as that. His feelings for Chevy, Izan . . . Flora . . . had nothing to do with it.

He would settle his debt and then go back to living his solitary, peaceful life.

TWENTY-EIGHT

CHEVY

Chevy sat in the middle of the minivan, feeling agitated and vaguely childish. No matter how she oriented her head, the early evening sunlight hit her straight in the eyes. If she actively focused on the present, all she could think of was that it had been her carelessness that had gotten them pulled over. It was like she was Whitehead, breaking his optic and forgetting his underwear, and Dolon was her corporal, unfucking her mess. She burned with shame.

It had been her mistake that jeopardized the safety of Izan and the device, but it had also been her mistake that elevated Dolon into a position of trust. Dolon had exploded out of the bed before she'd gone for the cop. He'd risked his own safety to save Chevy and Izan, and now that she'd seen that, she *knew* he was on their side. Now he was part of her team. Her job now was to protect Izan, the device, *and* Dolon. She couldn't fuck it up again. She was the one with battlefield experience. She needed to act like it. They were her flock to protect, not the other way around.

She needed to do something. She needed a task.

She glanced around their stolen ride. The car was . . . crunchy. Rotting avocados, a string of prayer flags, some brightly colored but poorly done drawings of a mountain range—all of it was emblematic of a foreign way of living. The van was trashed and smelled. She counted to four. She needed order over chaos right now . . . She could only control so much, but that didn't mean everything was out of her control.

"We should change," Chevy said, looking at her unfortunately memorable shirt, the cartoon AR-15s dark against the red fabric. She glanced back at Izan who lay on the back bench seat, eyes closed, chest moving with sleep.

"Yup," Dolon agreed. "One of those bags has the stuff I bought for you. Might as well familiarize yourself with what we brought. Shame we had to ditch the truck, but I expected it."

Chevy pulled one of the bags to her. It was a shapeless duffle with shoulder straps. She opened it and saw a rifle stock and shotgun barrel.

"Guns?" Chevy liked this bag.

"My Ruger and 870 are in there. You could assemble them while you're back there. There's a cleaning kit in the brown bag."

Chevy felt her world realign. This is what she needed, a task where she could make lists and then check things off in an orderly fashion.

"Why are they disassembled?"

"Didn't know if we would have to hoof it or not. I had Izan disassemble them just in case. Thank God for hippies leaving their keys in gas caps."

Chevy set the bag of guns down and opened the other three bags. Inside of one she found the plastic bag from the thrift store. She pulled it out and rooted around until she found a black tee that was obviously her size. She shucked the angel and assault rifle shirt, letting it fall over some incense sticks, and pulled the black one over her head. She found a dark blue shirt for Owl. She set it on the seat next to him and went back to looking for the gun cleaning kit.

"They're clean, but they'll need the dust wiped off after rattling around in that bag," Dolon said.

"Sure thing." Chevy didn't need to be told how to care for a long gun.

Dolon didn't respond, and Chevy went about inventorying what gear they had. When she found two rotten avocados under her seat, she chucked them out the window. Tactical minivans didn't contain rotting hippie fruit.

TWENTY-NINE

THE CRANE

The Crane stood in the back room of the Love's Travel Stop, just off of Highway 6. The space was crammed with overflowing supply shelves, and the only empty wall was consumed by a huge, crumbling poster of some long-forgotten Ace. The little room reeked of curry and bleach. The stench mingled with the humidity of too many people in too small of a space, and it caused the Crane's stomach to flip.

"I need to see your footage from this morning, just prior to seven," the Banker told the two truck stop employees.

"You got it," the older one exclaimed, his face the color and texture of a shriveled raisin.

"Yeah," the Banker purred. "Do you mind?"

He pushed the younger man away from the keyboard and began to type. The Crane sighed.

"People think they can disappear into the desert," the man continued. "Not so. This is a good town, with good people. We look out for each other."

"Sir," the Crane interjected. "My partner works better without distractions. Do you and your associate mind waiting outside? We'll be out of your hair in a moment."

The man looked abashed, but after a second, he nodded. He and the younger man left the office, the door hanging open long enough for the Crane to see the TV above the register showing footage of Launch Tech gaining ground on Jinzhan.

The door swung shut, and the Crane turned his gaze back to the computer screen.

"I'm downloading the footage, but it's not great." The Banker slapped the cracked computer tower. "Look at pump seven, at six fifty-one."

The Crane nodded and stared at the screen. He watched a battered Ford Ranger pull into pump seven. A figure got out, a man, but he couldn't make out much more. The footage was grainy. He walked inside to pay. The Crane glanced at the truck's plate, but it was too pixilated to see.

"Are there any credit card transactions for that pump at this time?" the Crane asked.

"I couldn't find any. That could mean there wasn't one. It could also mean there's a glitch in the system and it wasn't recorded, or the guy paid in cash."

In the video, the man walked outside and began to fuel. He stood near the tarp-covered truck bed and looked at something beyond the gas station. The Crane couldn't make out his face. He wore a big, brimmed hat that shaded his features. His clothing was obvious though, green pants, a tan long-sleeve shirt, and a coyote-colored sun hat.

Once the man was done fueling, he got back in the car and drove off.

"Can we hear the audio for that pump?"

"It's pretty garbled. I know he said, *space sick*, but the rest is gibberish. Too much background noise." The Banker didn't look at him as he typed into the computer.

The Crane reversed the video to the best image of the man and truck. It was fuzzy, and not much to go on, but from it he had a general vehicle and clothing description. He tried to peer into the passenger side of the truck, but an RV blocked the camera's view of the truck's cab.

"That's a truck that could use Goodyear Wranglers," the Banker said.

The Crane nodded, his eyes on the screen, trying to tease more information from it. Then the Banker's posture changed. The Crane knew he was looking at data on his retinal display.

"What's up?"

"Cop radios are still transmitted over frequencies off the network, so I've been monitoring all of them in a one-state radius," the Banker said, his eyes still far away. "An Idaho Trooper pulled over a vehicle on 86 East, just outside of Twin Falls. Someone attacked him, knocked him out, stole a bunch of his gear, and is in the wind."

"Is there any information on the attacker?"

The Banker's eyes roved the ceiling.

"He ran the plate before he made the stop. Came back to a Ford Ranger out of Nevada. Whoever it was took the cop's body cam." The Banker rolled forward, his eyes again seeing the Crane. "Looks like they're headed north."

The Crane looked at the Ford Ranger frozen on the screen.

"Let's get out of here. We can blast this image to surrounding agencies . . . and do you think anyone would miss these two donkeys running the gas station? The old one talks too much."

"I like the cut of your jib." The Banker tapped his fingers. "I'll make the call from the car."

"Some days chaos is all we're capable of."

"Some days," the Banker agreed.

THIRTY

CHEVY

Chevy sat on the passenger side middle bench, Dolon's gear bags spread around her. Dolon drove, and Izan still lay across the back bench seat, snoring softly. She was in the middle of inventorying their ammo when Izan went silent. She turned and saw he was awake, his dark eyes on her. Her stomach jumped when she realized he'd been watching her.

"You're up," she whispered.

"Yeah . . . What happened?"

"You passed out again. I gave you one of those pills a while ago."

She'd forced his mouth open and tilted the water bottle to his lips to chase the pill down, but he hadn't been fully conscious. The memory made her skin bristle.

"Where'd we get this car?"

"We stole it."

Panic flashed across Izan's face. "What happened to the cop?"

"Don't know. His buddies reached him and then we ditched the radio."

"Where are we going now?"

"Back toward Ely."

He nodded and pulled himself to the middle row of seats. Chevy moved the guns off the seat so he could sit. She watched him take in the weapons. Even though he was an elite super soldier, Aces didn't use guns. Obviously shooting guns in space was not ideal. He regarded them warily.

"Here." Chevy handed him a new shirt. "You should change out of that."

Chevy had changed earlier, and her old tee now wrapped Dolon's truck's license plate. It all sat on the floor, ready to be tossed when the timing was right.

Izan pulled off his shirt, and Chevy's eyes snapped to his exposed torso. She angled her head so it looked like she was counting ammo.

"Yes?" Izan asked.

Her jaw tightened. "What?"

Izan let out a small laugh. "Guess it's true what they say."

"What who says?" Chevy pointedly did not look at him.

"That marines aren't subtle about anything."

Chevy felt her checks go red, and Izan laughed again. She marshaled herself, whipping her head toward Izan. He choked off his laugh.

"You're right." She leaned at him aware of how her breasts pushed at the fabric of her shirt. "There is *nothing* subtle about me, but in terms of what you're implying, no one's ever complained. Not that you would know."

Izan went pale.

Chevy stretched her neck and rubbed the back of her shaved head. Izan seemed to have stopped breathing.

"There."

Chevy and Izan both looked at Dolon, the moment broken. Dolon tilted his chin at the oncoming lane. Chevy couldn't see what he was talking about.

"A black SUV going over a hundred just passed us, headed the way we came," Dolon said. "I would put money on it being Exoterra."

The silence in the van was deafening. Finally, Chevy said, "It's always sobering when you finally see the ghost."

"The ghost?" Izan asked.

"My grandam, when no one else was around, used to tell me we all have a ghost following us. But seeing it, that's the rub. When you finally have proof that it exists, things become much, much harder, and much, much easier," Chevy said.

"Ghosts are just another word for memories," Dolon said. "That's mind over matter. It's the living that I'm worried about."

THIRTY-ONE

DOLON

Dolon saw the exit for Wells and signaled. They'd get on I-80 and go up through Salt Lake. He hated city driving, but he was playing the hand he'd been dealt.

"Are we getting off the highway?" Chevy asked.

"We're going to cut east and go north on 15," Dolon said. "Hopefully we can blend into the sprawl of Salt Lake."

Chevy shifted uncomfortably. "Lots of people mean lots of cameras."

"I know, but we don't have a lot of choices right now."

"I hate to add another issue into this mess," Chevy said. "But I'm hungry. Those service station snacks left my system hours ago."

"There's a town on the border with casinos." Dolon flipped down the visor. The setting sun drilled into his eyes. "We can get an actual meal there."

"I imagine casinos have a lot of cameras," Izan said.

"We can get gas station food instead," Dolon replied.

"I'm going to die if I don't eat at least two thousand calories," Chevy snapped, "and not from three bags of pork rinds."

"It smells like there's food in this van," Izan said.

"This van smells, period," Chevy said.

"Amen," Izan agreed.

Dolon glanced in the rearview mirror and saw the two of them rooting through the stuff that the vehicle's owner had left. He had packed MREs in his go bags, but he respected that Chevy was smart enough not to dive into those when there were other options.

"Here's a half-open bag of chickpea chips." Izan held up the bag.

"Ugh," Chevy groaned. "Can't be worse than chow hall eggs."

Dolon heard the crinkly packaging being passed to Chevy. A period of brief but intense crunching followed and then Chevy said, "Well, that was a wonderful ten calories. What else can you find, Owl?"

Dolon quit listening to their chatter. Instead, he set the van's cruise control and did his best not to think of Flora. After all, ghosts were mind over matter. But they'd crisscrossed this state more times than he could count. She loved to stop at odd pull-outs and read the sunbaked signs that hadn't been replaced in decades. They'd be in the middle of nowhere, and suddenly a faded *Exhibit Ahead* sign would appear, and she'd insist they stop to see it. They'd pull off the road, the air hotter than hell, and attempt to read them, but half the time the signs were so old and weather-beaten that Flora would just wing it.

And here is where the Original Star Trek *was filmed. They painted over actual pictographs so that the rocks looked more futuristic when they projected purple light on them while using copious fog machines.*

God, he missed her. He wished he didn't feel her everywhere he went. His fingers tightened on the steering wheel. She was gone. But Izan and Chevy weren't, not yet. And last he checked, he was still alive too. Or at least going through the motions.

He swallowed. The sun was setting, so he folded the visor up and stared straight at the falling ball of fire. Maybe he could burn out all lingering memories lurking in the far corners of his mind.

Roughly an hour after passing Wells, the sky now dark, they pulled into West Wendover, just over the state line on the Nevada side. The state line meant everything to these towns, and this side boasted casinos and brothels, the Utah side, a Mormon Stake Center.

Dolon eased into a service station. The van needed gas. He got out and went inside to use the bathroom and pay. On his way out of the bathroom he saw a stack of cheap gallon jugs of water. He grabbed three and put the money down for the gas and water.

He went back outside and unceremoniously dropped the water next to one of the to-go duffels.

"Thirsty?" Chevy asked.

"Prepared," Dolon said, shutting the door.

He filled the car then drove toward the Wendover Nugget, the town's main casino, and pulled into a large, yet mostly empty, parking lot.

"Okay," Dolon said. "I'm going to go get us some food. I won't take long. Any requests?"

"No mayonnaise," Chevy said.

"That it?"

"Yeah. I don't like mayonnaise."

"Noted," Dolon replied. He handed the Conlow bag to Chevy, who took it and stuffed it into her pants. "If I'm not back in twenty minutes, something's up. Got me?"

Chevy stared at Dolon for a beat, unreadable. "Copy."

Dolon pulled his hat down low and got out of the van. The night air was still hot. He walked across the floodlit parking lot, where a few people milled around but paid him no mind, then up the casino's probably once-grand and now crumbling front steps, before stepping into the revolving door.

Once inside, a heavy blackness punctuated by flashing neon screens washed over him. The air smelled like stale cigarettes and disinfectant. He blinked, and a holographic woman wearing a bikini appeared.

"Welcome!" she said, her breasts bouncing in sync with each syllable.

"I don't need help."

"Of course you don't. But maybe you'd *like* some?" Her lips pursed and her eyes widened.

Dolon's vision finally adjusted to the haze of smoke. He walked through the hologram, following the faded carpeted path between rattling slot machines until he found a diner. A girl, a real one in way too much makeup, stood at the front podium.

"Do you do take out?" he asked.

"Of course." She handed him a menu.

Dolon studied it. He had no idea what Izan ate, and he knew that whatever he got Chevy he would have to order in triplicate. He ended up ordering three cheeseburgers, a steak, three side salads, a side of mashed potatoes, and a meatloaf, along with three cups of coffee, some Cokes, and some apple pie.

"Wow." The girl batted her eyelashes at him. "You must be hungry."

"The wife and kid too." Dolon smiled and handed her the money. "Keep the change."

She smiled coyly and told him it would be fifteen minutes.

"SIR. STOP."

Dolon turned to see three armed security guards march around a corner. They walked straight at him. He pushed away from the wall, and they sprinted at him. He thought about running, but he knew his old knees wouldn't beat all three of them in a foot race.

They reached him in seconds.

"Please come with us, sir," a young, fat-faced guard said. "Don't make this harder than it has to be."

"What's wrong?" Hands clamped onto Dolon's arms.

"This way please," the fat one said.

They led him away from the diner. He looked back at the girl, her eyes wide. It looked like she might actually feel bad for him.

THIRTY-TWO

CHEVY

"Something isn't right," Chevy said.

They'd been waiting for Dolon to come back for over half an hour. The parking lot floodlights burned into the black pavement, but without a moon, the night seemed oppressive.

"What do you think we should do?" Izan asked.

Izan moved next to Chevy. They crowded the window that faced the door where Dolon had entered. Chevy could smell Izan. It was distracting.

"I guess I need to go in there," Chevy said, then realized she believed what she said. She did need to go in there. Dolon was her responsibility now.

Izan tipped his head. "You're fairly noticeable."

"I think we might be past skating through unnoticed." Chevy turned and grabbed the 10/22 case. "You ever shot one of these?"

Izan shook his head, and she snapped the barrel and stock together.

"It's easy. Point and squeeze the trigger. No recoil, very accurate. This is a fun gun."

He stared at the gun hesitantly. "I take it we're sieging the castle."

"I'm a grunt." Chevy loaded the magazine into the rifle. "It's time to send me in. Can you drive?"

"I learned when I was a kid, but it's been over ten years."

"Okay, well look. This is the shifter, the gas, the brake. Sit in the front seat, with the van idling, and cover me. When I get out with Dolon, drive as soon as we're in."

"What exactly is your plan?"

"I don't know, but I'll figure it out when I get in there."

"It appears you're going to blow our cover."

Chevy pushed the gun into Izan's hands "If Dolon's captured," she said, handing him the Conlow bag, "that cover is probably gone."

Izan held the gun and the bag awkwardly. "Well then, it sounds like you're just going to blow it up for good measure."

"We need him."

And, Chevy thought, *he's on my team.*

"I know, but there's no going back if I have to start shooting people." Izan seemed inordinately distressed by this. Chevy wasn't sure what to make of that.

"The moment you launched that lifeboat there was no going back," she said.

". . . I guess it's different when it's civilians who aren't involved at all." He turned the gun in his hands like he'd never held one before.

Chevy shrugged. "I suppose it is, but if it comes down to us or them, I choose us."

Izan climbed into the front seat and turned on the van, the 10/22 and the Conlow bag in his lap. He squared his shoulders, his bearing changing, the weirdness gone. He spoke confidently, although with regret. "You aren't wrong, but it sucks our choices keep getting worse."

Chevy shrugged again and tucked the cop's gun in her waistband, which wasn't as fun as the movies made it seem. She didn't like that it wasn't secure. She pulled a shemagh from one of the bags, wrapped it around her head and face and opened the door. She waggled her eyebrows at Izan then lifted her fist.

"Oorah!" she cried and walked toward the casino.

Ten minutes later she was back at the van, bags of takeout in hand. She'd made it to a diner and the hostess told her, in not so many words, that her friend was probably in security, on the back side of the building. She'd also given Chevy the food Dolon had apparently paid for.

Inside the van, Izan was still in the front seat, car idling, rifle on his lap. Chevy put the food on the floor.

"Security has him. I think we can drive back there," Chevy said.

Izan put the car in gear and eased the van forward. He was a tentative driver and the van bunny hopped.

"How do you make it roll smooth?" Izan asked.

"Stop driving with two feet . . ."

A woman stepped into the parking lot about twenty yards ahead of them. Izan slammed on the brakes. Chevy's forehead hit the seat in front of her. She peeled her face from the back of the headrest and felt her nose.

"Ahhh . . ."

"Sorry," Izan said.

Chevy grunted, still feeling her nose. It wasn't broken.

Finally, they got to the back of the parking lot, and Chevy saw the dumpster and an unmarked door.

“I think that’s it.” Chevy pointed from the back seat.

Izan swung the car around, so it was facing the parking lot’s exit. He parked it in a shadowed space the industrial floodlights didn’t reach.

“Ready?” Chevy asked.

“As I’ll ever be.”

Chevy hopped out of the van and left the door open. She moved to the back of the van and twisted the license plate bulb. It flickered out. She’d seen that in a movie, and it seemed appropriate here. She then trotted to the door, gun in one hand, pulling the shemagh close around her face. The door was metal and flush with the wall. She tried the handle. It was locked. She knocked. Nothing happened. She knocked again, this time faster, and the door clicked open.

Chevy grabbed the handle and ripped it backward. A stunned security guard in an ill-fitting uniform stood inside. Chevy grabbed him by the collar and pushed him into the wall.

“Where is he?”

The guard didn’t say anything, and Chevy threw him to the side. She looked around the room. Cluttered and dark, the room had a few banged-up desks littered with crumpled papers. On the far side of the room was another door.

Chevy picked the man from the ground and hissed, “Take me to him.”

The man had vapor locked, so Chevy pushed him toward the far door. He stumbled forward and they entered a fluorescent hallway. To her left, Chevy could hear voices. She pushed the man before her and toward the sounds. At the end of the hallway, they came to a closed door.

Chevy tried the knob, but it was locked. The door was wood, so she brushed the shaking guard aside and kicked next to the handle.

The door splintered, and Chevy grabbed the guard and plowed him through the door.

He fell to the ground, and Chevy found herself in a small holding room. Dolon sat handcuffed to a bench inset into the wall, and two other guards stood before him. Dolon's wallet and cash lay on the room's sole table.

The detail that caught Chevy's attention was Dolon's puffy face.

They. Had. Hit. Him.

Her teammate.

They had hurt him on her watch.

Her world erupted into red. She rushed to the closest guard and threw a left hook. The man went down like a bag of rocks. She rammed into the second guard, driving him into the bench where Dolon was chained. The guard's head knocked into the metal edge. He went instantly limp. Chevy whirled back to the guard who she'd driven through the door, gun out and on him. He lay on the ground, crying.

"Nice to see you," Dolon said, with the mildness of commenting on the weather.

Chevy's heart beat with the adrenaline of battle. She turned her back on the sobbing man and grabbed the nearest guard. On his belt she found a set of keys on a retractable wire. She ripped the entire thing off the man's pants and moved to Dolon, stuffing the cop's pistol into her belt.

"What did they do to you?"

"They roughed me up a little, nothing too bad," Dolon said, again, with way too much chill.

Chevy found the key to the handcuffs and freed Dolon. They quickly cuffed all of the guards using their own handcuffs. Dolon grabbed his things from the table and stuffed them back into his pockets. They ran down the hallway. Chevy kicked open the outside door, and they ran to the waiting van.

They reached the van, and Chevy practically threw Dolon inside. She grabbed the doorway handle, pulled herself in, and Izan hit the gas.

THIRTY-THREE

THE CRANE

The Crane and the Banker moved down the hallway of St. Luke's Hospital in Twin Falls. The Banker walked with a scrappy swagger. The Crane's movements were so precise they were almost sterile. They made an ostensibly odd pair, which worked in their favor. They intrinsically made people uncomfortable. Nurses, patients, even doctors, scurried out of their way.

The trooper, Brumas Kelley, was in room 504. They turned the corner and saw a cop sitting in a chair outside of a room halfway down the corridor. He quickly sized them up, his face tensed. He stood, his hand slipping to his sidearm.

"We're here to speak to Officer Kelley." The Crane flashed his Exoterra badge. "I believe you're expecting us."

The cop glanced at the Crane's badge and then at the Banker's. He relaxed and motioned them past.

Officer Kelley lay on a bed in the darkened room. A machine beeped softly next to him. The docs had wired his jaw shut. A tablet lay next to his hip on the sheets.

"Hello," the Crane said.

Officer Kelley's eyes fluttered open. He saw the Crane's and the Banker's badges.

"We would like to talk to you about what happened." The Crane's voice was butter. "We believe you were attacked by a group we've been tracking. They're extremely dangerous and possibly possess a stolen weapon of mass destruction."

Officer Kelley's eyes grew wide. Was that satisfaction—maybe vindication—that the Crane saw settle on his face?

"We'd like you to do your best to describe everything you can remember," the Crane said.

Officer Kelley nodded and picked up the tablet. The Crane and the Banker sat.

An hour later, they left Officer Kelley's room.

"This is good information." The Crane led them toward the elevators. "We have a Launch Tech marine, a *male* Ace, and, dare I say it . . ."

The Banker whistled. "A phantom."

"A male Ace and a phantom . . . Strange times indeed," the Crane said. "Launch Tech is pulling out all the stops to get the device to a safe location without us vaporizing it. Their plan is so analog, the only circumstance under which it could possibly succeed is the one we're in. Network down, no connectivity. Hence, the phantom."

They reached the elevators. The Crane hit the button. The Banker grunted and pulled out a knife and scraped under one of his fingernails.

"But, Exoterra sees us as the contingency plan," the Crane said. "They'd like us to get the device, but not if it takes too much time. With the hostile takeovers Launch Tech just committed . . . They can't take over four of the Big Six *and* get the device."

The Banker's nostrils flared, and the elevator doors opened. The Crane understood the Banker's annoyance. Exoterra had tasked them with recapturing the device, but if they were unable do so, the Crane was to order a space strike that would vaporize it. And, depending on the Crane and Banker's proximity to the device, that space strike would possibly take them out too. Of course, it was hard to order a space strike while the network was down, so the Crane and the Banker had some extra time. But not that much. High risk, high reward. The elevator doors opened on a floor that was not their stop. A woman started to enter the elevator but stopped when she saw them, backed out, and walked away.

"I think Officer Kelley's career is over," the Crane said, the elevator moving again. "It's absolutely abhorrent he would attack a veteran and her sick passenger. Cops like him are the reason people don't trust the American government anymore."

The Banker smiled. "Agreed. I'll call the sheriff with our official statement." He tapped his fingers.

The Crane enjoyed destroying people, even if they didn't really need it. It was why he was good at his job. Empathy was weakness. If he was able to destroy those who didn't deserve it, he would never falter when he caught his prey. Every life he destroyed only further confirmed his professionalism.

Pushing Officer Kelley from his mind, he pulled up a saved video of Lucy walking through her habitat. Through his retinal display, he watched Lucy trundle her little tortoise legs through the sand while the Banker called the sheriff through one of the encrypted radio channels he'd set up.

But the call didn't go as the Crane anticipated. The Banker just listened, said *I see* several times, and then thanked the sheriff and ended the transmission.

"What was that?" The Crane blinked away the video of Lucy so he could clearly see the Banker, his cauliflower ears prominent in the elevator's dim light. This was a *slow* elevator. He was impressed the Banker had been able to get a call out in this vertical coffin.

"The Wendover Nugget, a casino on the border of Utah off of highway 80, just called the Troopers who then called the sheriff. They have a guy matching our photo, same clothes at least. He's being held by the casino security staff." The Banker tapped his fingers again. "The timeline makes sense. These guys could be in West Wendover by now, if they doubled back."

The Crane let out a sharp breath.

"I've got a small plane on standby. I can route it to Twin Falls to pick us up. The flight will take less than half an hour . . ."

The Crane smiled. The snare had sprung.

"Good work, Banker."

THIRTY-FOUR

CHEVY

Chevy was thrown backward when Izan floored it toward the entrance. The Conlow bag rested between his legs and the 10/22 sat on the floor between the front seats. Dolon climbed into the passenger seat.

"I'm gonna take over," Dolon offered. "I imagine you haven't been behind the wheel in a while."

Izan hit the brakes, and Dolon scrambled to not pitch into the dashboard. By this point, Chevy had put on her seatbelt. Izan threw the car in park and slipped out the side of the seat as Dolon stepped over him. They were back up and driving within seconds. Izan sat in the seat next to Chevy, holding the device.

"What happened in there?" Chevy asked.

"Security found me. They took me back to their office and hit me a few times. Said that Nevada didn't tolerate terrorists. I got the feeling they were holding me for someone." Dolon merged onto Wendover Boulevard.

"Hmmm," Izan said. "I wonder who that could possibly be."

Dolon pulled onto I-80 East. He punched the gas. "Welcome to Utah!"

"How did they recognize you?" Izan asked.

"Dunno," Dolon replied. "They took my photo, though."

"It could be the fact that you appear to have only one set of clothes," Izan said. "You make an impression in that getup."

Chevy and Dolon both looked at him. Chevy hadn't thought of that.

"I . . ." Dolon glanced at his pants. "I . . . I don't have the need for a lot of clothing."

"You got us new clothes, but you didn't think about getting any for yourself?" she asked.

Dolon threw up one hand.

"It's fine," Izan said. "We got you out of there. Do you have any other clothes with you?"

Dolon shook his head.

"I don't think anyone is coming after us." Chevy peered through the back window.

"This car is hot," Dolon said. "We've got to change it out as soon as possible. Unfortunately, there isn't much between here and Salt Lake City."

"I unscrewed the plate light," Chevy said, proud at having thought so far ahead.

"So, some Trooper is going to pull us over for having no plate light?"

Chevy's cheeks colored. "I figured it was better than their cameras getting our plate!"

"It's a gamble either way," Dolon said.

Headlights passed them on the other side of the highway. In the dark, they couldn't see what kind of car the lights belonged to. Chevy felt a creeping paranoia clawing at the base of her spine. Any of those headlights could be the cops. Had she really fucked up again?

The roar of engines cut through their minivan.

"What the . . . ?" Izan said.

Chevy pressed her face to the window, which looked out at the blackness that was, according to a road sign, the Bonneville Salt Flats. The lights of a low flying plane passed over the van. Chevy watched the plane parallel the road then set down on the salt flats, the roar of its engines so loud she flinched.

"Oh fuck," Chevy said. "You know they're here for us."

"They don't know we're here, in this car." Dolon glanced at the landing plane then back at the highway.

"They know we're near enough!" Chevy said.

"Well, they still have to get to a vehicle that lets them travel on the highway," Dolon said.

"I imagine our blacked-out plate will be a neon sign to all the cops in the area," Izan muttered.

"I WAS DOING THE BEST FOR THE MOMENT WE WERE IN," Chevy screamed.

No one said anything. Dolon stared straight ahead. Izan twisted backward to look at the plane, which was now rolling to a stop. Soon it was lost in the black of the night. Blood pumped in Chevy's ears. She had to get a hold of herself. But they needed to quit ribbing her. She had made a choice, and not all choices were one hundred percent gold. Sometimes you had to choose between shit and slop, and those had been her options.

"What's the plan?" Chevy finally managed.

"Get to Salt Lake City," Dolon said.

"We need to get off this road," Chevy said.

"I know, but there haven't been any exits."

Chevy opened her mouth, a rejoinder on the edge of her tongue, but instead took a long breath and sat back in the chair.

"Let's eat," Izan said.

Chevy felt her face twist into a sneer. Izan held a bag out to her, an olive branch to prevent a war. She pushed her face into a frown and nodded, tearing into the plastic bag. She opened a box, picked up a burger, and ripped a bite out of it.

"FUCK! I fucking told you I hate mayonnaise!"

Chevy spit out the burger. She threw the bun at the seat in front of her and punched the back of the front passenger seat so hard it broke.

The silence in the van wasn't brittle but tired. Chevy's chest heaved. The occasional set of oncoming headlights lit her up, and she could see her body moving. She began to box breathe. Beside her, Izan opened the other bag and cracked the top container. It held a steak.

"Here." He held out the steak's box and took the hamburger from her. "Looks like no mayo on this steak."

Chevy didn't move but let Izan take the hamburger box from her. Another set of headlights hit them, and Chevy saw just how much bigger than Izan she really was. If she had a total meltdown, Izan would be scared.

"Great," she said, mostly to herself. "Great. I'll eat this. Thanks."

She picked up the slab of meat and bit into it. Izan stared at her for a moment then took a bite of the burger he'd taken from Chevy, his movements subtle and compliant.

Chevy had seen that kind of behavior when she was a kid and her dad or an uncle would get angry. All the women would flip and become quiet and still. Here she was, suddenly in the place of the drunk, stupid uncle, and an Ace had turned into a scared wife. She could feel the primal anger wafting off of her, and the shame of it only added to her rage.

She wanted to scream, to cry, and to hit something else.

THIRTY-FIVE

DOLON

Dolon sighed and tried to push away the headache that was threatening to overwhelm him. He could feel its sharp tendrils wrapping around his brain, and he did his best to let go of the tension now clamping his shoulders to his ears.

Chevy . . . Chevy . . . Chevy. He watched her in the rearview. She was back there, having a temper tantrum and eating a steak like a caveman, grease smeared across her cheeks. In the beginning of this road trip from hell, Dolon felt that having Chevy around was a bit like getting a baby tiger as a pet. Initially an interesting and entertaining idea, then one day it grew up and tried to eat your thigh for breakfast.

But now, now she was the daughter he'd never had but needed to save. This is what having a teenager had to be like. He was old enough to be her father, and she obviously needed some sort of parent. How had this overgrown killing machine twisted him up like this? He shook his head and flicked his attention to Izan.

Izan's body language suggested meekness, but Dolon had begun to notice that with Izan's slowly restoring health, his eyes had started to shine with something else—calculation. Dolon could see it now. Izan's eyes were too sharp, too fearless, despite the submissive hunch to his shoulders. This sent a loud ping through Dolon's brain, even though Izan still made him think of Flora. He knew Chevy was fascinated by Izan. He could feel her dripping pheromones when she and Izan spoke (as if Dolon couldn't hear them). But Izan . . . There was something a little off, something a little passive and manipulative about him. Dolon couldn't put his finger on it. Everyone loved Aces except for Dolon, fair enough. And he didn't like that there was a current zipping between Izan and Chevy. But Chevy could break as many car headrests as she wanted, and Dolon would still find that less suspicious than Izan's ineffable magnetism.

Dolon pushed a stream of air through his nose. They were all tired and stressed, him included. Izan was obviously better than the monsters they were running from. So what if he wasn't totally transparent? Neither was Dolon. Izan was on their team. Maybe Dolon needed to eat a steak with his hands and he'd feel better too. A set of oncoming headlights pinged up the volume on Dolon's growing headache. He needed to get off of this road, but he hadn't seen an exit in miles.

Finally, one appeared: a low prime number and the words NO SERVICES. It was perfect. He pulled onto the ramp and slowed. They came to a stop sign and Dolon put the van in park. He got out, went around to the back, and screwed the light back into the rear plate display. It flickered on, weak but true. He returned to the driver's door and got in without saying anything, then put the van into gear and got onto the frontage road, still headed east toward Salt Lake.

He looked in the rearview mirror again. Chevy was now shoveling a salad into her mouth. Izan stared out the window with his burger forgotten on his lap.

"You want some food, Dolon?" Chevy said, her voice gruff. Dolon checked the rearview and saw her holding a box out to him.

"Thanks." He set it on his lap and took out the other burger and took a bite. Cold hamburgers usually turned his stomach, but this one did the trick. More than a chickpea chip could have, anyway.

In the distance, Dolon saw what looked like a refinery. Lit up smokestacks grew larger, and soon they passed a sign that said, SOLUTIONS RECYCLING CENTER. Below that was another sign. HORSESHOE KNOLLS OHV AREA NEXT RIGHT.

Dolon took the next right.

The fringes of a plan began to knit together in Dolon's mind. He'd been here, ages ago, with a buddy of a buddy. He'd hated it, but it'd made an impression. It was the kind of place he never wanted to go back to. But it was the kind of place that actually might save them right now.

"Where are we going?" Chevy asked.

"A no rules, off-roading area up here. We can leave the van. We'll go cross country to the edge of Salt Lake."

"Like walk?" Chevy said.

"No," Dolon scoffed. "We're not walking anywhere. I have an idea."

THIRTY-SIX

CHEVY

Chevy wished she was back with her marine buddies. With her meltdown, the proverbial curtain had been pulled back on all the lies she'd been telling herself. She wanted Izan, bad. And she wanted him to want her back. Yet, she'd just shown herself to be nothing but a big, dumb, dangerous idiot. No one wanted that. Including her. She wanted to curl up and die.

But dying wasn't really an option, so she just went back to work box breathing. Because she was a big, dumb grunt, and that was what she'd been trained to do. And gallingly, it helped, like always. She hated she was so predictable.

She opened another box and found a slab of meatloaf, then went to work on that while avoiding looking at Izan. They were both professionals. They could work together and get this done, even if she was embarrassed as hell. It wasn't like she hadn't been turned down before, although not by anyone she'd given a bath to . . . Damn it, again. She needed to just eat and breathe and quit fucking thinking.

"Start gathering up our stuff," Dolon said.

Chevy glanced at Dolon. "You want the guns broken down?" she asked.

"Leave the Remington out. Pack the rest of it up. Keep the water accessible."

Izan glanced at Chevy. He looked at her quizzically, and something fragile inside of her was fortified. They could wonder together about Dolon's crazy plan. Izan might not be into her, but they were still teammates. He wouldn't let that go at least. Maybe she had been a little worried about that too.

She began to pack up their gear. "So just my rifle and shotgun stay functional?"

She wasn't going to ask to keep her rifle out, but she wasn't going to start a fight over it either. They were a team, and she had messed up. She could show deference.

Dolon's eyes moved to hers in the rearview. He stared at her in a way that she'd never seen before, and she felt, like a kid . . . who had a dad who . . . cared? She froze. Her brain was assigning dad vibes to Dolon? She didn't know what to do with that feeling. She looked away.

"Actually," Dolon said, "keep out the 10/22 too."

Chevy's shoulders relaxed. Dolon had accepted the peace offering.

"You got your pills, Izan?" Dolon asked, his eyes no longer on Chevy.

Izan held up the bottle and shook it, then put them in his pants pocket.

"Where's the device?" Dolon said.

"I have it." Izan handed it to Chevy. "But Chevy's got it now. Her pockets are bigger."

Chevy took the device from Izan, her fingers grazing his. Now she felt it, even though it was just a flash. The energy between them was sizzling, yet soft. Like silky electricity.

That woke her up, and not in the way she needed, so she thought of PFC Gandres vomiting. She dug into her memory and recalled the fetid, humid air of the drop ship, the stupid way PFC Whitehead said "click" every time he fastened his harness straps, the way her Kevlar chonies gave her diaper rash. She thought of the last time she was in the med unit and a guy had been there with trench foot, literal fucking trench foot, and she thought of the smell of PFC Tan's skin after it had been burned off. She thought of every horrible thing she could to dampen down the rising pressure in her stomach.

The van slowed. Chevy gulped air.

"Okay," Dolon said. "This area is real popular with the worst kinds of people. There are idiot meth heads out here just trashing this place. They're shooting anything that moves, humping anything female, some things not, driving their dirt bikes and side-by-sides across the desert, ripping up critical habitat to sensitive species. I hate these fucking people. We're going to ditch the van, and they'll torch it in no time. Then we're going to steal some rides and keep heading east."

"What?" Izan said. "How are we going to just steal someone's ride?"

Dolon tapped the clock. It showed nine twenty-seven. "They've started to tie one on. We just need to wait 'til they pass out."

Chevy stiffened. The sound of gunfire and screams cut through the van. She peered out of her window and saw they were approaching what looked to be several RVs surrounding a bonfire. Dolon turned onto a dirt road and drove past the fire. A group of men stood by the flames, firing guns into the darkness. A woman screamed, and Chevy wasn't sure it was because she was having fun.

They drove past the RVs, the road bumpy and rough. Dolon didn't say anything, and they passed several more camps made up of RVs, drunken men, the occasional woman, expensive off-roading vehicles—quads, dirt bikes, Jeeps, jacked-up trucks—and huge fires of every kind, from bon to oil drum. Everyone they passed was armed with at least one visible weapon.

"I see why you hate this place," Izan said. "This is why I went into space."

They passed one guy who looked a lot like Chevy's cousin, and one of the RVs was the same kind her favorite uncle had lived in.

"These people are not good people," Dolon said. "They have very little regard for life that isn't their own. The stuff I saw here the first time I came; it makes me sick to think about."

Neither Chevy nor Izan asked for details.

They drove for twenty minutes and groups became more and more spaced out, before they rounded a curve and saw a cluster of RVs positioned behind a hill. Dolon slowed as they drove by the camp. Unlike a lot of the other groups they passed, this little convoy seemed to be made up of families. Several women were herding children into the RVs. A few men sat in lawn chairs around a flaming oil drum. A side-by-side, two dirt bikes, and an ATV were parked between the road and the fire. Several trucks could be seen in the flickering shadows of the RVs. The men were talking but weren't as animated as the other groups. Chevy noticed beer cans littered the ground between the men. Music played from a portable speaker.

"Ladies and gentlemen," Dolon's voice was grand, like an announcer's, "I think this is our group."

THIRTY-SEVEN

THE CRANE

The Crane stepped out of the plane and onto the packed earth of the Bonneville Salt Flats. The desert air prickled at his nose. His suit felt wrinkled after that flight, and he tugged it so it hung properly. In the distance, he could see I-80 and the headlights of cars bright against the moonless night.

The Banker had called Wendover Nugget security guards before they took off. The security team said they would come pick up the Crane and Banker when they landed. The Crane scanned the blackness now and saw a rapidly approaching set of headlights, swirling dust announcing the vehicle was no longer on a paved road.

A few minutes later, a sweaty, soup-sandwich of a man popped out of a dented fifteen passenger van.

"Welcome. I'm Marvin." He thrust out a damp palm. "I'm the sergeant in charge tonight."

The Crane felt his eyebrow rise at this. So, he was giving himself a rank for tonight? Did this man think he was an actual officer?

"Thank you for coming to get us." The Crane ignored the fleshy hand that hovered before him. "I think you can appreciate our need for speed here, Marvin. These people are dangerous."

"You bet." Marvin bobbed his head, wiping his hands on the front of his disheveled uniform. "Let's get you to 'em."

The Crane and the Banker folded themselves into the van, the Crane taking the front seat. Marvin pulled his roly-poly self into the driver's seat and said, "Everyone in and buckled?"

Neither the Crane nor the Banker responded.

"Well . . . Right then. Let's get to it."

Marvin put the van in gear and pulled away from the plane.

"How did you identify the individual as the man we're after?" the Crane asked.

Marvin perked up at the question. "We have a real slick guy who works the cameras."

Marvin beamed at the Crane. The Crane didn't smile back.

"Well, anyway, he got your APB. He's always scanning those and found someone who matched the guy in the picture. Same clothes, same height, same everything. Even had the same white beard. We've got him in our holding cell."

"What is his name?" the Crane asked.

Marvin screwed up his face.

"It's a weird one. And the last name is foreign sounding. You know, with two capital letters. I can't remember off the top of my head, but we've got his ID. We're only a few minutes away."

The Crane sighed and leaned back into the chair.

They drove in silence for the rest of the trip. When they pulled into the Wendover Nugget parking lot, the Crane felt his pulse quicken. There was a chance, however unlikely, that this bowling ball of a human had actually managed to capture the Launch Tech phantom. He licked his lips.

"Now that's odd," Marvin said, stopping the van.

"What?" the Crane said.

"The outer door is open. It shouldn't be. That's not how I run my ship."

Marvin wiggled out of the driver's seat and moved as fast as his form would let him toward the open door. But the Crane and the Banker were at the door, guns out and entering, before Marvin could say another word.

The Crane and the Banker flowed into the room. They hit the hard corners, cleared behind the ramshackle desks, entered the hallway and worked systematically, door by door, until they came to the last room, which was not an open door, but a splintered one. Inside, the Crane saw three men, handcuffed together. One out cold, one crying, and one clearly dazed.

His heart both flipped and fell. The phantom, the grunt, and the Ace weren't here, but they *had* been here. He heard a scrape behind him. He turned and saw dopey Marvin, staring, mouth agape, at the door and his men. The Crane was so impressed at what Marvin's guys had almost managed to do, he had to take a deep, long breath.

It was almost beautiful, except that his prey had escaped once again.

The Crane wanted to break someone. And he would. When he caught that Ace, because he would, he would show no mercy.

THIRTY-EIGHT

DOLON

Dolon drove past the obviously drunk men, the pressure in his head a little less now that he'd choked down some cold burger. He rounded a bend. They found themselves in a forest of burnt cars, their metal skeletons twisted, black, and eerie in the van's headlights and against the nighttime sky.

"This is our stop. Get the stuff," Dolon said.

He pulled off the road, nestling the van between a partially burned sedan and a gutted pickup truck. They gathered their things.

"How you want to carry all this water?" Chevy poked at the jugs Dolon bought at the service station.

"Keep those out of the packs. We're going to use them here soon."

Dolon saw Izan glance at Chevy, his eyebrows twitching in conspiratorial questioning. It was a look meant for Chevy, and Chevy alone. But Dolon caught it. It made him want to grab Izan and drag him into the darkness and beat him until he told Dolon what his angle was. Maybe that's what having a teenaged son was like? Jesus. No. This was what having a teenaged boy hang around your teenaged daughter was like. Izan was the little shit trying to get in Chevy's pants. And as much as Dolon hated that, he also wanted to, needed to, believe in the kid. He wanted to hug Izan and accept him, trust he was the good thing Chevy believed he was, but deep down, men were men, and Dolon was one too. He got it. And, what enraged him more, now that he was on the topic, was that he *knew* he would fight for Izan. Izan was *his* little shit stirrer, not Exoterra's. That was the tribalism wired into his brain. Dolon would do what he had to protect both of them, even if Izan was a little turd stick he'd like to knock some sense into.

Fuck. Dolon rubbed his temples. Chevy had calmed since she'd eaten approximately five thousand calories, and now Dolon was hyperfocused on Izan. Maybe Dolon was the issue. He grabbed a few soggy fries from the takeout container.

Chewing, he grabbed the license plates from the truck.

"We should have ditched these a while ago," he said through a mouth full of fries.

He got out of the van. The stars bathed him in a muted glow, and he unscrewed the van's stolen plates then walked into the darkness, all of the plates in hand. Dolon found an overhanging rock and used the plates to dig a hole under it, then tossed them in and covered them with dirt.

He walked back to Chevy and Izan. Their soft whispers floated through the heavy night air but stopped when he was close enough to make out their words. Dolon pushed down his irritation.

"You got everything?" Dolon asked.

"Yup." Chevy hoisted one of the bags onto her shoulder.

"Alright, let's torch the van."

"Really?" Chevy was excited. "I thought you said other people would do it."

"Yeah, given enough time."

"I don't want to leave it to chance," Izan agreed.

Dolon pulled a blackened pot, a hammer, and a nail from one of his bags, then stuffed himself under the van. He nailed through the fuel tank and let the liquid spill into the pot until it was full, then shimmied back out and opened one of the doors. He doused the inside of the van and stepped back.

"Ready to move?"

Chevy had the majority of their gear. It looked uncomfortable.

"Here, give me the device. You've got enough to keep track of."

Chevy didn't look pleased by this, but she dug the Conlow bag out of her pocket and handed it to Dolon.

"And I'll take the Remington," Dolon said.

Chevy handed him the shotgun. Dolon cracked the chamber and noted, "Great. You loaded it."

Bewilderment clouded Chevy's features. Of course she'd loaded it, she was a marine. Dolon grabbed a last handful of fries from the box Chevy had set in the sand. Izan held the .22, and Dolon knew better now than to ask if it was loaded. His Ruger was zipped into one of the go bags. On their drive out of Twin Falls, he'd watched Chevy clean each piece then wrap the pieces in their discarded T-shirts.

Dolon reached into his pocket and pulled out a matchbook. He lit one and threw it into the open van. Fire whooshed across the interior, and Chevy let out an excited huff.

"Let's move," Dolon said.

They took off across the dry ground. Dolon led, followed closely by Izan. Chevy had their six, humping enough stuff to make two of Izan. She held her rifle naturally. Dolon realized she was finally in her element.

The group of drunk men slowly came into view, laughing now. Dolon could hear the sounds of children coming from the RVs and guessed the women were putting them to bed.

They stayed on the other side of the road and moved quietly, the men never glancing their way. Soon, they were against the hillside.

"I should have asked," Dolon whispered, looking at Chevy, "but I assume you can ride a dirt bike."

Chevy gave him another bewildered look but simply managed, "Yeah."

"Great. I'm going to secure our rides. Stay here and cover me."

Chevy nodded at the top of the hill. "I'll cover you from up there."

Dolon nodded back, and Chevy began to move. Izan lay behind a rock and propped the 10/22 in the direction of the RVs.

Dolon picked up the three gallons of water and slung the Remington across his back. He set off toward the men's vehicles, the pressure in his head receding with each step. He proceeded slowly and deliberately, made all the more awkward by the sloshing of the three gallons of water. He kept his focus on the men, but they were too absorbed in whatever they were doing to notice him . . . yet.

He got to the parked quad and slowly undid the straps holding the gas can lashed to its back. It was full, thankfully. He opened the vehicle's gas cap and tipped one of the gallons of water into it until it was gone, then another until the tank began to overflow. Then he moved onto the bikes, watering down the smaller of the two.

He emptied the gas can into the undamaged bike and the side-by-side, which mercifully had the keys in the ignitions.

He moved on toward the three trucks parked behind the RVs, popping the hoods on the first two and snipping their spark plug cables with his multitool. The third truck had the hood release in the cab, so he punctured its driver side tires instead.

He took a satisfied step back, watching the truck list to the side when a voice behind him said, "Stop right there."

Dolon turned, his hands raised.

A woman in a dress stood behind him holding a shotgun, its muzzle pointed at his head.

Before he could say anything, she yelled, "I CAUGHT A GUY FUCKING WITH OUR STUFF."

THIRTY-NINE

CHEVY

Chevy lay on her stomach on the back side of the top of the hill, her rifle propped on the ridge and aimed at the circle of RVs. The men and milling women moved as if no one were watching. Then it happened. A woman screamed, and seconds later Dolon was being marched into the circle of men, a woman in a long dress holding a shotgun to his head.

This was bad.

For a moment, the camp didn't react, then the families erupted into action. Women and kids hemorrhaged from the RVs. The men jumped up and pulled pistols from their waistbands, leveling them at Dolon. Everyone seemed to be screaming. Then, the mass of people stilled and went quiet. They all watched one man.

He stepped to Dolon, his pistol pointed at his forehead. "Get on your knees." He had scarred cheeks, bad teeth, sallow skin, and a ratty beard.

Dolon said nothing but lowered himself to the ground. Another man took the Remington off his back. The woman continued to hold the shotgun on Dolon. Chevy could hear her muttering what sounded like *motherfucker* on repeat.

Scraggle beard barked an order at one of the men to go see what Dolon had been doing behind the RVs. Another man moved forward and roughly patted Dolon down and pulled out the Conlow bag. He dropped it like it was hot and screamed. Everyone but Dolon flinched backward. The woman with the shotgun tracked the bag to the ground, seemingly confused about what she should be aiming at.

The leader kicked the Conlow bag toward the oil drum.

Chevy's body went tense. Her senses erupted to a new level of alertness and focus. The sand against her stomach became sharp. She felt blistering potential in her trigger finger. All she had to do was let it go. The scent of the burning oil drum separated, and she could now smell wood and chemicals, could taste the baking rust. The world didn't feel slow. She felt fast.

No one touched the Conlow bag.

"Who the hell are you?" the man said.

"I'm no one."

The man who had patted Dolon down kicked him in the back. Dolon folded forward.

"You're traveling with something like that," the bearded man pointed at the Conlow bag, "and you have the balls to say you're *no one*. You think I'm stupid? You think I didn't do my time inside? I remember. Secrets get kept in Conlow bags." He laughed, the pitch crazed. "Yeah. Dangerous secrets, valuable secrets, get kept in Conlow bags."

The group murmured in response.

"Who the fuck are you with?"

Dolon groaned.

"Maybe we should ransom you. To the highest bidder." The group seemed enthusiastic about that. "Or maybe we just destroy whatever is in the bag and kill you. I mean, no doubt whatever it is is some major shit. Only going to further poison the world." The group seemed more excited about that. "That what you want? To poison the world?"

Dolon sat up. "I wouldn't do that if I were you."

"What?"

"Destroy it."

The man stiffened. Chevy's heart rate went up, but her brain stilled. This was not the kind of guy to tell what to do, Dolon. But Chevy had an answer for that. The man moved toward the Conlow bag.

"You dare tell me what to do? I'll throw you and your devil bag into this fucking fire! You're not in control here."

If the device touched fire, Chevy didn't need to be a fucking scientist to know they and probably all of Salt Lake were dead. Maybe Earth with it. Who knew? But she wasn't going to sit around to find out. The likelihood of her shooting all of them before one of them shot Dolon was low, but she could try. She hoped Dolon was feeling spry.

Rat beard took another step toward the Conlow bag, and Chevy double-tapped him in the chest before raising the sights to his head. She let the third shot fly and his face disappeared. The group exploded into screams. She pivoted the rifle's barrel and took out another man, and then two more. The kids and women, including the lady with the shotgun, disappeared into the shadows. They had probably drilled this, Chevy realized. Dolon was off his knees, attempting to scoop up his Remington when a man grabbed him from behind. They went to the ground, wrestling over the shotgun.

Chevy did not have a shot, and the rest of the group had faded into the darkness. She threw herself to her feet and ran over the crest of the hill and straight at the oil drum. The Conlow bag still lay where it had been kicked.

The moment she stepped into the firelight, she heard the shots. Someone in one of the RV windows was chucking rounds at her. She plugged several rounds at the window, pushing herself faster. The shots stopped.

Dolon was still scrambling on the ground when Chevy reached the Conlow bag. She smashed it into her pocket, and someone grabbed her and yanked her backward. She spun, grabbed the man's arm and dropped her weight, tearing his shoulder and driving her knee into his neck as they hit the ground. He gasped for air, but his trachea was shattered. She left him to die on his own time.

Chevy pivoted to where she last saw Dolon, but a shotgun blast redirected her. She saw the frontier wife in the dress racking the gun. Chevy shot her in the neck then in the nose. The frontier wife collapsed with the downward violence Chevy had only ever seen in lights-out kills.

A strangled cry caught her attention, and she saw a man on top of Dolon, the shotgun barrel across Dolon's neck. The man struggled to maintain the choke and reach for his pistol. Chevy leveled her sights at the guy's left eye, and a moment later his torso followed his brain backward and off of Dolon.

Dolon slithered his legs out from under his dead attacker when the sound of a handgun caused Chevy to dive behind one of the RVs. She turned and saw a kid, a fucking elementary school-aged kid, holding what looked to be a giant pistol in his tiny hands. He shot toward her again. Chevy drilled several rounds into the RV above his head. He dropped the gun and ran inside crying.

Chevy loped to a different RV, tucking out of the firelight, and surveyed the scene. Six men and one woman lay dead between the

RVs and oil drum. Dolon had disappeared, and she didn't know if he'd been hit. She knew the women and kids were somewhere, and they were clearly dangerous. This was a nightmare.

Circling behind the RVs in the shadows, Chevy ran through the dark desert and back to Izan. He jumped as she slid beside him. Chevy opened her mouth then caught sight of Izan's eyes. He looked haunted.

"Are you hit?" Chevy hissed, immediately padding Izan's body.

Izan stared at her for a few moments, at the mercy of her aggressive injury sweeps, then shook his head.

"What's the matter with you then?" Chevy turned her attention back to the RVs. No one had appeared. Where was Dolon? She looked back at Izan. He looked too pale. Maybe he was hit and he just didn't know it. She went back to checking for blood.

"Stop," he finally said. "I'm fine . . . I . . ."

Someone was coming up on them. Chevy spun on her back, rifle up, finger on the trigger. Then she recognized that white beard. Dolon. She lowered the rifle.

"Jesus, old man. I nearly fucking shot you."

Dolon collapsed next to them, panting. Chevy refocused on the RVs. Still no movement.

"We gotta get out of here," she said, scanning their peripheries.

"There's a side-by-side and a big bike, it's blue. That one's for you. The side-by-side is for Izan and me. We get in them and go," Dolon wheezed. "Izan, you're navigating. I'll drive. I poured water in the small bike and quad, took out two of the three trucks' spark plugs, and wrecked the tires on the third."

Chevy nodded. "Well good job on doing that *before* this all went down. I'm sure this group in particular would have appreciated the guerrilla tactics, assuming they weren't trying to kill us."

"It's . . . it's why they hired me," Dolon managed, getting his breathing under control.

"If you can call it that," Izan muttered.

Dolon's face tweaked at that, his features going sappy, but Chevy didn't have time to dwell on it.

"You good?" she asked.

Dolon nodded.

"You get hit?"

"I don't think so."

"We can check when we get out of here. We should go before those hill wives reemerge with their gun-toting spawn. You two ready?"

Dolon mumbled something, and Izan simply stared at Chevy like he'd never seen her before. She stood, yanked up Izan, shouldered all their gear, and pushed Izan between her and Dolon. She took point to the waiting vehicles. No one appeared.

They reached the UTV, and Chevy threw bags into the back. Izan climbed into the passenger seat like a shadow. Chevy kept her rifle only low enough to see just over the sight. The desert gloom seemed alive with hostiles, but every time she swiveled to what she thought was an enemy, she found nothing.

When Izan and Dolon were in the side-by-side, Chevy went to the bike Dolon indicated. Still no movement from the RVs or their curtilage. She slung her rifle so it was in front of her, but there was no way she could ride the bike and shoot. She did not like this, but this was her reality.

Chevy straddled the bike, turned it on, flipped the gas line to open, pulled out the choke, and shifted the bike into neutral. She looked at Dolon. He nodded at her.

Dolon turned the key, and Chevy twisted the throttle.

The dirt bike didn't immediately purr to life, so Chevy cranked the throttle again. The side-by-side was moving. She wasn't.

Fuck, she thought.

Another rip of gunfire. A woman was back by the lawn chairs, what appeared to be a .357 Magnum pointed not exactly in Chevy's direction, but close enough.

Then the roar of a shotgun split the air, and the woman dove toward the nearest RV. The bike leapt to life, and Chevy did a Kegel and kept her balance. She took off after the UTV, which had moved out of the range of the firelight.

Chevy zoomed into the desert, breathing hard. The buzz of adrenaline sounded in her ears. She smiled wildly into the desert night. She had lived through another battle. Every nerve in her body sang with life.

This was when she was most alive.

Nothing could top this feeling, right here, right now.

She opened her mouth and howled at the moon.

FORTY

THE CRANE

The Crane stood behind the Banker studying the security footage on a monitor screen. The marine was frozen, mid door kicking, with a shemagh covering most of her face. Somehow, even after all the smashing and damage she'd done to the inside of the security office, it had never slipped from her cheeks. The best image they had of the woman was this one, as she bulldozed through the door. The low-res camera still managed to catch the predatory light in her irises.

The three security guards who'd been in the office when the marine came barging in were of almost no help. Marvin's "superstar" of an employee was so traumatized he couldn't speak. The other two weren't much better. What was even more frustrating was that they'd never recorded the phantom's name, even though they'd been in possession of his ID.

This made the Crane angry, yes, certainly angry, but they did have a better photo of the man. For some unknown reason, the security guards had photographed him prior to getting a conclusive ID.

The Crane looked at that photo now.

Eyes the color of weak green tea stared at him from a windbeaten face. A white beard, trimmed, but not fashionable, obscured the man's jawline. It was clear from the flat way he stared into the camera that he was unimpressed. His hair was limp and drained of color. It reminded the Crane of muddy river water. A network of lines spread from the corners of his eyes, branching out like the channels of a river delta.

The Crane himself couldn't have picked a better archetype for a phantom.

"So far, no hits," the Banker said, typing into the ancient Wendover Nugget computer. "Nothing is recognizing his face. I mean, he's out there, for sure. You can't get to be his age nowadays and not have had your face on a camera at some point in your life. But the most obvious places, social media, check-ins at stores, restaurants, police files, etc., are coming up empty. I'm going to have to dig for him." The Banker smiled and tapped his fingers above the keyboard. "And, thanks to this lovely casino contracting with Jinzhan, we can use their setup to surf the web. Even with the war, their customers still have connectivity."

The Crane tore his eyes from the phantom's face and walked to the metal bench where the casino processed their detainees. He held a scanner over the surface. A clear thumb print materialized on the machine's screen.

The Crane smiled. They couldn't stay hidden forever. The hunt continued.

FORTY-ONE

CHEVY

Burping giggles, Chevy stopped her bike next to Dolon and Izan in the shadows of a hill. The noise and lights from the RV camp were long gone now, and she could just make out Izan in the UTV's passenger seat, his head thrust to the side in sleep. Chevy laughed again.

"What is wrong with you?" Dolon said.

He looked wiped. His hair was matted and his eye was puffy from either the security guards or the shotgun death wrestle, maybe both. She wanted to hug Izan and Dolon. Dance with them in a field of flowers. Yell at the stars. They were together, and alive. In this moment, Chevy loved them.

"Thanks for the cover. I didn't know if the bike was actually gonna start."

Dolon waved her away. But Chevy couldn't help it. Her blood was *rushing* through her veins. They were *alive.* Another giggle escaped her throat.

"Fucking marines," Dolon mumbled. "Are you all children?"

Chevy worked to marshal herself and inhaled slowly. After a few moments of silence, Dolon dug into one of his bags.

"We need to get to Salt Lake."

"Then what?" Her voice had an edge to it. The wave of ecstatic silliness had rushed through her and left. The euphoria dried up as suddenly as it had come. Classic crashing after a battle. She now felt tired and cold.

Dolon considered her. She knew he was waiting for her to laugh again, but she'd come back to Earth. She was done. He held out an MRE serving of instant coffee. She grabbed it, and he tore the corner off of his own paper sleeve before dumping it into his mouth.

"We find somewhere to bed down and recharge. I'm not twenty. I need some actual sleep. I'm barely hanging on as it is."

"You think you can keep driving? I mean, maybe Izan can drive for a while."

Dolon snorted and poured more coffee crystals onto his tongue. "The fact he survived that drop . . . And the fact that he's been improving so quickly outside of medical care . . . He should be dead. He's a tough little bastard, but we need to tax him as little as possible."

Chevy nodded, her eyes on Izan. Watching him made her skin crawl with worry. She turned her focus to getting the coffee packet open.

"I'm not saying he's going to die, but he should be in a hospital. Not hightailing it across the desert in a stolen UTV."

Dolon's voice was gratingly gentle. He'd read her face like a book. Chevy let out a defeated sound and tossed the coffee grounds into her mouth.

"So, the plan is, I drive, he sleeps. I'll wake him in a little while to take his med, and when we get to civilization, we crash."

"Copy," Chevy said.

They drove for what seemed like days. Then when it seemed the night couldn't get any blacker, the horizon began to shine.

They were nearing Salt Lake. They passed dilapidated houses, run-down shacks, ramshackle sheds, unending fields of junk and rusted metal. A sign that said, HOME SWEET HOME dangled from a wagon wheel. An RV full of bullet holes, a toilet bowl full of fake flowers. Then, a lawn of rotting vehicles spread before them. A trailer with an exterior light sat about a quarter of a mile in the distance.

Dolon stopped the side-by-side, pulling it behind a crumbling fifth wheel. "See what you can find."

Chevy parked the bike between a spray-painted SUV and a crushed teardrop trailer. Swinging a stiff leg over the bike, she got both feet on the ground. Bowlegged and unsteady, she took a few steps before moving into the mass of vehicles.

Some of the cars were so old she didn't recognize them, which was saying something because like any Southern girl, she was pretty good with vehicle recognition. Some of these were from the twentieth century. Most were newer, but they'd clearly been trash when they were made and were now nothing but shapeless bundles.

Finally, she came across a red KIA Futuro, which, unlike the burned-out hulks around it, actually seemed like it might run.

She folded herself to fit and got in. She was spiritually opposed to KIAs. No military member ever wanted that acronym in their file. And KIAs were made for people Izan's size, not hers. The entire vehicle seemed to touch the ground when she sat in it.

It had a push button start, and when she hit it, the dash display showed enough charge for two hundred and fourteen miles. She opened the center console and found the fob sitting inside. She nodded at her luck: A second-generation self-driving model. She let it ease itself backward, then directed it back toward Dolon and Izan.

Dolon already had the bags out of the cargo net and tossed them in when Chevy popped the trunk. Dolon gently shook Izan awake and guided him to the back of the KIA. He crawled in and went immediately back to sleep.

"I wiped the bike and UTV down while you were finding this," he whispered, pulling the passenger door shut. "While they took my photo back at the casino, I tried not to touch anything. When they were giving me the what for though, I think I probably grabbed onto something."

Chevy hadn't even thought about her fingerprints at the casino. She'd smashed through a door for God's sake.

"Good thinking." Chevy nodded, not knowing what else to say.

Chevy touched the drive button, and the car pulled away slowly. She'd twisted the headlight knob to manual and kept them off. Maybe they could get away from the trailer unnoticed.

They eased onto a gravel road and eventually found pavement. She turned on the Futuro's headlights.

"Let's find a hotel that doesn't look like it'll ask questions and isn't right off of I-80 or I-15," Dolon said.

"Alright. I'll direct the car, you spot."

"Got it," Dolon said.

And in that moment, Chevy felt the warm embrace of having him on her side. It was them against the world, and maybe, just maybe, they would win.

FORTY-TWO

THE CRANE

The old man was certainly a phantom. The Banker still hadn't managed to pull up anything concrete on him, and he'd been looking for hours. There was no way that naturally occurred. Launch Tech was curating his visibility.

The Crane paced the Wendover Nugget security office, the Banker typing away loudly into one of their ancient computers. They had taken over the space, sending the three traumatized guards to the hospital. Marvin went with them in a show of solidarity and the casino sent a maintenance guy to install some OSB as a temporary exterior door. About an hour after that, a sleepy-looking guy in a wrinkled uniform showed up to cover for Marvin while he was gone. The Crane told him to find a different office to sleep in and slammed the makeshift door in his face.

While they hadn't unearthed anything about the phantom, they did know who the grunt was thanks to the fact she seemed to have touched everything in the room. Chevy Llewellyn Cole. Born in Biloxi, Mississippi, to Abraham and Linda Cole. It appeared that Abraham believed in a certain brand of Americanism. He was xenophobic, nationalistic, large, loud, white, and proud. He'd taken part in a myriad of civil disturbances in his twenties. Linda seemed to be exactly what you'd expect of the wife of a man like Abraham—meek, sheltered, no job history (the Crane refused to count making bath bombs as a career). And based on her social media posts, she didn't seem to have any critical reasoning skills.

The Crane's picture of Chevy Cole was starting to coalesce, though. Cole appeared to have been a bright enough kid, but she'd never gone to an actual school. From what they could tell, Cole had never used any of her leave to visit her family. She had never reached out to them via any mode of communication. She joined Launch Tech at eighteen and that seemed to be the last time she'd interacted with them at all.

She'd used her last shore leave to visit a retired marine in Winnipeg. When they'd called him about her though, he'd just laughed at the notion that he and Cole were seriously involved. The Crane knew from the smile in the man's voice that sending someone to Winnipeg to interrogate him wasn't going to help. Otherwise, Cole had a few social media posts about the Big Six and space, but nothing useful. Other than the corporation that gave her an out from her backward family and was now claiming their return on investment by knowingly placing her directly within the sights of the Crane and the Banker, it was clear she meant nothing to anyone, anywhere.

Beyond Cole and the phantom, they still had no concrete evidence of the Ace. There was the absence of human remains in only one of the two lifeboats that made it to Earth (two hadn't successfully reentered the atmosphere). There was the account of the Idaho State Trooper. But otherwise, they had nothing. No photographs, no grainy videos, no partial fingerprints, nothing. He was more of a ghost than the phantom.

The Crane felt frustration creeping up the back of his neck. Exoterra's and Launch Tech's lack of networks was not making this easy. If they had been up, the Banker could have hacked into Launch Tech's data stores and found something on the Ace. No, the Crane knew that was fanciful. Breaching Launch Tech's network was something done on specialized tech from secure areas. Not from the rent-a-cop office of a third-rate casino.

The Crane wondered what knowledge existed that could help him. What didn't he have access to? He pivoted and idly considered if he'd wear away the Nugget's linoleum with his pacing. He reached the far wall and turned again, swiveling his neck so a series of pops clicked up his spine and granted some relief.

Once again, they had disappeared.

The Banker's fingers made loud clicks on the brittle keyboard. The Crane was a professional and a sportsman. He had to give it to Launch Tech. They were exceling in an impossible situation.

The network would be fixed soon, and when that happened, everything would change.

Time was running out. For everyone.

FORTY-THREE

CHEVY

"You shouldn't carry anything," Chevy said.

They'd found a motel, a seedy hole-in-the-wall tucked away on the disheveled edge of town. Dolon had stumbled from the car to one of the beds, and Chevy was pretty sure he'd started to snore before his head hit the pillow. Now she and Izan were shuttling their bags into the room. But Chevy didn't want Izan carrying anything. After her conversation with Dolon, she was scared for him. She couldn't let Izan die. Her objective was clear. Protect him.

"It's fine. This duffel bag is so light, it practically floats. You take the heavy stuff. I'm not competing." Izan lifted the bag like it was drifting away.

"I'm not saying you're trying to out ego me." Chevy took the last bag from the trunk. "I'm just saying, you need to be careful. It's not like you've recovered from falling out of orbit."

"I know." But he kept carrying the bag anyway.

They were in the room now, their voices hushed. The room was small, too small for the two beds and the table and chairs jammed into it. Every time Chevy wanted to take a step, Izan had to move, or a chair had to be adjusted or one of their bags had to be pulled out of the way. Then the AC clunked on, so loud it reminded Chevy of a drop ship. Luckily, it seemed Dolon wouldn't wake up if a train came through their front window.

Scratchy sheets and plastic laced comforters adorned the beds. A microwave sat on the tiny table. Chevy unplugged it and stuffed it under one of the beds then pushed the table to the window. It now blocked most of the path to the bathroom, but their security was more important than immediate toilet access. Chevy set her rifle on the table and propped it on an extra pillow from Dolon's bed. She moved the curtains so she could see through their gap.

"You hit the sack," Chevy said. "I'll take first watch."

"Why don't you sleep, and I'll take the first watch?"

Izan moved to her side, his lithe stride causing Chevy's heart to jump. He tipped his chin up and looked out the window. Chevy could see the soft, underside of his neck . . . Her stomach jingled.

"You need to rest," she swallowed.

He turned his knowing brown eyes on her. Gone were the pale cheeks and slack jaw from their brush with the hill people. An Ace was once again in her presence, and she couldn't help but feel his power.

"So do you. I've gotten several hours of sleep, and we all know neither you nor Dolon are going to let me drive tomorrow. I can sleep as long as we have a car."

"Your body needs time to recover."

"Yup. So does yours."

He pulled the 10/22 from its case.

"I . . ."

"It's not up to you," he said. "I outrank you. Go to sleep. I'll wake you when it's your turn."

Her mind hit a wall. He was pulling rank on her? Could he do that? She'd never actually looked at the rank charts in terms of if an Ace *actually* outranked her. Since she'd never interacted with an Ace at work prior to pulling him out of the pod, it had never been a piece of information she needed to know.

"I . . ."

"You want to review the chain of command with me? I do. Even an entry-level Ace ranks as a major when interfacing with marines." He smiled. "And I'm *not* an entry-level Ace."

"But . . ."

"Nope. It's your turn to sleep. I'll use this baby rifle so yours doesn't break my fragile space shoulder."

Chevy opened her mouth and closed it. Her memory banks had finally fired up and she realized he was right. In the unlikely event that an Ace somehow ended up entangled with grunts, they automatically assumed the rank of major even if they had zero ground experience. That part was particularly fitting to the entire bureaucratic system. Of course an elite space fighter should outrank a ground fighter when on the ground. How could that not make sense?

Outside of her ego rankling, his words dug at her. It was true the only time they'd let him drive was when there had been no one else, but she and Dolon were right to do that. He was sick. He needed to be protected. It was logical. He hadn't been Earthside in over a decade. He probably wasn't a very good driver, but they had just made the decision for him.

But she knew, her protectiveness wasn't just professional.

So, here she was, at an ungodly hour, in a sleezy motel with an old man snoring behind her, getting outranked by a male Ace whom she both wanted to fuck and protect. Her ego and life suddenly seemed to be crumbling around her ears.

Izan checked his rifle's magazine, his movements fluid now, even though he'd never held a 10/22 until a few hours ago.

She stood, knocking over her chair. "I . . . I just . . . You can still die."

The air in the room changed. The conversation went from a work disagreement to a personal plea. Chevy heard it in the timbre of her voice.

He picked up the chair she'd knocked over and sat.

"I know." He set his rifle on the table, settling the barrel against the pillow with intention. "I knew before I dropped. I could keel over in ten minutes or two days or sixty years. We didn't sign up for safe. This is just the hand we've been dealt."

"But . . ."

He met her eyes. "But what?"

But I don't want to lose you, she thought.

"Nothing." She broke eye contact. "You're right. I'm tired."

"Go to sleep." He looked at her like a teacher would a favorite pupil. That twisted her stomach into a knot. "I'll wake you in a few hours."

Chevy stared at him, the intense longing to go to him and grab him, kiss him, and pull him onto the bed overtaking her. She didn't breathe for what seemed like years, then she felt the air moving out of her lungs.

"Okay." Her shoulders sagged. Her adrenaline had left her. "Okay."

FORTY-FOUR

THE CRANE

The corporeal nature of the human condition plagued the Crane. He did not like having to rest and feed his body, but he existed in a time and place where that was necessary. In some future he would be able to augment himself past the base needs of the unevolved human, but not now. Begrudgingly, he lay down in bed in the suite the Wendover Nugget had provided him.

"TV," he said.

A digital jungle erupted around him. The room became hotter and more humid. This TV was top of the line. Its hologram technology put older models to shame. And pairing that with climate intensification, the Crane really did feel like he was in a jungle. An annoying bird trilled by his ear. He wouldn't have guessed such tech would be in the Wendover Nugget. He stood corrected.

"News."

The air became pleasant, and the jungle and the bird disappeared. A crisp, clean smell filled the room. A newscaster with bad body mods stood before the Crane.

"And this is the terrorist . . ." the too-symmetrically faced man said.

The face of the nameless phantom floated before him, the green eyes burning through the dark room.

"Mute."

The room went quiet. The newscaster's mouth opened and closed silently, and the just too-clean-smell seemed even stronger without the audio. The Crane's lips cracked upward into a smile.

The Banker had asked the Idaho Troopers to blast the phantom's face to every media outlet and influencer worth their salt. The Crane had Cole's information along with her line of duty death photo primed and ready, but he and the Banker held on to it. With four of the Big Six having now fallen to Launch Tech after Jinzhan had thrown in the towel that morning, it was better to keep Launch Tech focused on their recent wins. Publicly calling one of their marines a terrorist would shift Launch Tech's focus to Exoterra even faster, and the Crane needed to delay that as long as possible. Hopefully, the gold-digging public would find the phantom before Launch Tech threw all their weight at Exoterra.

Exoterra was offering a reward for credible information, although the public didn't know Exoterra was behind the reward. It was easier to let the world think the phantom was an unaffiliated bad guy who was a threat to *everyone* regardless of allegiance. All the public needed to know was the reward was straight global credit, no taxes, no fees, no deductions, directly wired to an account of the tipster's choosing. Straight credit was something most civilians could only dream about in a world of hidden fees, subscription surcharges, and corporate fine print. No one got paid straight credit anymore. Let the sharks find them.

"Bring up Lucy's feed," the Crane said.

The air around him changed. It became hot and dusty. And then, Lucy's reptilian head appeared, her black eyes wide, her shell's patterns distinct and symmetrical. She swept forward, her belly hovering just above the sand. She was under her enclosure, headed toward a plate of lettuce and flowers. She blinked, something ancient and ineffable passing through her gaze.

"My little battle wagon . . ." the Crane said.

He watched her crunch a purple flower, and for a moment, the fusion device was the furthest thing from his mind.

FORTY-FIVE

DOLON

Dolon opened his eyes to see Izan setting several bags onto the table. Chevy stood next to him, looking at Izan like he might be an alien. Something was off.

Dolon sat up. "What happened?"

Chevy swallowed but did not speak. She looked gagged. Izan regarded her coolly. Without taking his eyes off Chevy, he said, "I went out and got us supplies."

Chevy looked mad enough to punch something. Dolon struggled to orient himself.

"You left? Alone? Why?"

Izan whirled to face Dolon. "Because you failed to bring a change of clothes and look what happened."

Izan dug in one of the bags and grabbed a folded piece of paper. He opened it and Dolon's face stared back at them, below it the word TERRORIST. The photo was from his brief stay in Wendover, unbruised and clearly from before they'd hit him.

"Fuuck," Chevy said.

"And," Izan said, flicking his eyes at Chevy in a way Dolon did not like, "the networks are still out. Supposedly you," he looked back at Dolon, "did it. Not only that, but apparently Launch Tech took Jinzhan, Tsiolkovsky, Lua Um, and Alpha Orbital in hostile takeovers. It's all real fresh, but it seems that now there are only two functional remaining members of the Big Six. If we succeed, there will only be one."

They all looked at the Conlow bag, which sat on the table beside Chevy's rifle. The room was quiet for a moment, then the AC roared back to life. Chevy sneezed.

Dolon turned his attention to his photo. He looked old, tired, and surprisingly sinister. The media would have a field day with this, but all Dolon felt looking at it was exhaustion. He took in the text surrounding the photos. A modern-day wanted poster. Armed and dangerous . . . He'd taken out the networks, yada, yada, yada . . .

"The lady at the pawn shop gave me this poster and also sold me this." Izan lifted his shirt to reveal a purple fanny pack. "This is *terrorist protection.*"

He unzipped the bag and pulled out a pearl-handled revolver.

"Whoa," Chevy seemed to temporarily forget her angst. She reached for the weapon, then remembered herself and snapped to an awkward standing position.

"She apparently hand sews these things." Izan stuffed the revolver back into the fanny pack.

Dolon still wasn't sure what was going on between Izan and Chevy.

"But you just left?" Dolon asked again. He looked at Chevy with a disappointed dad look. "Chevy?"

"He pulled fucking rank on me." She looked down as she said it. Embarrassed. "An Ace always outranks a grunt. What was I supposed to do? Put hands on him? He woke me up for my watch and fucking left."

Dolon turned back to Izan, who watched them intently.

"Don't be mad at her, Dolon. She did what she was supposed to do. And I did what I was supposed to do. You all are treating me like I'm some fragile doll, but you know it wasn't all unicorns and rainbows before you found me, right? We had to fight to get the device, and I did that lifeboat drop. I know the risks. And I know my responsibilities. I went out and got us supplies because that's what needed to be done. It was the right play, to keep the marine on guard duty and send the guy who can pass as a civilian into town. We need this stuff to get the fuck out of here."

Izan pushed the bags toward Dolon. Dolon hesitated, then opened one of them—takeout. He poked into the next—clothing. Another bag held what looked to be hair dye, some scissors, and a pack of razors. Dolon glanced at Chevy. She glowered. Izan wasn't wrong. He had been burned, and Chevy couldn't pass as a normal person if her life depended on it. This stuff would hopefully get them across the finish line.

"Well done. You take your pill?" Dolon said, finally.

Izan nodded, his features folding flat. "I did, but thanks for checking."

They quit talking, but the air was still charged, still awkward. Dolon tried to sort it out. He'd let go of his anger at Izan. He'd agreed he'd been right. Why . . .

Then Dolon saw it. Or he felt it. Chevy was staring at Izan in a way that could have blown a door from its hinges. And Izan . . . He was decidedly not looking at Chevy. Dolon coughed. He was choking on the sexual tension.

"Oh, fuck you two," Dolon breathed.

He rooted through the bag of clothes, pulling out a faded blue tee and a hat with a poop emoji. He ripped off his work shirt, threaded his arms through the tee, and then smashed the ball cap on his head. He grabbed his wallet and ripped open the door.

"I'm getting my own breakfast. Figure your shit out."

He stepped into the mid-morning sunshine and slammed the door behind him.

FORTY-SIX

THE CRANE

"Interesting," the Banker said.

"What?"

They were back in the security office of the Nugget. After waking, the Crane had lifted, working a brutal cardio session between his sets, and now his mind felt clearer. He was more focused. The fact they were swimming in data but had no clear path forward didn't tug at him the way it had when he'd woken.

"Looks like Launch Tech got their fingers into our third-party press release."

The Banker spun his monitor to face the Crane. A video of a newscaster greeted him. He hit the play button.

"We've got a breaking story to share with you," a woman in a puce blazer said. "The apparent terrorist, the so-called Nameless Man," the screen cut to the photo the Crane had released, "is actually a Launch Tech agent who may have just saved millions of American lives.

"An individual high up in the Launch Tech chain of command, who chose to remain anonymous, stated that the Nameless Man is working in their counterterrorism division. He is central in derailing a plot involving Exoterra. The Big Six corporation allegedly planned to destabilize the American government by detonating a weapon of mass destruction in a large American city."

The newscaster paused for effect.

"As you are no doubt aware, since Voyager 3, the infamous former Big Seven member who launched a nuclear assault on northern China and was then dismantled by today's Bix Six, no mega corp has ever threatened nuclear war. In the last several days, Launch Tech and Exoterra troops battled throughout the southwest, resulting in both corporations losing their network connectivity. In an unprecedented military hostile takeover, Launch Tech then initiated assaults against Jinzhan, Lua Um, Tsiolkovsky, and Alpha Orbital. Launch Tech claims everything they've done in the past few days has been aimed at stopping Exoterra from detonating a nuclear device on American soil, as the other members of the Big Six were complicit in Exoterra's nuclear plot. The Nameless Man stole the device during one of the ensuing skirmishes, thereby preventing the annihilation of millions of innocent Americans.

"President Hellman has weighed in on the events, stating that the Nameless Man's involvement saved countless American lives. Had he not stolen the WMD, it is unknown what could have happened. A true hero indeed.

"The president is asking anyone with information regarding the whereabouts of the Nameless Man to report to the tip line listed below. It is believed that Exoterra is pursuing them, and they may be in danger.

"And, finally, both Exoterra and Launch Tech report they are working around the clock to restore data to their customers. We will keep you updated on the estimated times of repair."

The Crane hit the pause button.

The Banker shrugged. "This was bound to happen."

"I know, but it's always annoying when it finally does."

"True," the Banker agreed.

"A WMD." The Crane chuckled and leaned back in his chair. "The rest of the Bix Six would eat us alive."

"The news is beholden to no truth but ratings," the Banker said. "Even if they weren't, it seems the rest of the Big Six are in their death throes. They probably don't have the energy to eat us."

The Crane started to reply but stopped when the Banker's eyes went to the ceiling. The Crane waited patiently. A few moments later, the Banker rolled his eyes back to the Crane.

"Utah Troopers just radioed me. A group of campers reported being ambushed last night. Several of them were killed. Their camp is just off of I-80, less than an hour from here. Here's the pin."

The Crane pulled up a map in his retinal display. The Banker's pin appeared halfway between Wendover and Salt Lake. The Crane smiled.

"Let's go. I have a feeling we might have worn out our welcome here anyway."

The Banker's fingers tapped his thumbs.

FORTY-SEVEN

CHEVY

Chevy stared at the door. Had Dolon just thrown a fit and left? She could run fast enough to catch him and could easily drag him back here. Then she felt Izan move.

She turned. Izan had squared off to her, his eyelids heavy. She was angry at him. She should have broken rank. He didn't know shit about ground warfare. She. Did.

She stepped to him, keenly aware of the size difference between them. Her bulk shadowed him. Energy zinged through her. Izan didn't flinch. She reached for him.

She hadn't meant to kiss him. Or had she? Her lips were on his. She pulled him to her. For a moment he didn't respond. Panic spiked through her. Should she retreat? Let go? And then Izan pushed back into her. She wasn't kissing Izan, they were kissing each other. *He* was kissing *her*.

She pulled back from him, her eyes wide. Her face bent into a grin. She grabbed him and kissed him again.

She was strong of course, but Izan didn't submit to her, and that made the rising energy inside of her that much more urgent. He grabbed the back of her head and pressed forward. She stepped back and hit the bed. She sat down and pulled him on top of her.

"Fuuck," she groaned. He tipped her backward.

He put his lips just above her lips, almost touching, but most certainly not.

"Corporal Cole," he breathed. "We don't have time for this."

She bit her lip. "Yes, we do."

He stared at her.

"Are you going to make me beg?" she spoke.

He held her eyes then backed up and slowly bent over to untie his boots. She watched him, transfixed. He kicked them off one by one then undid his pants. They fell to his ankles, and he stood in front of her, the white of his boxers highlighting the caramel color of his legs. He turned, her eyes going straight to his ass, and slid the locks on the door.

He faced her.

"Where were we?" he asked. "Oh right, lie back down."

Chevy did what she was told.

FORTY-EIGHT

THE CRANE

"One woman. And then the old man."

The Crane nodded. The skinny woman shook her head at the homely one. The pear-shaped one and the short one just watched the two argue, their faces puffy from crying.

"No, Elma, there had to have been a few of them in the shadows. It couldn't have just been the one monster!"

The Crane looked at the sad circle of rusting RVs, the dirt before them dark and sticky. This group of losers—Elma, Eliza, Emily, and Elba—why all their names started with E he couldn't begin to fathom—told them all their men and one of their fellow sister-wives had been killed, in what looked to the Crane to be a very efficient ambush. Oh, and a side-by-side and a dirt bike had been stolen. The women had cleaned up the bodies, wrapping them in sheets and stacking them like cordwood in the backs of the trucks.

"I shot at them," the one with a face like a pancake sobbed. "What the fuck did the rest of you do?"

The Crane looked at the Banker. The Banker flicked his eyes and a message appeared on the Crane's retinal feed.

Kill them and leave them with the others? At least then they would quit crying.

The Crane seriously considered it, then tabled the idea. They had a seething horde of kids smashed in the RVs. It wasn't that he was opposed to snuffing out the kids too; it just seemed like a lot of effort right now.

"Thank you," the Crane said, cutting off whichever E woman was crying. They'd gotten the gist of what had happened. "My associate and I are going to walk the perimeter of your camp. I think we have all the info we need from you currently."

He and the Banker walked back to their vehicle, leaving the distraught women behind.

"A Conlow bag, an old man, and a giant woman, who sniped half of them from the dark before engaging in some hand-to-hand combat," the Banker said.

"I'll get the drones. Maybe we can follow their tracks. See if we find an abandoned van around here. They probably ditched their last ride not too far. Maybe they left something in it we can use."

The Banker looked at the Crane sadly. His malformed jaw and shiny eyes were twisted into what the Crane knew was meant to be a look of compassion, but the Banker couldn't look compassionate. He looked like a swamp monster melting in the sun.

"You feeling okay, Boss?"

The Crane sighed. "I'm ready to find them."

"Me too. You sure you don't want to shut these incompetents up? Might make you feel better."

The Crane frowned and looked across the blistering desert. Even with his sunglasses and hat, he felt like he was burning. His retinal display logged the temperature at 108. He scanned the desolate sweep of nothing that stretched before him. Lines of heat disrupted his vision, causing the entirely too bright nightmarescape to seemingly fold in on itself.

If they were still out there, they were in a rough place.

He hoped they were.

Sweat trickled down his back. He was going to have to get this suit professionally cleaned. That was annoying.

"Let's kill them and then break out the drones," he said.

The Banker smiled, his fingers dancing. "For you, Boss. Anything."

FORTY-NINE

DOLON

Dolon had calmed down. He found himself standing at a corner with a pharmacy and a taco truck, his new hat pulled low over his eyes. The taco truck had a cheap hologram projector next to it, and Dolon mindlessly watched a hologram of a guy in a sombrero holding a taco ride a rocket to the moon.

He couldn't take his rage about this situation out on Izan, or even Chevy. They were lucky to have someone to hold on to in this moment. Being jealous of their connection wasn't productive. And maybe that was all it was, jealousy. Maybe that's all it had ever been. Being around both of them made him aware of how alone he'd been the last fifteen years. Their proximity forced him to remember what it was like to share a connection with someone. He both craved that and hated it.

He missed Flora. He wished he could hold on to her for a final time. He usually did so well at keeping the pain, the longing for her, locked away. Sure, he thought about her. He even felt her at times, but he didn't like to consciously acknowledge the gap she'd torn in his life when she'd died. That jagged maw was always there, locked deep within him. Normally, he kept his feelings for her light. Remembering the way she smiled or the way she cocked her head. When he thought too much, though, when he fell too deep into who she was and what she was to him—the way she made him feel relevant, like his existence mattered, like if he disappeared he'd be missed, how she made him a part of something, not apart from everything—when he thought about those things . . . those were the things he shouldn't think of, couldn't think of.

He needed to get hold of himself. The last time he'd gone to this precipice, he'd stepped off, letting himself free-fall until three months later he'd woken up on his kitchen floor, Captain Picard licking his eyelid. He'd drunk everything in the house and nearly suffocated face down on the floor he'd built for Flora. He'd never felt so alone and worthless as he had in those few months.

He didn't have time for that right now. He needed to lock it up. People were complicated. Izan obviously was. Even Chevy was. And so was he. All three of them were many layered messes. But right now, they were a mess together, even if he was out here, and they weren't.

"Hey, señor! Tiene hambre?"

Dolon looked toward the voice. A woman waved from the taco truck. He walked to her.

"You look hungry," she said, her English lilting. "You need some food. We have prickly pear tacos. And coffee, from Mexico. You should buy some. You need it."

He stared at her, his eyes watery.

"I give you two churros, gratis. You look bad, señor. You should take more care."

The hologram reset, and the guy with the taco began walking between long-armed cacti. Dolon was thankful the hologram's sound wasn't activated. He watched the guy stumble across a rocket nestled between tumbleweeds.

"Thirty-three, seventy-eight," the woman said, punching her device.

Dolon quit watching the hologram and gave her two twenties.

"What did I order?" he asked, feeling lost.

"You want change?"

He shook his head.

"You sit over there. I bring it out to you."

She pointed at a sad collection of plastic furniture in the vacant lot next to the truck. He nodded and shuffled to the closest table.

He felt like he'd just sat down when the woman burst through the back of the truck. She held a basket of tacos and a basket of churros.

"I come back with the coffee."

He looked at the food before him. It smelled delicious. He picked up a taco and bit into it. He'd devoured it by the time she'd brought him the coffee. She set it down and said, "You like?"

He nodded. "It's great," he managed, his mouth full.

"Good. Good. You need to eat. Like I say, you look bad."

Dolon tipped his head again, marveling at the fact this woman, whom he'd never met, had somehow extracted forty dollars from him. But she also provided him with the nourishment he clearly needed.

"If you need more, you yell," the woman said, stepping back into the truck.

"Thanks," he said, covering his full mouth with his hand.

He ate the three tacos and the plate of five, not two, churros. He was still hungry. He drained his coffee, but something had changed. The darkness that had been creeping into his veins seemed more distant. Was beating that tattered wound in his soul as simple as eating fresh churros? Maybe he was simply low in calories? Maybe this lady was a sorceress? Maybe she was sent by Flora? Did he believe in such things? Did it matter?

He went back to the woman.

"What else do you have?"

FIFTY

THE CRANE

The micro drones were surprisingly effective at finding their prey's tracks, although killing the women and their seemingly inexhaustible supply of prodigy had delayed their use. The Crane and the Banker hadn't bothered burying them, just left them as the apparent victims of yet another random desert killing.

The Banker had been right; the Crane felt a little better now. Not quite as good as a workout that squeezed him dry, but still pretty good. He'd also snuck in a moment to watch a recorded video of Lucy walking through the rain, and that, too, sanded away some of his frustration. Now, they followed two sets of tire prints into the desert, using a side-by-side they'd bought off of another camper. The Banker drove while the Crane flew the drones.

Before they'd embarked on their ride, the Banker had found a plain of torched cars, one of which was still burning. It was a van, but nothing usable had been found inside of it.

The tire tracks, though, first went east, then turned back north toward the highway. The longer they followed them, the more convinced the Crane became they were on the phantom's trail.

"Smart," the Crane said, looking at his display screen. "There's a bunch of mountains between here and Salt Lake. I-80 goes through them, but if they'd simply punched east from that camp, they would have had to navigate them."

The Banker nodded and tugged at one of his bulbous ears. They now paralleled the highway.

"You think we'll find them at the end of these tracks?" the Banker asked. "Like a pot of gold at the end of a rainbow?"

The Crane let out a dry cough that could have been a laugh.

"I think out of the two of us, their luck is better than ours."

"Luck is fickle," the Banker said. "It runs out eventually."

FIFTY-ONE

DOLON

Someone shook Dolon's shoulder. He startled then calmed when he saw it was Izan.

"Dolon, it's zero three thirty."

He nodded, blinking. Chevy was at the window, the rifle trained on the crack in the curtains.

"I'm up."

Izan nodded and stepped back from the bed. Dolon watched him move to the table and begin to put things into a tote bag. His body language wasn't different from the last time they'd spoken, which had been before Dolon had left. When Dolon had eventually made it back to the hotel, Izan had been asleep. Chevy had let him in and given him a sheepish grin. Dolon had gone straight into the bathroom to dye his hair and shave his beard. Then he'd gone right back to bed, leaving Chevy on watch. He dragged a hand across his freshly shorn jaw, its smoothness alien.

Out of Izan and Chevy, Dolon figured Izan would be the less emotional one. Dolon knew, and he now felt it was confirmed, that if there was going to be drama regarding Chevy and Izan, it was going to be with Chevy and not Izan.

Dolon navigated the beds and table to the bathroom. His reflection's violently black hair and pale jawline disturbed him, so he quit looking at himself. Once he finished in the bathroom, he helped check the room for anything they'd overlooked. Chevy held up the Conlow bag, making it obvious in what pocket she put it, and then at zero three forty-six hours, they stepped into the early morning Utah air.

Dolon sat in the driver's seat, Izan next to him. Chevy didn't really fit into the back of the KIA Futuro, but she was so easily recognized, she couldn't be in front. And while she'd bic'ed her head while Dolon had been sleeping, it hadn't really helped her look less like a marine.

Dolon instructed the car into reverse.

"Here," Izan said.

Out of the corner of his eye, Dolon saw Izan pass something strangely lifelike to the back seat.

"What is this?" Chevy asked.

"It's a wig. Wear it. I got one too."

Izan pulled out a long gray wig and put it on his head. Dolon glanced in the mirror and saw Chevy now wore a long blond wig. She appeared ridiculous and totally different. She was like an out of focus image Dolon couldn't make sense of.

Next to Dolon, Izan hunched forward and jutted out his neck. For a split second, he looked like an old woman, then he smiled, and the spell was broken.

"I look insane." Chevy stared at herself in the rearview mirror.

Izan turned to her and began to laugh. "You look like a meathead who time traveled from the 1970s. We should get you a bandana and some short shorts."

"We don't need the shorts," Dolon heard himself say.

Chevy glanced at Dolon, then said, "He's right. I'll keep my pants, but a bandana might be cool."

Dolon felt a ping of relief. Chevy was no longer acting like a caveman. Izan wasn't being a prick. Maybe they could do this.

They stopped for a supercharge before they merged onto I-15 North. Dolon elected to pay extra to top off the battery in fifteen minutes. The charging port projected an ad with an Ace, the woman so gorgeous Dolon wondered if she were just AI, onto their windshield. Dolon paid an extra fee to shut off the sound for the ad.

They sat in stressed silence, waiting for the battery to fill. Ten minutes into the charge, Chevy said, "Too bad we can't plug this into the car." She waved the Conlow bag.

Dolon just wanted to go back home and see Captain Picard. After the last few days, taking a nap with that cat in the afternoon sun seemed like paradise.

Dolon borrowed Izan's wig to pay for the charge, and they all let out a long breath once the car merged onto I-15. Fifteen minutes wasn't that long, but it had felt like an eternity. He hoped they hadn't been recognized.

He'd checked a map yesterday and estimated they had to drive about four hours and some change before reaching the Sinclair station. This assumed there weren't any major delays, which was a bold assumption.

Four more hours. He couldn't believe it. They were so close he could taste it. They had been close before, outside of Twin Falls, but this time, their chance of reaching the Sinclair felt more real.

He knew the others could feel it too. The mood in the car was tense, not fragile, but after the joke about the fusion device, no one spoke. The air was heavy. With each mile they passed, Dolon felt his stress levels ratchet higher. They were getting closer, but his anxiety wasn't lessening. And Dolon realized, it wasn't just the anxiety of getting there that was filling his insides. It was the after. What would happen to the three of them once they made it, assuming they did? Chevy and Izan hadn't been anyone to him a matter of days ago, and now, now they were everything. As much as they drove him insane, was he expected to just . . . go back to how things were before? Forget he'd met them? Forget they'd pulled him back into the world of the living, even if only for a few days? He'd spent fifteen years forgetting what it meant to be connected to another living person. He didn't want to spend the next fifteen years forgetting that.

They passed the blue sign that said WELCOME TO IDAHO.

"Man," Chevy said, "I don't know about you guys, but I am tense."

"Yeah," Izan agreed. "I keep holding my breath without realizing it."

"I'm also in it," Dolon said. "I guess I just can't believe that we might actually make it. By eight thirty this whole thing could be over."

He felt their eyes go to the vehicle clock. Four fifty-one.

"That's not that far away," Chevy said.

"I wish it was closer, though," Izan said.

"Agreed," Dolon said, although he wasn't sure if he did.

No one spoke after that. The air became thick and weighted, and all Dolon could do was monitor the car as it drove.

FIFTY-TWO

CHEVY

Chevy watched the signs for Pocatello come and go. She alternated between watching the mile markers pass and the clock. It was excruciating. The clock changed from six forty-five to six forty-six. This sucked.

And she didn't want to bring it up, but when they made it to wherever Dolon was bringing them, because they would make it—she was an L Tech marine, she didn't fail missions—what would happen? Would she get sent back to her unit? Would Dolon just go back to being a hermit? Where would Izan go? She hadn't wanted to say it, but his spacefaring days were probably over. No doubt his insides were all fucked up, and she doubted L Tech would want to chance putting him back on the roster.

Would she see either of them ever again? The grumpy old man who now looked at her the way dads in movies looked at their daughters, where would he go? Her real dad had never looked at her like that. What would happen to the Ace with whom she'd crossed so many lines? What would become of their team of three?

Then she felt it. It was subtle, but when it happened again, she knew it was real.

"What's wrong with the car?" Chevy's voice was a sledgehammer.

"I don't know, but something's not right," Dolon said.

"Is it out of charge?" Izan asked.

"The gauge shows we're fine, but this thing was rotting in a field when we found it, so who—"

The world spun. The sounds of screeching tires and collapsing metal whipped through Chevy's ears. She hit the side of the car and felt something pop in her right arm. The world closed in on itself.

FIFTY-THREE

DOLON

Dolon did his best to drag Chevy, who was heavier than any human had a right to be, away from the now fully engulfed car. Izan tried to help, but he was so weak the only help he really offered was moral support. Dolon got her about ten feet from the car, her blond wig gone, her head covered in blood, before saying, "I have to stop."

They were on the shoulder of the highway. A wall of jersey barriers prevented them from getting farther off the road. The air was warm even though the sun had yet to rise, and the car fire only made Dolon hotter. The flames from the Futuro blazed in the last moments of night, the lightening horizon dim compared to the pyre of their former vehicle.

"Fuck." Izan gulped air. "What happened?"

Dolon felt like he might pass out. "I . . . don't know." Dolon wiped his face. "It was driving fine, then I felt something change, a little wiggle in the suspension. Then we were spinning. We hit the wall, I think on Chevy's side, then . . . fire."

"No wonder we found that thing in a junkyard." Izan finally had his breathing under control. He looked down at Chevy. "Chevy! Chevy!"

Her right shoulder hung at a strange angle, and she didn't react when he called her name. Her eyes were closed, but he could see her chest rise and fall.

"Shit." Izan knelt beside her.

Izan ran his hands over her body, checking for blood and deformities. Izan seemed injured too. Dolon worried the Ace might also pass out.

"Her shoulder is jacked up, and something cut her head." Izan's voice came out feathery, but he pulled the shemagh Chevy had wrapped around her neck to her head. He tied it and the bleeding lessened.

"Does she have the device?" Dolon asked.

Izan pulled it out of her cargo pocket and handed it to Dolon.

"Well at least this isn't in the car right now." Dolon took the Conlow bag. "You know, the farther we get from where I met you two, the more ridiculous this thing seems."

"What do you mean?" Izan fussed with the shemagh.

Gunfire erupted from the Futuro.

"Fuck!" Dolon ducked. "The rounds are cooking off!"

He grabbed Chevy and pulled her farther from the roiling car. Izan acted like he was helping. They didn't get far before having to rest again. The car rattled like a popcorn cooker for a few more moments and then the explosions ceased.

"You get hit?" Izan asked, his hands moving over Chevy again.

"I don't think so." Dolon patted his torso.

"Good."

"I think our stuff is toast."

"Do you have your wallet?"

Dolon put a hand to his back pocket. "Got it."

"Well, at least there's that."

Dolon was watching the burning car when a wave of light washed over them. He turned and saw a vehicle had pulled onto the shoulder behind them.

"Are you okay?" a voice called.

Dolon couldn't see anything but the headlights, then several people appeared. A man in overalls, a woman in a long skirt, and a teenaged boy with a homegrown haircut hurried to them.

"What happened?" the man asked.

"The car lost control and we hit the wall," Dolon said. "Can you give us a ride?"

"Of course," the man said. He saw Chevy and gasped. "Oh! Your companion!"

The woman pushed Izan aside and knelt next to Chevy. She pulled out a small bottle from her blouse and began to mutter as she tipped the container over Chevy's body.

"What are you doing?" Izan asked.

"My mom's a healer," the boy said. "You'd best let her work. Help her if you want."

"What? How?" Izan asked.

The boy looked at him like he was an idiot.

"Pray." He said the word loudly, like he would to a deaf dog.

Dolon glanced at Izan, who stared at the now rocking woman. She had her hands up and was wailing.

"JESUS. HELP ME SAVE THIS POOR WOMAN."

"If you could bring us to Idaho Falls . . ." Dolon said.

"We will," the man said, "but you'd do right by letting my wife work. She's a known medicine woman. Able is right. We should help her by praying."

And with that, the man and his son got to their knees and began to pray as well, their voices rising to meet the woman's. The whipping car flames amplified their high keening.

"Shit," Dolon said.

"HELP US," the woman screamed, her eyes open and on Izan and Dolon. "She needs your help!"

The teen grabbed Izan and pulled him to the ground. The man did the same to Dolon. Izan locked eyes with Dolon. For a moment the world seemed to stop, and then Dolon lifted his hands skyward and called to Jesus.

Dolon did his best to participate in the fundamentalist roadside prayer meeting he'd just been thrust into, but really, they just needed a ride. They needed to get to Idaho Falls, and he knew they weren't far. If they could just get there, he could figure out the final step. They were less than two hours from Driggs. They were so fucking close. And now here they were, the Futuro on fire, no other cars stopping to help, Chevy unconscious, and the only people that could get them to Idaho Falls were wailing like banshees.

"What . . ."

Dolon looked at Chevy, whose eyes were now open and on the howling family.

"She's awake!" Dolon yelled.

"PRAISE JESUS," the father called. The son echoed him.

The mother began to rock on her knees. "Merciful Jesus! You are our savior who works miracles both big and small. Today we have seen one, and we are further assured of your heavenly presence."

"I think we should get her off the road." Dolan stood.

"Can you walk, hon?" the father asked, reaching for Chevy's left arm.

"What . . ." Chevy repeated.

"She can walk." Izan's voice was rough. "She just needs help. Thank you."

"Wait . . ." Chevy grabbed at Izan. "What about my rifle and the . . ."

"Your rifle is toast," Izan whispered. "Dolon's got the stuff that was in your pocket."

Before Chevy could respond, the father and son helped her up. Her arm bent at an unnatural angle. Blood coated her eyelashes and face. She looked frail. Weak. Powerless. Dolon wanted to reach for her, but instead, he slipped his hand into his pocket and touched the Conlow bag. This mission, this *device* had done this to Chevy. It was too late to reverse course, but seeing her so broken, it made him want to drive the device in the opposite direction. Throw it off a bridge. Uninvent it. Keep that fifteen-year debt.

From the moment Chevy told him what was in the Conlow bag, he'd known, deep down, that getting the device to Launch Tech was a fool's errand, but he hadn't had to face the truth until now, when he looked into Chevy's bloody, dazed eyes.

Of course, Launch Tech wouldn't do good with the fusion device. Sure, they could make clean energy and save the world with it, but they could just as easily make it into a bomb and destroy the world. He had thought settling his personal debt would be enough to erase this fact, but now, watching Chevy fail to stand on her own, Dolon knew, he'd been an idiot. He'd let his supposed moral compass obscure the fact he was delivering ultimate power to an evil corporation. He'd tried to pretend it was a noble cause but look at what had just happened to Chevy. How many more Chevys would be eaten by this thing once they got it to the Sinclair?

He was just as bad as Launch Tech.

"What are you doing?" Izan said.

Dolon looked up to see the son taking photos of his dad helping Chevy. He then pointed his phone at the burning car, capturing the flames and Izan's face.

"Documenting this," the boy said. "I'll post it to our church's site. This is a true miracle! There's a forum for this kind of thing."

"Oh, we don't believe in being on the internet." Dolon said, jerked from his reverie.

"Get in! Let's get you to I.F.!" The woman pulled herself into the van.

Dolon was the last to get in.

Once they were moving, the father said, "I haven't seen a car go up like that in a while. Not since my cousins' Futuro exploded."

"Ours was a Futuro," Dolon said.

"What?" the father said.

"You all are surely blessed," the son said. "Those are death traps!"

"Did y'all miss the recall on them?" the father asked.

"I guess?" Dolon struggled to recall anything he'd ever known about Futuros.

The boy laughed. "They said they don't believe in the internet!"

"Well, you should maybe pay a little more attention to the world's goings on," the father said. "Futuros blow up. They aren't even legal anymore. It *is* truly a miracle you survived!"

"Truly." Dolon's voice was dry.

"This will be the best miracle post of all time!" Dolon glanced over his shoulder and saw the boy clicking away at his phone. "A Futuro. I bet this goes viral!"

Dolon locked eyes with Izan. They needed to get out of this van ASAP.

"How far are we from Idaho Falls?" Dolon asked.

FIFTY-FOUR

CHEVY

Her rifle was gone. She'd seen the car on fire, or she'd seen fire. Her eyes kept crusting in blood, so it was hard to see. Izan said her head was bleeding. Someone had wrapped something around it, but she couldn't stop thinking about her rifle. Losing it unnerved her. That rifle was a part of her. It having burned in the car, that was bad.

She no longer had the cop's pistol either. Not having the pistol didn't rub her as badly as not having the rifle, but now she was totally unarmed. At least they had the bag though. But more immediately, she was injured. Her head hurt, her thoughts swam, and her right shoulder was dislocated and painful. On her list of immediate needs, she needed her shoulder put back in.

This had happened to her before. She'd gotten injured in boot, as had everyone, and she knew the drill. She needed to relax and then she needed to get someone to put it back in place.

The problem was she was jacked. She wasn't trying to be egotistical about it, but she had a lot of muscles, and they got real cranky when she did this. If she was lucky, she could get the shoulder back in with a massage and maybe a heat pad. If she was unlucky, she would need muscle relaxers to get the job done. And she guessed they didn't have time for that.

But the pain. It was a screaming klaxon in her mind. She teetered on the edge of consciousness. She counted to four and held her breath. She let it out, counting to four again.

"How's it going?" Izan's voice was soft, just for her.

"I'm in a lot of pain. Can you, can you massage my shoulder?"

"Sure."

"This . . . happens to me. If I can relax enough, I can talk you through putting my shoulder back in place."

"Okay."

He reached up and grabbed her trap. She felt the briefest spark of excitement, and then the pain swallowed it. But he kept squeezing, and soon, she felt the tension in her neck relax. She could hear the driver prattling on about the ways the Lord worked, but all she could concentrate on was Izan's touch. She felt like she was melting, and she wanted to melt.

"I'm going to get into the seat behind you," he said. "I think that will make this easier."

"What's going on?" the woman asked.

"I'm trying to get her shoulder back in place." Izan's voice was ragged. "The car accident dislocated it."

"Oh!" the woman said. "We can pray for you."

"Thanks."

Izan settled behind Chevy.

Chevy closed her eyes while Izan's hands worked her traps. They moved into the spaces between her scapulas. He dug at knots that seemed to have taken up permanent residence under her shoulder blades. He ran his fingers parallel to her spine. She felt the tension leaving her. She was breathing easier. He kept going. Finally, she said, "Come back to this seat."

He climbed to her.

"Okay. I want you to hold on to my elbow and then put my arm at a ninety-degree angle."

He did so, moving her hand so it hovered over her belly button.

"Now, keep holding my elbow, and rotate my arm out toward you, like you're slowly opening a door."

Chevy was only dimly aware of the family praying around her. Izan began to move her arm, keeping her elbow pinned in place, and then *pop!*

She exhaled.

"Whoa," Izan said. "That was crazy. I could see it happen."

"Did it work?" the woman asked.

"Yes." Chevy felt lighter.

The son cheered.

The pain wasn't totally gone, but it went from a nine to a three within seconds. She knew she needed to baby it, though. This frustrated her. They weren't at their objective yet. She couldn't afford to be hurt.

"You need to tie up that shoulder and take it easy." The woman reached into a bag in the space between the two front seats. "Here."

She held a long piece of calico fabric. Izan took it and folded it in half to make a sling.

"I remember the first time I was taught how to do this," Izan said. "I never thought I'd ever actually make a sling in real life."

Chevy smiled. It was part of boot camp, field first aid. Despite that having been over ten years ago for Izan, he did a good job. He tied the final knot in the sling, and Chevy felt immense relief at not having to hold up her arm any longer.

"Where do you need to go exactly?" the father asked.

Chevy looked out of the window and saw buildings. Were they in Idaho Falls?

"Oh, anywhere is fine," Dolon said. "But we were going to the Walmart to get supplies."

"We can drop you there, no problem!" the father said.

Ten minutes later the van pulled up to the Walmart.

"Thank you all for your help," Dolon repeated, opening the door. "Is there any way we can repay you?"

He got out of the car, and Izan followed. Chevy gingerly maneuvered to the pavement.

"We are humble servants of the Lord," the man replied. "You owe us nothing."

"Look! Look!" The teen bounded to the front bench seat. "My post is the top post in the Miracle Forum! This is awesome!"

Chevy and Izan paled.

"Well then." Dolon nodded. "Have a good rest of your day."

He shut the door and the van drove away.

"Fuck," Izan hissed.

"Let's go." Dolon pushed him toward a row of parked cars. "We need to steal a car and move."

"Wait," Chevy said. "That kid posted us on the internet?"

"Yeah," Izan said.

"Is Launch Tech's network back up?" Chevy hissed between clenched teeth.

"I don't know," Dolon said. "But right now we need to look for a car."

Chevy realized the pain in her shoulder had been replaced by fear. She preferred the pain.

FIFTY-FIVE

DOLON

Dolon found their car. A late model PT cruiser so weather-beaten, Dolon wasn't sure what color it had originally been. He let out a somewhat birdlike cry and Izan appeared.

"This'll do," Dolon said.

Without fanfare, Dolon popped the driver's door and went to work on starting it. The car was old, so old, it wasn't self-driving. This was good.

Chevy shuffled toward them.

"I'm a bit slow," she wheezed.

Dolon glanced up from his work, catching Izan's eye. He could feel Izan's worry. And Dolon understood. Chevy looked bad. He had to keep it together though. Be the adult. Not let Izan see that Dolon was also afraid for Chevy. For all of them.

"Get in," Dolon said.

Izan opened the back door, and Chevy hefted herself in without speaking. The car rumbled to life.

"Ha!" Dolon shut the driver's door, grinning.

Izan got into the front passenger seat.

"It's got half a tank." Dolon shifted it into gear. "Hopefully that's enough."

Chevy groaned and laid across the back seats. Junk piled the floorboards, and a menagerie of stuffed animals and lace doilies decorated the dashboard.

"Get this shit off of here." Dolon swept an arm across the sun-faded toys.

Izan tossed them into the backseat.

"I think Chevy needs a doctor," Izan said.

Dolon glanced into the rearview mirror.

"We're less than two hours from Driggs. She'll have to hold on, and so will you. You look like you're at death's door. Have you taken your pill?"

Izan opened his fanny pack and pulled out the pill bottle from beside the revolver. He swallowed the white tab dry.

They approached Highway 20, and two police cars with lights and sirens passed them, headed the way they had come from.

"They might be here for us," Izan said.

Dolon hit the gas. "Let's disappoint them."

He guided the car north and onto Highway 20 and tried not to think about all of the implications of the morning.

First, he chose not to think about Chevy, who was possibly dying in the back seat. There was absolutely nothing Dolon could do other than get her to the Sinclair station. Going to the hospital was out of the question. The fastest way to help her was to end this Godforsaken road trip.

Then, he chose not to think of Izan, who was completely stoic about the fact that Chevy was in dire straits. But Dolon could feel that, under that calm exterior, he was in pain. Add onto that, Izan's face had taken on a grayish tint in the last hour and his movements had become clunky and torpid. Dolon knew his space sickness was starting to show.

Which then led him to not thinking about Flora, whom he missed more than anything. She'd looked like Izan did now before she went downhill for the last time.

And by not thinking about Flora, he obviously wasn't thinking that in less than two hours he could be free of his debt to Launch Tech for trying to save her.

And that meant, he wasn't thinking about the fact that by paying his debt he was allowing Launch Tech the technology that could remake the world, for better or worse.

No, he needed to just concentrate on getting to Driggs without any more issues. One mega corp was as good as another. Who cared if Exoterra or Launch Tech had the device? What mattered was settling his debt and getting Chevy and Izan help.

Chevy groaned in the back seat.

"She seems worse than when we were in those people's van," Izan said.

"She does."

"I'm no doctor, but she could be bleeding internally," he added.

"Seems probable."

"She's got a head injury."

Dolon waited for him to say more, but he didn't. Dolon heard himself blurt, "Do you think this has been worth it?"

"What?"

"Everything this mission has cost. The other Aces, the battle at Zola, all the things we've done—the people we've hurt, the things we've stolen—all for what? This device? And we're just going to hand it to Launch Tech and trust they do the right thing with it?"

"It's a little late to be having buyer's remorse." Izan's voice was flat.

"Is it? We could destroy it. I could throw it off a bridge."

"First, you know that would just vaporize most of the state, but if we did destroy it and somehow survive, Chevy would still die. The only way to save her is to get her to medical, and that means get her to Launch Tech. We can't go to a hospital."

"I just . . ." Dolon's voice stalled in his throat. "Is she worth it? Are you worth it? Are any of us, me included, worth it? What if they do something terrible with it?"

Izan and Chevy had showed him what it was to find meaning in others again, and now they were going to give the world's most dangerous object to a mega corp, who could potentially use it to wipe out millions of people. Launch Tech could, if they chose, inflict the same grief he felt at Flora's absence on the entire world. And he would have given them the tool to do that. Were the three of them worth that when weighed against that level of ineffable suffering?

Izan's face took on an expression Dolon had never seen. Then, that unsettled feeling Dolon had gotten while watching Izan consider Chevy as she howled about mayonnaise, it hit Dolon like the Futuro exploding. Dolon hadn't been seeing things. Izan was hiding something.

"What aren't you telling us?" Dolon asked. His voice was soft, but his tone was not.

Izan's lips twitched like he was about to speak, but he stayed silent.

"We saved you," Dolon continued. "*She* saved you. Chevy, the woman who has never been anything other than what she's shown you, saved you, carried you off a fucking battlefield. We risked our lives to get you this far. And now, she might die. So tell us the actual truth."

Izan's mouth flicked into a smirk, and something inside of Dolon flipped.

"If I wasn't driving this car, I would beat you until you breathed your last words. I would beat you with the same artistry I used to build my late wife our house. I would use every bit of skill I've learned in my sixty years to yield maximum pain. And I would do it not because I felt moved to, but because that is what you have earned with your bullshit. But I'm not going to do that because Chevy's life, while it may not be worth the price of fusion, isn't worth the price of me teaching you a fucking lesson."

The PT cruiser hummed at an awkward octave. "Tell me what you've been hiding. Now," Dolon demanded.

Izan stretched his neck then cocked his head at Dolon. He smiled the smile of a competitor who had finally met a worthy match.

"They say," Izan's voice was bereft of its usual warmth, "that Aces are special. That we aren't like other people. And that's true, but it seems, so are phantoms."

"Nah. I'm not special."

Izan took a breath, and it belied his physical state. He was decompensating, Dolon could see that, but he also was finally being honest.

"I told you all I joined up at eighteen. To escape a life of migrant farming, like my parents. I wear this, as a tribute to them." He held up his wrist, showing Dolon a bracelet of thin, unadorned leather. "That is my truth, but there is more truth beneath it."

Dolon felt dizzy.

"Aces aren't tracked in at eighteen. Launch Tech sequenced my DNA when I was in utero. My mother went to a Launch Tech clinic for prenatal care. They identified me as genetically promising. I was born and was raised by Launch Tech. My parents were paid well for the exchange."

Dolon let that sink in, but he wasn't going to cave to Izan. "So? You never had a choice. Tough shit. You got to be an elite soldier. An Ace. Most people would kill for that."

Izan laughed, and it ended with a hacking cough. "I'm not the 'soldier' you think I am."

"What's that supposed to mean?"

"I was chosen to be a public face."

Dolon felt the car closing in on him. He cranked down his window.

"I'm not an elite space fighter, Dolon. I'm a pinup. The fighter Aces, they have a different genetic profile. Mine is magnetism, charm. Most people, phantoms aside apparently, can't help but like me. They parade me around to distract the public from what's really going on up there." He pointed skyward. "You think the fighter Aces retire to become pop singers and adventure athletes? No one can do it all, Dolon. And no one does."

Dolon's vision swam. A burning anger flushed from his stomach to his cheeks. "So, you're a what? A doll dressed up as a soldier? That doesn't explain anything. If you're not a real Ace, how did you get this?" He held up the Conlow bag.

Izan smiled. Calmly, he took the bag from Dolon. Dolon let him take it, but he felt like he'd just stepped off a cliff and there was nothing he could do but wait for impact.

"This. Is not the fusion device."

Dolon almost hit the brakes. Almost quit speeding forward, but he didn't. The car kept going, Dolon and Chevy and Izan in it, but not in the same way they had been moments before.

"What?" Dolon finally breathed.

Izan, his movements cold and intentional, spun the bag.

"We were a distraction. Me and the other three Aces."

Izan hefted the bag.

"Launch Tech has had the fusion device for days, Dolon. Our little road trip? It's been distracting Exoterra's best black-ops teams. The actual device was swapped out before I was even in the lifeboat, smuggled off the ship using the lifeboat launches as a distraction. Launch Tech has no doubt duplicated the device by now, making them superior to Exoterra. Jinzhan, Alpha Orbital, Lua Um, and Tsiolkovsky have fallen. Launch Tech is the *only* global power now. Exoterra and the rest of the world, they just don't know it yet."

Dolon felt like he'd been stabbed.

"You . . . You're . . . So none of this, everything we did . . . All of it, was a lie. None of it matters?"

Izan's face fell at that.

"That's not true. We, Launch Tech, did it this way because this mission, our mission, Dolon, gave them the space they needed to duplicate the device without having to defend it. These past few days have been the most successful geopolitical feint in all of human history. Launch Tech is making more fusion devices as we speak, putting the pieces in place to deliver the killing blow to Exoterra, and Exoterra still thinks they are fighting an analogue Hail Mary. They have no idea what's actually happening, and it's because you, me, and Chevy are keeping the ruse alive. Do you know what it means to have an extra few days to prepare for the final battle that will end in the control of the entire planet? Dolon, we are the reason Launch Tech is going to be the only one standing by the end of the week."

"So, none of this was real?" Dolon felt dizzy. "You've been a double agent this whole time?"

Izan shook his head. "I'm not a double agent, Dolon. I have always been, and still am, a Launch Tech Ace. And in terms of us, this little team, you and Chevy matter more to me than anyone I've ever met. My whole life has been curated. Everything I've done has been scripted and planned for. But you two, you are the first *real* people I've ever met. You're my first real friends."

Dolon's blood boiled.

"You think we're your friends? After what . . . You manipulated Chevy into . . . everything. Liking you, sleeping with you, thinking you saw her as a person and not just an objective."

Izan's frown deepened.

"I may have a certain inherent attraction that Chevy is drawn to, but my feelings for her, and for you, are not manufactured. I've never been a part of a group who wasn't specifically selected for a predetermined outcome . . ."

"But that's exactly what we were! We've been manipulated from the beginning."

Izan shook his head. He looked clammy, but Dolon didn't care.

"The three of us should have never gotten this far. I should have died, you were activated to further cloud the water for Exoterra, and Chevy, Chevy was never part of the plan."

"So what? None of this fucking matters? Chevy is dying back there for nothing . . ." A horrifying thought hit Dolon. "Wait . . . Is there even a safe house? Or are we going to get caught by Exoterra no matter how fast and far we run?"

Izan's face fell.

"Dolon, I don't think you understand what I'm telling you. Our only chance is to keep running toward the safe house. I want it to exist. It could exist. It might not, but what is certain, is that if we stop, we are most certainly dead. Exoterra has been chasing us with everything they have because if they don't stop us, they know they die. My life has always been for Launch Tech to spend. How that happens I have yet to see, but it will come to pass. And when it does, I will be remembered as a hero. I am a fucking *male* Ace, Dolon. I'm useful. I'll be a legend. But you. You *could* survive. And you *could* save Chevy too. If the safe house does exist, and you get us there. That script isn't written yet."

"You're disgusting," Dolon managed. "This has been nothing but a game to you."

Izan shook his head. "Dolon, it's not a game. It's just business."

FIFTY-SIX

THE CRANE

The Crane ran through the darkened streets of Salt Lake City, his footfalls becoming louder as he pushed himself faster. It had taken him hours to fall asleep, despite watching a live feed of Lucy drinking water, and even that sleep had been restless. Finally, at zero four hundred hours, he'd gotten out of bed and started to run.

The Crane knew his prey had disappeared into the Salt Lake area, but where exactly, he didn't know. And with every passing minute, Exoterra was closer to restoring their network. If he had nothing to tell them when it was back up, he knew they would want to scuttle the device as soon as they had a bead on it. It had been days since Launch Tech took it. They couldn't be far from disappearing it. Assuming, of course, they hadn't already.

The Crane hoped his prey had bedded down, not made it to their safe house. If they were just hiding, at some point they'd have to poke their head out, be it to get food or supplies. And for that eventuality, he was ready. If plastering their faces everywhere had pushed them beyond Salt Lake, though, or their safe house was in Salt Lake, well, then the Crane had made a significant error.

He quit running and looked at his watch. It was nearly zero seven hundred hours. He'd been running for over two and a half hours. Not bad.

He made his way back to the hotel suite and opened the door.

"BOSS!" the Banker yelled. "You're going to want to see this."

The Crane moved to his desk and opened the computer the hotel had provided him upon learning he was an Exoterra subscriber. The Banker, in the suite's other room, typed loudly on a keyboard.

"Click the link!"

The Crane minimized the Lucy feed and clicked the link. A church website populated. The page was labeled "Miracle Forum." The Crane skimmed the first post.

Complete with photos, the author, who seemed about as intelligent as a fairly dull teenager, chronicled the "miraculous miracle" of the spontaneously combusting KIA Futuro. On the page, the Crane saw them. There was a photo of an unknown man helping Chevy Cole, now with a head injury, into a van. Another photo showed a small man, his face too dark to make out, next to the phantom. The phantom had dyed his hair and shaved his beard, but none of that distracted from his eyes. They were the same watery green, alive and piercing.

It was his prey.

"It's geotagged in Idaho Falls," the Banker said, now standing next to the Crane, "from seven minutes ago. It places them at the Walmart."

A call came into the Banker's comm system. He answered and nodded with a smile. His focus shifted to the Crane. "It's the Idaho Falls police. They have a lead. Transferring to you."

This was one of the best parts of modern-day America, at least as the Crane saw it. No one had allegiance to anyone. The Banker had "promised" more than what Launch Tech was offering for information regarding the "terrorists." And now, the cops were calling them.

The audible ping of the call transfer rang in the Crane's comm.

"Sir? This is Captain Kyle with the Idaho Falls Police Department."

A woman yelling punctuated the background of static.

"Yes, have you found the terrorists?" the Crane asked.

"Well, sir, it appears they stole a vehicle. A PT cruiser, brown in color."

The Crane motioned for the Banker to join the call again.

"I've got the owner here," Captain Kyle continued. "She says her car's chipped, and she's got an app that lets her see where it is. It's northbound on Highway 20. They're about fifteen minutes south of Rexburg."

"I see," the Crane said. "Are you able to have the Rexburg police meet us at the airstrip?"

"I'll call them now, sir."

"Thank you. You've been very helpful."

The Crane cut off the call before the policeman could say more.

The Banker laughed. "A PT cruiser?"

"Let's go," the Crane said. "The plane is ready. We're going to Rexburg."

FIFTY-SEVEN

DOLON

Dolon didn't know how to respond to everything Izan had just said, so he focused on driving. It was actually real. He was in this car. He could feel the steering wheel on his palms. The pedal under his boot.

Chevy groaned, and Izan climbed into the rear seat. A red-hot spike of anger tore through Dolon, but before he could snap at Izan to get away from Chevy, she vomited. Through the rear-view, Dolon watched Izan mop her face with a formerly cute tea towel.

When Chevy was re-situated, Izan crawled back into the front seat, his hands trembling. Dolon watched them, caught between compassion and vindication. If Chevy died and Izan lived . . . Dolon took a breath. But if Izan died, maybe that was just.

Dolon felt his jaw flare. He was clenching his teeth. What choice did he have? To stop now? With or without Izan's lies, they were being chased. Running to a sliver of hope was better than waiting for certain death. Dolon slowed to get off the highway.

"What's the town called again?" Izan asked.

Dolon didn't want to answer the little prick. The silence stretched. Dolon tried to hold on to the betrayal, but really, everything was so fucked. He could rage against the position Izan had put him in or . . . "Driggs," Dolon exhaled.

"How far is it?"

Dolon unclenched his fingers. "Maybe an hour."

An hour. Nothing compared to how long they'd been trying to get to Driggs, but forever in terms of what Chevy needed.

The road's yellow lines stretched endlessly toward the horizon.

Dolon realized that everything he felt back at the Futuro no longer mattered. If Launch Tech already had the fusion device, the quandary of Dolon delivering it to them in hopes that they chose good over evil was no longer an issue. But Izan was right. He was in the actual driver's seat of not just his fate, but the fates of Chevy and Izan.

Izan broke their silence. "If we complete this mission, even if it is not the mission you initially thought it was, and the safe house is real, Chevy might live."

Dolon didn't have anything to say to that. He simply looked in the rearview mirror, saw Chevy with her slack jaw, bloody, vomity head, and slinged arm, and it was all he could do not to burst into tears. Thankfully, Izan had turned to stare out his window. Dolon felt a modicum of privacy.

They drove in silence down Highway 33 for almost thirty minutes. He'd been regularly checking his mirrors and scouting the road for waiting cops. When he finally saw the approaching red and blue lights, he almost felt relieved. This was something more immediate to focus on than the conversation that was bouncing in his brain.

"Cops," Dolon breathed.

"Where?"

What his face was doing, he wasn't sure, but his eyes were locked on the rearview mirror. Izan turned, squinted, and saw the lights.

"Well, it might be time to step on it," he said, matter-of-factly.

Izan's calm pierced the chaos in Dolon's brain. Izan might not be who Dolon thought he was, but they were in this fucking car together, and like it or not, that made them some sort of team. Dolon punched the gas.

Chevy hadn't made a noise since they merged onto 33, but as the car accelerated, she let out a pained moan.

"We got company, Chevy," Izan said, turning to look at her and the approaching cruisers.

"They must be tracking this car," Dolon said.

"This is the car, out of all the cars we've borrowed, that has a tracker in it?" Izan held up what looked to be a grocery bag full of quilting squares.

Dolon shrugged. "We're lucky our luck lasted this long."

They passed a sign that said TETONIA 10 MILES.

"If we can make it there, maybe we can ditch the car," Dolon said.

"Ten miles seems a lot like forever."

The lights were gaining, but slowly. Dolon had the pedal floored. He watched the dashboard tick down the miles.

"How are we going to deal with Chevy?" Izan asked.

Dolon hadn't thought of this.

"Can she not walk?"

"I don't know. She seems like she's mostly unconscious."

"Fuck." Dolon ran a hand through his stupidly dyed hair.

He watched the mileage counter spin down the miles, and when he looked up, he saw buildings. They were nearing Tetonia.

"You see any parking areas? Big stores, that kind of thing?" Dolon asked.

"This looks pretty rural . . . Wait, look . . ."

Dolon followed Izan's shaking finger and saw a large brick building—a Fred Meyer. He changed lanes and hit the exit ramp way too fast.

The PT Cruiser fishtailed, but Dolon got it under control by the time the ramp ended. With a rolling stop, he sped through the intersection and entered the parking lot.

"Okay, we want older model cars . . ."

"Fuck that, we don't have time for this," Izan said. "Stop."

"What?"

"Stop the car!"

Dolon did so but only because the tone of Izan's voice scared him. None of the cars they were near would do. They were too new which meant he couldn't hotwire them. Izan opened the door and nearly fell out of the car. He pulled himself to standing and hobbled to a single man standing outside of a newer model SUV. Dolon saw Izan pull something out of his waistband.

"Oh, sweet Jesus," Dolon heard himself say.

Izan held the pearl-handled pistol. He was carjacking the man.

The man put up no fight. Within seconds he handed Izan his wallet, keys, and phone. Izan waved Dolon over, and Dolon drove to the SUV.

"PLEASE DON'T KILL ME," the man screamed.

Dolon felt like he was having an out-of-body experience. He opened the back door of the PT cruiser and did his best to pull out Chevy. Luckily, Chevy helped somewhat and was able to get into the back of the SUV.

"Keep it down," Izan hissed at the man.

People were staring at them.

"Let's go." Dolon realized he was speaking again.

Izan got into the passenger seat, and Dolon got in the driver's seat. He shut the door, and the man took off running.

"Go," Izan ordered.

Without a word, Dolon hit the drive button, and the car leapt to life.

FIFTY-EIGHT

THE CRANE

The Crane sat in a vehicle with the captain of the Rexburg Police Department, a corpulent man with an outdated mustache. Despite his passé hair fashion, the man could drive.

"Grew up on dirt bikes with my brothers and cousins," Captain Rigby chuckled. "Love this kinda thing."

They screamed into the Fred Meyer parking lot.

"It's here," the Crane said. The captain's dash screen showed a blinking dot that was the GPS of the PT cruiser. "It hasn't moved in the last three minutes."

"They might have left it," Rigby said.

"It's that way," the Crane indicated with his chin.

They turned down a row and saw a brown PT Cruiser, doors open, abandoned.

"Well heck," Captain Rigby said. "They can't be far. Oh dang. Let me switch the radio. We're outside of our jurisdiction." Rigby spun a dial on his center console. The radio crackled at them.

"Any unit near Fred Meyer," came the dispatcher's voice. "A carjacking occurred approximately five minutes ago. Stolen vehicle is a white GMC SUV, Idaho plate."

Captain Rigby's eyes lit up.

“Sounds like your terrorists!”

“It does.”

The Crane was again thankful for the age of misinformation. The fact that Launch Tech had issued statements declaring Exoterra the bad guy had made zero impact on Captain Rigby or any of his backwoods peers. As far as they saw it, it was all a game. If they helped a member of the Big Six, *any member*, even the members that Launch Tech had bested or was trying to best, the prize could be great. It also helped that the Rexburg Police were Lua Um subscribers and therefore still had a working GPS.

“Vehicle last seen getting on Highway 33, eastbound.” The dispatcher’s voice was tinny over the radio.

“You wanna follow it?” Captain Rigby’s caterpillar eyebrows waggled at the Crane.

“I do,” the Crane said.

“Well hot dog! Let’s do it then!” Captain Rigby punched the gas.

The Crane activated his ear chip. The Banker was in a car behind him and therefore should have been within range to talk over their impromptu mesh network.

“Banker, we’re going east on 33.”

The Banker responded with a single *copy*.

“I don’t know where they’re goin’,” Captain Rigby said. “This leaves Idaho over Teton Pass, and that’s a pinch point.”

The Crane pulled up a map on his retinal display.

Captain Rigby was right.

The Crane could feel it. This chase was about to end.

FIFTY-NINE

DOLON

"You used your terrorist protection set to carjack a guy?" Dolon slammed the accelerator, despite the vehicle's self-driving capabilities.

"The vehicle is exceeding the speed limit," purred a British woman's voice.

The vehicle attempted to slow, but Dolon kept his foot on the gas. The car seemed to hesitate before accelerating. Dolon jabbed at the vehicle's screen.

"Fuck these self-driving cars." Dolon mashed his finger across the glass. "There has to be a way to disable the autopilot."

"It's not like I shot him."

"The vehicle is still exceeding the speed limit," the car repeated.

"Jesus." Dolon clicked through the screen. "I can't believe you held that guy up. You know, with you being an actor and all, or whatever, I didn't figure that."

Izan pinched his lips. "Actor is a bit too fluffy of a term. I've been training to complete objectives my whole life."

Dolon grunted. "Well thank God for that, and thank God this guy disabled some of the more restrictive parts of the AI. I think he took the governor offline."

Izan put his head between his legs. "We just didn't have time to futz around with stealing a car."

"I don't disagree about the timeline, but still . . ." Dolon stared at the console. He pushed an icon that looked like a steering wheel.

"Dolon." Izan's voice was soft, "if they catch us, Chevy'll die."

Dolon took a breath. "We *all* might die, goddamn it."

"I know, but I don't want *her* to."

"You're a real fucking gentleman."

They passed a sign that said, DRIGGS 5 MILES.

"We have to go a little east of the town center," Dolon said. "The station is on the border near the town of Alta."

"Okay." Izan raised his head.

Dolon realized Izan might not be functional much longer. Very soon, Dolon might be the only one of the three of them capable of finishing this. He felt his throat go gummy. He couldn't think about that. Especially when he wasn't even sure what finishing this now actually meant.

Buildings became more frequent. Then a sign appeared. ALTA, NEXT RIGHT.

Dolon kept pressure on the pedal, and finally, after having cycled through several menus on the car's display, Dolon was now able to mostly drive the SUV. He made the turn onto Ski Hill Road and edged the pedal down. Izan groaned.

Chevy and Izan were hanging onto life by the skin of their teeth. Dolon centered himself. He was the only one who could save these two, if saving them was actually possible. He wasn't pleased with Izan, but if what Izan said was true, none of this mission had been his choice. Dolon might not like the bastard, and Dolon did think Izan could have told them the truth prior to this point, but that didn't mean Izan deserved to die. Even if that seemed to be what he wanted. Dolon was calm enough now to see that.

What Dolon needed was more speed.

They passed a construction crew. The two guys in hard hats and orange vests yelled at them angrily then pulled a barricade across the road behind them, closing the road to any more uphill traffic. Dolon liked that. He accelerated up the two-lane road. The car complained, but it didn't attempt to override him. He willed the car faster. The Sinclair station was supposed to be on the border. His throat felt dry.

It would be there, wouldn't it?

He checked his mirrors again and saw the cop car at his rear bumper.

"Object approaching from the rear," the car said, her voice eerily calm.

Then the SUV began to spin.

SIXTY

THE CRANE

They followed the white SUV into downtown Driggs. When it turned to go up toward Alta, the dispatcher came through with the missing vehicle's license plate. It was a match.

"Oh, heck yeah!" Captain Rigby's excitement was almost infectious.

The Crane plugged the plate numbers into his retinal display. He discovered nothing useful in their saved database. He flicked his eyes back to the road. A construction crew had dragged a metal and wooden barricade across the road in front of them.

"I don't brake for terrorists!" Captain Rigby screamed.

The cop car smashed through the barricade, sending the construction guys scrambling. The Crane watched one of the men scream into a radio. He let out a tight breath. This was all about to end. He could feel it. He'd have bet his life those men knew nothing about road repair. Then he realized, he'd bet his life two days ago.

"This is wild!" Captain Rigby laughed. "Heck with it! Let's PIT 'em!"

The Crane wasn't inherently opposed to the captain's plan. A PIT maneuver might very well stop their prey's car. But he knew it might also stop their own vehicle.

Captain Rigby smacked his lips in anticipation.

He went for the PIT, aiming to knock the SUV's back panel so that the car spun out. Unfortunately, the SUV hit the brakes just when Captain Rigby committed to the move, and the cruiser hit too far forward.

The SUV tipped, and the cruiser containing the Crane shot past it.

When they hit the tree, the Crane heard nothing. Later, he would reflect that the lack of sound was simply a precursor to him losing consciousness.

SIXTY-ONE

DOLON

Dolon lay for what seemed like an eternity, just focusing on breathing. When he finally opened his eyes, the bright sunlight blinded him. Then he took in the carnage before him. A police car was wrapped around a tree, and two men, one dressed like a cop and the other dressed like an Exoterra agent, were running from an intact cop car to the compacted police car. They hadn't noticed him, yet. Dolon knew they would soon.

To his right he saw their stolen SUV. It was on its side, crumpled, a Dolon-sized hole in the windshield. In the chaos of Izan pulling out that gun, he'd forgotten to clip his seatbelt. He let out a groan.

"Dolon!" Izan skittered to a stop next to him. "Dolon, can you hear me?"

Dolon nodded. Izan looked no worse for wear. He was still pale, and his hands were trembling, but his bones didn't seem broken, and he was up and talking, which was more than Dolon could say about himself. Briefly Dolon wondered where Chevy was, but Izan was saying something.

"I need the device."

"What does it matter? It's not real . . ." Dolon felt tired, and he was sick of running. He just wanted to take a nap, maybe with Captain Picard. Where was that cat?

"I'll give it to Launch Tech in exchange for them helping you guys. Dolon, it's the perception that matters. It's all a shell game."

Izan patted Dolon's pockets and removed the Conlow bag. Shaking, Izan unzipped his terrorist protection kit and pulled out his pills. He managed to get the top off. He poured several in his mouth, chewed, and swallowed them.

"I'm not leaving you. I'll bring the world."

"Sounds good." Dolon's voice was feathery. "Get to the dinosaur."

Izan stood and ran into the trees, the two men still focused on the cruiser. Dolon put his head back against the ground and closed his eyes. How long he had them closed he didn't know. But he eventually realized someone was standing next to him.

Dolon let out a sigh and opened his eyes. One of the men, the one in an undertaker suit with neck tattoos that crawled above his collar line now stood over him. Dolon waited. He wasn't excited about whatever was about to happen, but he was very, very tired, and as such, he had very few fucks to give.

"Where is it?" The man grabbed the front of Dolon's shirt and hefted him into a sitting position.

He wasn't a big man, but he had that methy strength. His skin was flaky, and his breath had a fishy stink, and most of the bones and cartilage in his face looked like they'd been broken at least once. Dolon knew this guy was a human cockroach. He was probably impossible to kill. The thought made Dolon even more tired.

"What?" Dolon snapped, realizing this man wore *way* too much body spray.

"The device. Where is it, phantom?"

"Who are you?" Dolon whimpered, easily slipping into the persona of a doddering old fart.

"WAKE UP, OLD MAN." The human bug shook Dolon.

"I think I was in an accident?"

"Don't play dumb with me." The man patted Dolon's pockets.

"I think my license and registration are in the car?" Dolon looked at the car. "Oh, my car!"

The man let go of Dolon in disgust. Another man appeared behind him. This one was tall, thin, and dressed in a well-fitted suit. He moved like an athlete.

"Boss," the first man said.

"Does he have it?"

"Not on him."

"Is it in the car?" the thin man asked.

This second man unnerved Dolon. He was clearly in charge. It appeared he'd come out of the totaled cop car, yet he had no injuries. Dolon wondered distractedly if he was even human.

"I'll check," the first man replied.

The bug trotted to the SUV, and the thin man eyed Dolon. He took a step toward him then crouched so they were at eye level.

"Hello. They call me the Crane. I take it you're the phantom?"

Dolon didn't say anything. He didn't think his wobbly old man routine would work on this guy.

"Not going to talk, I see." The Crane bent his neck. A chain of pops erupted, and his too narrow face broke into a cold grin. "Ahhh, good as new. I must commend you, this was a very fun hunt."

Dolon focused on keeping his face neutral. It was important this Crane did not see how much he unnerved Dolon.

"BOSS!"

Both Dolon and the Crane looked toward the other man's voice.

SIXTY-TWO

CHEVY

Chevy could hear someone yelling. It was a man. She didn't know him. Chevy realized she was in a car. It looked like she'd been in an accident. She wasn't on the seat. She was on a window. But it was broken. Where was her team?

"The grunt's in there," the voice said.

"And the Ace?" Another voice.

"I can't see him, but it's possible he's in there crushed and dead."

Chevy felt a surge of panic. She knew the Ace. She couldn't remember his name, though.

"What about the device?" the second voice said.

"I'm not getting any readings on it, but it could be lost in there. I think we need a wrecker."

Chevy heard an expulsion of air.

"Move. If the Ace isn't in there, it's probably with him, wherever he is."

Chevy heard some scratching and then a thin-faced man stuck his head through the windshield. They locked eyes. Chevy did not like this man. He took in Chevy's situation and smiled coldly.

"Well, Ms. Cole, you aren't going anywhere."

For a brief second, fear eclipsed the pain in Chevy's head. She wasn't sure who this man was, how he knew her name, or why he was in this car, but an undercurrent of anxiety chilled her.

The man looked around the rest of the car before returning his focus to Chevy.

"You might die in there, Ms. Cole, so allow me to be the last person you ever meet. My name is the Crane. I'm the one who killed you."

SIXTY-THREE

THE CRANE

The Crane pulled his head out of the wrecked car. He hoped the grunt's internal trauma killed her slowly. He could have shot her, but in the off chance she knew where the Ace was, and he couldn't find him, he didn't want her dead, yet. Still, it felt good knowing he'd been the cause of her life-altering, if not life-ending, accident.

"The Ace isn't in there," he said to the Banker. "We need to look for him. Let's see if your driver will help."

They walked to the crushed police car that the Crane had somehow managed to walk away from. Captain Rigby wasn't so lucky. He was stuck inside and wasn't responsive. The cop who had driven the Banker was tugging on the mangled car's driver side door.

"Officer," the Crane started.

"I can't help you right now!" the cop yelled. "Captain Rigby needs to go to the hospital. An ambulance is coming."

"The two people in the other vehicle are the terrorists. The third one is still at large. We need to go look for him."

"Yeah, okay. Go then." The cop waved a hand at them.

The Crane sighed. He would have liked to leave someone with the phantom and Cole, but he needed the Banker with him.

Still, Cole was entombed in that car, and frankly, the old phantom might keel over at any minute. Leaving them wasn't ideal, but they were in ideal conditions to be left.

"Boss."

"What?"

"The network's back up."

The Crane whipped his head at the Banker. His eyes were skyward, skimming. The Crane flipped his retinal display out of offline mode. A single message pinged before him. It was from his bosses at Exoterra.

If you don't have it yet, order the space strike.

They were out of time.

"Wherever they're going must be linked to Launch Tech's tunnel network. If they get the device to it, it's gone. I think we should order the space strike," the Banker was saying. "We can back out from here. We need three minutes to be out of range. This is perfect. We can scuttle the device and make it out."

An awkward pause extended past the Banker's words. The Banker was right. They could complete their objective and live. But that wouldn't be a sporting end to a thrilling hunt. His prey wouldn't make it out alive, but he also wouldn't be the one to claim the victory. They were so close . . .

"No, we almost have it."

"Boss—"

The Crane flicked his hand. The Banker went silent. They stared at each other, the moment brittle. Finally, the Banker said, "What's the plan then?"

He had bent to the Crane. The hierarchy was intact.

"They were headed toward Wyoming. So, he's going that way, and I doubt he's dumb enough to walk on the road . . ."

They scanned the edge of the roadside. Overgrown grass and trees made visually clearing the area difficult.

"This grass is long. Do you see a trail leading from the accident site?"

He and the Banker fanned out and began to sweep the area for broken grass. Large animals left trails in grass. The Ace was a large animal.

"Here."

The Crane moved to the Banker. He saw a faint but true path through the tall grass that led away from the wreckage and into the trees that paralleled the road.

"And the hunt continues," the Crane said, his pace quickening.

SIXTY-FOUR

DOLON

Dolon watched the Crane and his henchman head into the bushes. He needed to move, and now, no matter how tired he was. He pushed himself to his feet, something was seriously wrong with him, but he didn't have time to deal with it.

Not ten feet from the SUV sat the un-wrecked patrol car. The driver's door was wide open. If he could get Chevy into that car . . .

He glanced at the other cop. He was still trying to get the door open to the totaled cruiser. Dolon stumbled to the SUV.

"Chevy," he hissed. "Chevy, can you hear me?"

"Yeah," came Chevy's voice. It was heavy and sick-sounding.

"Can you get out of there?"

"I . . . I don't know."

"Try."

Dolon heard rustling and the sound of something breaking.

"Can you kick out more of the windshield?" Chevy asked.

"Yeah. Watch yourself."

Dolon kicked at the remaining windshield. It folded on itself. He pulled it out of the car with his shoe.

Chevy crawled out. Her head was still wrapped in the bloody shemagh, and her homemade sling hung uselessly around her neck.

A new set of cuts and bruises covered her body, but Dolon didn't see any new serious injuries.

"I have the worst headache of my life." Chevy's voice was slurred.

"Okay. We need to get to that cop car, and we need to do it fast."

Chevy wobbled to her feet.

"I think I'm dying." She looked into Dolon's eyes.

"Probably," Dolon said. "Are you ready to run?"

"I'm ready to keep fighting, and if that means running, sure."

"Alright, one . . . two . . . THREE."

SIXTY-FIVE

CHEVY

Chevy didn't know how she was moving. The pain from her footfalls, from the sun, from the sound of her breathing . . . it all reverberated in her brain like buckshot. She felt she was shattering into a million pieces.

Yet she made it to the car. She collapsed inside and threw up on her lap.

Dolon was in the front seat. Someone was at the driver's window. A guy in an orange vest. The guy was screaming at them to stop and then the car was moving.

The cop spun to face them, and for a second, he just stared at them. Then he drew his gun. Dolon hit the accelerator and sped past the cop. The gun cracked. The sound was too loud. Dolon flinched. Chevy felt like she might die.

"Are you hit?" Dolon said.

"Ahhhh! Why are you yelling?"

A frantic voice came over the radio. "The terrorists stole my car! Where's my backup? Where's the ambo?"

Just the click of radio made Chevy puke again. When she finished, she slammed the off button on the radio console.

"Just hang on a little longer," Dolon said. "We're almost there."

SIXTY-SIX

THE CRANE

They lost the Ace's trail, but the Crane knew he was moving east. There was no reason for him to go any other direction now. So he pushed forward, too, the Banker trailing behind. And soon, he left the Banker. The Banker was strong, but the Crane, the Crane was a runner.

And then he saw an intersection. He knew that was the state line. On the other side of the road was a gas station that looked abandoned. The parking lot was empty. Graffiti-coated plywood covered the derelict building's windows. The sign was broken—its translucent panels hung from its frame. Dirty covers draped the pumps. A tumbleweed, a real-life tumbleweed, rolled over the broken concrete between the pumps. The sign, swinging in the wind, made a screeching noise. No one was in sight. A weather-bleached dinosaur shined in the sunlight.

A small form neared the road.

It was him—the Ace. The Crane could feel the hunt pulling him. His hand moved toward his sidearm, holstered at his hip, then he jerked it away. His arms began to pump and he sprinted.

He was going to snare this Ace with nothing but his mind and body. Using a gun on him would be like baiting a deer.

He was a fair hunter, and in this gravity the Ace was a shark on land. If he were to best an Ace, he wanted it to be because he was better than the Ace, not because he blew him away from a cowardly distance. Also, he didn't want to accidentally hit the device. Which meant no guns, no space fire. This would be a fair fight.

He ran faster, excited.

He reached the road. The Ace, who was clearly injured and barely on his feet, turned when he heard the Crane's footfalls. The Crane though didn't give him a moment to prepare. He launched at the Ace, slamming into his side in a perfect tackle, which took them to the ground.

The Ace threw his shoulders to the pavement, preventing the Crane from taking his back. But that was okay. The Crane could feel the Ace's strength; it was laughable. The Ace was weak, deadly weak. The Crane was in control. He could take his time. With intention, he shifted his weight and pinned the Ace to the ground. He didn't grab for the Conlow bag though, which the Ace still clutched. Instead, the Crane considered the Ace like a cat might consider a mouse.

The Ace, it seemed, was struggling to stay conscious. The Crane had mixed feelings about this. He didn't want this final fight to be over without any effort, but this confrontation was the result of a long, demanding chase, and the Crane could be proud he had pushed so hard, the Ace had run himself to death.

The Crane smiled, settling so his weight was best used to keep the Ace under control. Then a sound found his ears. A car. It was coming up the hill, fast. It came into view and screeched to a stop only feet from them.

"Izan!"

The Crane looked up to see the phantom, bloody and skeletal, standing at the driver's door of the cop car. The man had stolen the working cop car. That was fairly entertaining. The passenger door opened and the marine, covered in blood and vomit, looking at death's door, hefted herself to standing against the vehicle.

"So," the Crane said. "We all finally meet."

The Crane heard someone breathing behind him. He twisted, without letting up on the Ace, and saw the Banker, doing his best to jog, enter the roadway.

"You're outnumbered," the phantom said.

The laughter that came out of the Crane was deep.

"You're funny, phantom. Very funny. Once this is over, I will miss you, in my own way."

The Banker, his suit a little worse for wear, stepped even with the Crane.

"You had a good run," the Crane continued. "Historic in a lot of ways. I have to give it to you three. You have pluck."

The marine vomited. The Banker sneered, and the Crane felt the same way.

"Too bad, in the end, it won't save your ragged little friend group."

"I can run you over. Right here, right now," the phantom said.

This time he and the Banker laughed together.

"That is funny, but you aren't the kind of man who can run over his buddy," the Crane said.

The Banker actually appeared to wipe a tear from his eye. The Crane appreciated that he found this as humorous as he did.

"They'll find us soon, Boss. We should do this and be gone," the Banker said.

The Crane sighed, feeling the Ace sag under him. The Banker was right. They couldn't play with their food forever. They were professionals. He gave the Banker a slight nod. The Banker drew his gun from his shoulder holster and pointed it at the phantom, the first gunshot sounding before his arms were fully outstretched.

SIXTY-SEVEN

DOLON

Dolon might not have been some sociopathic killer, but he wasn't a pushover either. When the cologne-soaked meatwad jammed his hand into his jacket, Dolon knew he had to move.

The angles weren't great, but he was pretty sure he could do it.

"Chevy, I'm driving!"

Chevy, despite dying, flung herself away from the car. Dolon ducked into the driver's seat and hit the gas. The man was shooting at him, and the crack of gunfire was loud but not at the forefront of Dolon's mind. Instead, Dolon spun the wheel, avoiding Izan by inches, and plowing straight into the tatted-up henchman. The man tried at some quick lateral movement, but his training plan was clearly more focused on the power muscles and not the twitch muscles. He folded like a snapping twig, the front of the car crumpling.

Dolon threw himself out of the vehicle. The man's gun was at Dolon's feet, and he lay, unmoving, several feet away from the bumper. Dolon gathered up the gun and spun to face the Crane, who still sat on Izan's chest, his focus now on Dolon.

The Crane was obviously stunned. Dolon raised the gun, hoping he didn't hit Izan, when several soft pops sounded. The Crane jerked, his hand going to his neck. He pulled his hand away, and saw it was coated in bright red. He stared at the blood dumbly then sagged backward, bumping off of Izan's chest.

Izan scrambled backward, a pearl-handled pistol in one hand, the Conlow bag in the other, the fanny pack at his waist open.

"Izan!" Dolon yelled.

"Fire on the gas station."

Dolon realized the Crane was speaking, his face slack, his voice scratchy and paper-thin.

Then a blast hit Dolon, throwing him backward. The gas station, which had been sitting placidly in the September morning air, was ripped away. In its place, a wave of flames, topped by a column of tar black smoke, billowed skyward. His stolen ride's windshield caved in. Chevy howled.

Dolon tried to pop his ears. He could hear, somewhat, but a high ringing sounded. He whipped his head back to Izan. The Crane now lay near Dolon, in the fetal position. He'd been blown backward as well, and blood shone on his face. He stared at the rising mass of smoke, his eyes so wide they were black.

Then the ground rose. Hulking forms folded themselves out of the landscape, reminding Dolon of the time he'd stepped on a ground wasp nest. Where there had been nothing, now there were dozens and dozens of marines.

Several explosions shook the Earth. *Space fire.* They were taking space fire! Dolon needed to get out of the open. He turned to see a figure towering over him, their face painted in greens and black, the whites of their eyes shining through the darkening smoke.

"Let's go!" the giant yelled.

Dolon scrambled backward. Had they really made it to a Launch Tech safe house? Dolon stood, stunned, before the mountain of a marine—why were they all giant?—reached out and grabbed him.

"Chevy and Izan!" Dolon yelled. "We can't leave them!"

Another round of space fire knocked him off balance. The iron grip of the marine squeezed his bicep.

"No one is getting left out here, but that smoke'll only hide us for so long." The marine pulled Dolon away from the gas station.

Dolon looked back and saw Izan, still clutching the Conlow bag, being dragged in the opposite direction. Two more ghillie-suited forms dragged Chevy, head limp, in a third direction.

"Where are we going?" Dolon struggled pointlessly against his captor.

"They'll target the gas station. We've got tunnels all over this place."

"But Chevy and Izan!"

"We've got them. We gotta move if you want to stay alive."

Dolon stumbled to the other side of the road, and the marine pushed him toward an outcropping of rock. Dolon saw a ladder peaking from a hole behind the biggest boulder. The marine pushed him toward it. He put his feet on the rungs and looked back to where he'd last seen Chevy and Izan. The smoke obfuscated everything beyond a few feet. Another explosion, this one closer, rocked him, and the marine shoved Dolon hard. Dolon scrambled down the ladder, his mind spinning.

He wasn't sure if Chevy and Izan had made it.

SIXTY-EIGHT

CHEVY

Chevy took in her surroundings. She lay in a bed, a machine beeping softly at her side. The world was white, clean, efficient. She was in a hospital.

"Hello?" she called. Her voice wavered like an old woman's. "Hello?" she tried again, this time with more confidence.

"Corporal Cole!"

A nurse popped her head into the room.

"You're awake. This is great!"

"What's going on? What happened?" Chevy tried to remember something, anything.

"Oh, you've been unconscious for a long time. You suffered a head injury in battle at the Zola mine. Do you not remember?" The nurse's face knotted in concern.

Chevy shook her head, memories crowding her brain. "No . . . I was fine after the Zola mine . . . Owl wasn't, but I was . . ."

"You saw an owl at the battle?" The nurse's lips formed an exaggerated frown.

"I . . ." Chevy stopped. She looked around the room again. Something wasn't right. "Where am I?"

The nurse smiled, seemingly happy Chevy was asking a rational question.

"You're in St. Milligan's Hospital in Barstow, on the Launch Tech base."

"I . . ." Chevy's brain swam. "How long have I been here?"

The nurse gave her a sad smile. "Three weeks. We weren't sure you were ever going to wake up."

"And . . . I was hurt at the Zola mine?"

"Yes, corporal. But you're safe now. And Private Tan is going to be fine. You saved him."

"I what?"

"You ran into space fire to save Private Tan. You're a hero."

"I . . . I don't remember any of this."

The nurse made another overly emotive frown. "That is expected. We don't know how much of your memory you will recover. But this is a great first step. You're awake and talking. It's practically a miracle. But I don't want you to tire yourself out. You need to rest."

Chevy noticed the nurse was fiddling with her IV tubing.

The room faded away.

* * *

"Sucks. Out of all of them, we got assigned her."

"I know. Big dumb grunt. Could have been on the team working the Ace."

"*Pfft.* You and I were never going to get to do anything as cutting edge as that."

Chevy wanted to open her eyes, but they were heavy. She was heavy. Hands jostled under her hips, her shoulders. They were pulling something from beneath her. Sheets. She was still in the hospital bed. Two people were changing her sheets. But she was so tired. She could not open her eyes. Her lids weighed more than she did.

"You should have screwed Major Williams. Then you'd be somewhere."

"Ha."

"You think he'll live?"

"Williams?"

"No, the Ace."

"The last guy they augmented didn't. But they say the Ace is special."

"What about the other guy?"

"The POW?"

"Yeah."

"Dunno. Sent me in to clean his room the other day. He's gone."

"Like dead?"

"Nah, just not here anymore."

* * *

When they finally let Chevy out of that hospital bed, she found herself in a new world. One where she had been diagnosed with having suffered a stroke and a traumatic brain injury. The doctors debated on which came first, but the result was the same. Chevy had brain damage and couldn't return to active duty.

They held a ceremony for her, awarding her some medal for risking her life and suffering an injury to save another marine. Her former platoon had made it out of the Zola mine and was now apparently training in Alaska. It was a long exercise, and she'd been told they were unreachable until its conclusion. But Chevy had been promised that Launch Tech couldn't let a hero of her status go unrecognized, so they insisted on giving her the medal even if the man she'd saved couldn't be there to see it. The ceremony had been sad and poorly attended, with a few desk jockeys attending the event. And that was that.

Launch Tech wasn't sure what to do with her. She'd been sharp before the brain injuries, but now they didn't seem inclined to give her any meaningful admin work. They said they were waiting until a good fit of an opportunity presented itself. In the meantime, she was to do the recovery work the doctors prescribed and get herself into the gym as often as possible.

So she did that.

It was clear they'd written her off. The days stretched into weeks, and she still did nothing useful. She continued to work out and go to the doctor. But she wasn't making any real progress. She still struggled to pick the correct words, angered easily, forgot things, and couldn't follow complex stories.

"I feel dumb," she told her doctor one day. "Like, I have a feeling of who I used to be, but I can't reach her."

The doctor nodded and typed into his device.

So, it wasn't really a surprise when she was called to the HR supervisor's office.

The HR supervisor, Major Lin, was a small woman who should have been smaller, but desk work had clearly restricted her fitness. Her uniform bulged where it shouldn't have, and the buttons holding her shirt across her chest flared, revealing her white undershirt.

"Corporal Cole. Major Lin said.

"Yes, ma'am."

"It has been decided you will be medically retired, starting today."

Chevy didn't move.

"You will receive a living stipend, and your retirement package will remain intact. Later this morning you'll meet with the Valhalla coordinator, and they'll go over your options."

Major Lin clicked a button on her computer.

"I've sent you all the paperwork and benefit explanation packets. Do you have any immediate questions?"

"I'm not a marine anymore?"

Major Lin waved a hand, her focus on her computer. "Once a marine, always a marine. Your appointment with the Valhalla coordinator is at oh-eight-thirty in Building F. Office 102. Now, if you'll excuse me . . ."

Four Months Later

Chevy bounced down the dirt road, the dawn light making the White Mountains shimmer. Her truck, a new-to-her Chevy Colorado, squeaked with every rut she hit.

She wondered if this was the road that would finally lead her to Dolon. It had taken her months to gather the little information she had, but now it was time to find him. She could only do so much alone.

She did believe she'd suffered a stroke and a TBI, like Launch Tech had said, but her lack of recovery had been her own fiction. Launch Tech claimed she'd been injured while at the Zola mine, and who was Chevy to disabuse them of that notion? If they could lie, so could she. Upon waking up and understanding that Launch Tech was lying, even if she didn't understand *why* they were doing that, Chevy knew enough to know Launch Tech played for keeps. One grunt's life was nothing if it stood between Launch Tech and their global grab for power.

Which seemed to be going well for them. By the time she was allowed to read the news, the Big Six was simply Launch Tech. The ramifications of that were still being sorted through.

But she remembered everything—Dolon, Izan, the device, all of it. She also remembered Izan telling Dolon that they didn't even have the device. The two of them probably had no idea she had been conscious and listening then, but she'd heard it all. She knew their mission had been nothing but a long, loud, messy distraction, and Izan, Owl, Izan, whoever he was, was both a victim and complicit in that.

But regardless of Izan's truth, Launch Tech wanted her and her knowledge gone, and she knew that if she didn't go along with their narrative, well, accidents happened to everyone. Aces, even the public-facing Aces, were worth more than grunts and look how that had turned out. So, she played into their fiction. She pretended to struggle with their tests, got angry at strange times, told her doc about her brain feeling fuzzy, but she knew what she had been through.

On a more philosophical note, and a less evil corporate one, this whole journey had caused her to reconsider her own life's value. She wasn't convinced her life was all that important, especially when juxtaposed against the trajectory of humanity as a whole. But she could never manage to talk herself out of the importance of her teammates' lives.

What had happened to Dolon and Izan? It had been her job to protect them, even if Izan hadn't been able to tell her everything. If he had been selected pre-birth to do what he did, that changed the feeling of betrayal. It didn't erase it, but it softened it.

She knew what she'd heard while on the nod from the opioids they'd pumped her full of. Launch Tech had Izan, and they were doing something terrible to him. *Augmenting* him. And that might kill him.

She couldn't stop replaying her first real conversation with Dolon. When he told her that Launch Tech was just another form of government, another form of monster. But she had pledged her life to Launch Tech because she believed in the mission it preached—that it would make humanity better. That it would save girls like her from lives without futures.

But now, after having been sent to start a battle over a mine that didn't matter, having spent days risking her life for a fusion device that didn't even exist, having killed people for a made-up objective, only to return to the fold to be told none of it happened, and then learn that the man they'd tried to sacrifice they were now experimenting on . . . She knew Dolon had been right. Launch Tech was a monster.

They had fusion. They had the world.

And they had Izan.

She wasn't sure how to steal fusion back from the only global power. She didn't do too hot the first time she thought she'd located fusion. But she did know she couldn't sit back and let Launch Tech take Izan apart toe by toe for whatever fucked-up thing they were attempting now. That was anathema to the Chevy Cole who'd started this mission. And while she was a very different Chevy Cole now, that kernel of her core was still there. She believed in doing what was right. And whatever they were doing to Izan was most certainly not right.

When she was first in, she'd had a drill sergeant who'd always yell at her about sphere of control. *What's in your sphere of control, Cole? Not what I do. What you do.*

And she felt, she just might have a little control over finding and rescuing Izan. He was on her team, and she didn't take that responsibility lightly. That team still had one behind enemy lines, and that was something she could not, *would not* abide.

She had been willing to die for an idea. Her identity had been being a marine, and even though she was no longer in, that fat retired-on-duty major who'd pushed her out to pasture had been right. *Once a marine, always a marine.*

Izan was still behind enemy lines. Her mission was not complete until he was home. And, outside of her identity, outside of her mission, she, Chevy Cole, also had some personal, unfinished business with Izan.

To find him, she needed help. She'd been cut off from everyone, and her ability to trust anyone had been trashed. But there was one person she trusted, even if she didn't know where he was. He was someone who understood doing something because it was the right thing to do, even if doing it was hard. That person was Dolon.

Tracking him down had required Chevy to look for information outside of the network of Launch Tech's loose lips. She'd had to get off the grid and into the desert. She remembered Dolon telling her he was a handyman who lived at the base of the White Mountains on the California/Nevada border. Once Chevy separated from Launch Tech, she drove to Eastern California and then into Western Nevada and talked to anyone and everyone who lived along the base of the Whites. Eventually, she ended up in Dyer. She'd asked around for a handyman, and some old guy named Jim had pointed her down this road. The road she was now on.

A cabin came into view. Chevy swallowed.

SIXTY-NINE

DOLON

Dolon watched the sun rise. Captain Picard purred happily on his lap. Dolon petted the cat and drank his coffee. The world before him glowed. The dawn light made everything seem alive and full of potential. Once the sun was high enough, though, the colors would wash out, the air would lose its hope, and he would settle into another day.

And today he didn't have anything to do. Yesterday, he'd finally wrapped up his work project at McGee's ranch. Old farmer Jim had asked him to help burn some slash piles next week, but until then, his time was his own.

He needed a project, not *more* free time.

He sighed. If only he had a second pair of hands. The things he wanted to get done were so much safer and faster with another person.

He supposed he could call Ms. Daisy, or June, as he had come to know her. He supposed they were sort of seeing each other, whatever that meant, but despite her and her company, which he did value, he had never felt lonelier. True, he had gone through dark times after losing Flora, but what he felt now, on a daily basis, it was bone cutting. For a brief week in September, he'd been re-exposed to the world of the living. Those precious, horrible, wonderful days he'd spent with Chevy and Izan had been his most meaningful days since Flora had died. They'd shown him what it was to live again, even if the entire week had been simply a gambit by Launch Tech. Now Chevy and Izan were gone, and he was still here, on his land, silent, and slowly dying.

Captain Picard purred louder.

A flash caught his eye. A truck bumped up the road to his house. Dolon tensed.

"Alright, Captain, it's time for you to go inside. Don't know who this is, and I don't want you getting hurt."

He picked up the cat and stepped inside. He grabbed the shotgun from the rack by the door and put Captain Picard onto the floor. He stepped back onto the porch and shut the door. Captain Picard let out an indigent meow.

"Yes, you're still a cat," Dolon agreed, watching the truck draw closer. "You passed the test."

Captain Picard gave another yowl.

The truck slowed then stopped next to the cabin. Dolon watched the driver's door open. He readied the shotgun.

"Old man."

Dolon didn't believe his ears.

"Chevy?" Dolon's arms relaxed. The gun's muzzle went to the floor.

Chevy stepped from the truck.

"Chevy. What are you doing here?" Dolon set the gun against the corner of the porch. "I thought . . . I figured you were out saving the world again. I didn't think you even remembered me!"

Dolon stepped off the porch to Chevy. He realized he was crying. Chevy reached out and hugged Dolon. He hugged her back.

"I—"

"I'm not out saving the world," Chevy said. "I'm done. Officially, I've been medically retired for brain injuries."

"What . . ."

A plaintive howl split the air.

"Oh lord, Captain Picard is mad about being locked up."

"Who is Captain Picard?"

"My cat."

"Right. You're a cat man."

"He adopted me. You want some breakfast?"

"Please."

Dolon led Chevy up his front steps and opened the front door. Captain Picard looked at him and then at Chevy and ran the other way.

"You're a fickle beast!" Dolon called. He turned back to Chevy. "Why are you here? Not that I'm mad. I'm glad. Very glad. They didn't tell me if you guys even survived. To tell you the truth, I've been going a little crazy wondering."

They entered the kitchen. Chevy dropped her bag against the wall. Dolon motioned her to sit at the counter. He pulled down his large cast iron.

"Well," Chevy said, sitting down, "they said I was injured at the Zola mine. No one ever mentioned you or Izan or the so-called fusion device."

"What?"

"They didn't want me to remember, Dolon."

Dolon's face went still. "Then why do you say 'so-called'?"

"I heard Izan's confession, from the back seat. I know it was all a ruse. I know he wasn't who we thought he was."

Dolon felt his heart creak. He had thought on this repeatedly. If he ever saw Chevy again, how to tell her. And then he hadn't needed to. She already knew.

"How do you . . ."

"What did they tell you?" Chevy cut him off.

Dolon hesitated. "That . . . my debt was paid, and if I ever spoke about any of it again verbally or digitally, they would hunt me down."

"They say what would happen if they caught you?"

Dolon shook his head.

"Yeah. That's probably enough. But they let you go. That's the important part."

Dolon nodded and set the cast iron down onto the stove. He drizzled oil on it and turned on the burner. "So, where's Izan? How's he?"

Chevy didn't immediately respond. Dolon turned from taking the eggs out of the fridge. Chevy watched him with a flat expression on her face.

"Well, Dolon, that's the thing. I didn't know. But I do know that Launch Tech has Izan, and they are doing something to him. Something that might kill him. *We* need to find him, Dolon. What we started isn't finished if Izan isn't home." Her voice was calm.

Dolon felt the egg carton slip from his grasp. It hit the ground with a telling crack.

"We?"

"What else are you doing?"

Dolon looked at the egg carton, a pool of yellow appearing around it. "I . . ."

"I came here to ask you for help, Dolon. We were a team. It was my job to protect you both. And that job isn't done."

Dolon watched the egg yolk blot out more of his kitchen tile. "He lied to us. He set us up and used us. Fuck, *he wanted* to die. He probably wants to be with Launch Tech now."

"Launch Tech used *all* of us. Izan was born into it. But our team out there, what we did. That wasn't a lie."

Dolon didn't like to think about Izan's confession. It caused him to wonder if the human connection he found meaningful from those days meant that the meaning he found in it was false.

"Dolon, they're experimenting on him. I heard the nurses say they are *augmenting* him. That it could kill him. He's still in danger. And you're the only person on the planet I can trust. Help me, please. Help me find him. Help me save him."

Dolon finally raised his eyes to Chevy's.

He thought of Flora. He'd spent fifteen years of his life waiting to close the chapter of her death, and he finally had. He was free from his debt. Free from anything to do with Launch Tech. He thought of Izan, and the betrayal that accompanied those thoughts. And then he felt deeper than the betrayal. He thought about the horror of Izan's existence. To never have had a choice. To have been made to die for something as soulless as a corporation. He thought of when Izan said he and Chevy were his first real friends. And how Dolon had thrown that back in his face. And he wondered if that memory crushed Izan as much as it crushed Dolon.

The silence stretched.

"Let's get some calories in you," Dolon finally said, scooping up the carton of eggs. Some of them had survived the fall. "Best to make decisions on a full stomach. We all know you're a bit twitchy when hangry."

"Dolon, I'm talking about Izan's life not fucking breakfast. I—"

Dolon held up a hand. Chevy snapped her mouth closed.

"We eat, then we talk. I'm making breakfast sandwiches. Any other condiments besides mayo on your blacklist?"

Chevy pinched her lips. Finally, she said, "No."

"Alright then." Dolon took out four of the surviving eggs. "Two breakfast sandwiches coming right up."

"Dolon, I know what you're doing, and delaying won't change the facts." Chevy said. "Are you in or are you out? Izan needs us. *I* need you."

Dolon held his hand above the pan. It was hot enough. He cracked an egg into the cast iron. It hissed when it hit the metal.

He could feel Chevy waiting for him to respond.

But he wasn't going to answer, not yet. He wanted to savor this moment. This moment when he was free from his debt and when Chevy was here in his kitchen, and they were doing nothing more complicated than sharing a meal.

Because when he gave her his answer, it would change everything.

ACKNOWLEDGMENTS

In September 2020, my husband and I were driving across Nevada, which, if you've done it, you know is mostly long swaths of open, mysterious land. At the time, we lived somewhere with hard-to-get, unstable internet. In fact, until my husband moved in with me, he had, for years, lived without internet or cell service. This wasn't by choice. He was just so remote, not even the internet could reach him. On that fall road trip, we were talking *what-ifs*. What if everyone had the internet? What if ubiquitous communication made governments irrelevant? What if private entities replaced the government?

And I thought, *I could write a book about that.*

And while *Cash & Gravity* isn't really about the internet at all, its origin story comes from living without connectivity and that long, long drive across the beautiful state of Nevada.

Cash & Gravity, born from a conversation with another human, continued—and continues—to be an endeavor of teamwork punctuated by bouts of solidary writing.

First, I'd like to thank O.C., Major, US Marine Corps Reserves, for buddying up with me on my first draft (and drafts beyond) to help construct the private military world in which Chevy exists.

O.C. assigned me reading, videos, and movies to watch, and he marked up my drafts with an eye for detail I will never have. While the military world in *Cash & Gravity* is not intended to exactly mirror the American military, anything I got right, I credit to O.C.

I would also like to thank my dad, Jim Pring, and my brother, Neil Pring, for helping me work through a variety of space-and physics-related issues. Neil in particular has a much firmer grasp on orbital mechanics than I will ever have, and I am grateful I can him call at a moment's notice for ideas on how to get myself out of whatever sci-fi corner I've just written myself into.

Next, the University of California Riverside Palm Desert MFA program. This program means everything to me. It took this novel from a fun hobby to a serious endeavor. The professors and students in the program taught me how to streamline my writing, and I learned so much about the publishing industry. Thank you, Stephen Graham Jones, for your workshop of this book. Thank you to all my peers who workshopped this book with me. Thank you, John Schimmel. Thank you, Ivy Pochoda. And finally, thank you, Tod Goldberg, for pushing me to pick *Cash & Gravity* back up.

Thank you, Rose King, Leena Pendharkar, Katy Hinterberger, Dave Oei, Kelly Tseng, and Emily Schleiger. Your feedback means the world to me.

Thank you to my agent, Jud Laghi, and to my editor, Toni Kirkpatrick, and to the awesome Diversion Books team. Also, thank you, Alan Dingman, for the awesome cover.

Thank you to Leah Maulucci, Alex Van Vechten, Josh Wentz, and Abby Childs. Thank you, Caleb Stefanovich, for being a supervisor who cared. Thank you to Janet Kelleher for always being the first to ask to beta read. Thank you to Dave Miller for then also asking to beta read.

Thank you to my mom, Lyn Pring, for always giving me unwavering support.

Thanks to my husband, Frank. You started the conversation, and I finished it with a book. I don't know how we ended up in the same stretch of mountains at the same time, but I'm glad we did.

And thanks to my muses, Po and Kefi. We all know you really wrote this book.

PRAISE FOR *RUBBLE*

"A witness to the hollowing of Palestine, Assi paints vividly on the inside of its carapace. Art is our final defiance of horror and death, and there is no better example than this."

—Meg Elison, author of *Big Girl*

"Vivid, lyrical, and compelling. Should be compulsory reading for those who are silent or inactive in the face of Gaza's huge tragedy."

—Ghada Karmi, author of *In Search of Fatima: A Palestinian Story*

"The name of the narrator is not important, because the world in which he lives has been torn apart by the forces of genocide. Life among the rubble isn't one, and survival is a matter of making it to the end of the day, and for the voice a matter of making it to the end of the next sentence. This novella is relentless."

—Nick Mamatas, author *Kalivas! or, Another Tempest*

"How does one while away one's time when lying buried under tons of debris from a bombed apartment building? That would seem to be an inappropriately facetious question except that it matches the tone of Seraj Assi's forceful new novel *Rubble*, in which the entombed hero often relies on wit to alleviate his misery. *Rubble* gives us a searing description of ethnic cleansing from the viewpoint of a victim who in his last moments is someone whose free-roaming thought is both nearing annihilation and verging on everything."

—Jim Feast, author of *Karl Marx Private Eye*

"*Rubble* is a tour de force, a remarkable journey of the besieged and restless mind. Trapped under the ruins of a bombarded cityscape, the narrator, like Samuel Beckett's locked-in antiheroic heroes, exists on memories and absurdist flights of fantasy. In the narrator's own words, 'The secret to surviving under rubble is to set your imagination free.'"

—JJ Amaworo Wilson, author of *Damnificados* and *Nazaré*

"Brilliant and harrowing. Assi's second novel begins as a silent song of survival and soon becomes a glorious symphony of the radical imagination. *Rubble* is timeless, essential reading."

—Cara Hoffman, author of *RUIN* and *Running*

"Poe's 'Premature Burial.' Jack London's *Star Rover*. Dostoevsky's *Notes from Underground*. Antecedents, perhaps, to this deeply moving tale of an individual's hope and despair after being trapped underground by an endless war. Using an easily grasped metaphor for the hopelessness of being caught up in the conflict, Assi buries his narrator alive, then lets him ramble beneath the rubble, meditating and hallucinating over the world that made him suffer and then brought him down below, into the rubble. Through all the musings, the memories, and the pain, Assi's everyman struggles for dignity. The dignity of a peaceful day-to-day existence. The dignity of just once having what everyone else takes for granted. The dignity of not living in constant fear. And finally, if it comes to that, the dignity of an honorable death. His story defines his humanity while restoring ours."

—Allan Kausch, author of *Warehouse Afternoons*